Also by John G. Hartness

The Black Knight Chronicles

Vol. 1—Hard Day's Knight

Vol. 2—Back in Black

Vol. 3—Knight Moves

Vol. 4—Paint It Black

And coming in 2014

Vol. 5—In the Still of the Knight

Paint it Black

Black Knight Chronicles, Vol. 4

by

John G. Hartness

Bell Bridge Books

Bell Bridge Books
PO BOX 300921
Memphis, TN 38130
Print ISBN: 978-1-61194-335-1

Bell Bridge Books is an Imprint of BelleBooks, Inc.

We at BelleBooks enjoy hearing from readers.
Visit our websites – www.BelleBooks.com and www.BellBridgeBooks.com.

10 9 8 7 6 5 4 3 2 1

Cover design: Debra Dixon
Interior design: Hank Smith
Photo/Art credits:
Cover Art (manipulated) © Christine Griffin

:Lbpl:01:

Dedication

This book is dedicated to my brothers, Bobby and Tom.

Thanks for all you've taught me and all the love and support you've given me.

Chapter 1

OKAY, I'LL ADMIT it. I was brooding. And not just the lay-in-the-recliner-staring-at-a-blank-TV-screen-with-REM's-*Everybody-Hurts*-on-repeat-on-the-stereo brooding. We're talking full-on, sitting on top of a mausoleum in the rain at midnight, wearing a trench coat and no hat kind of brooding. The kind of brooding that makes preteen girls swoon and RuPaul question *your* masculinity.

I was drunk, too. And given the peculiarities of my metabolism these days, that's saying something. The bottles scattered around my feet ratted me out to the tune of a handle of Bacardi 151, two pints of Jim Beam, half a gallon of Patrón, and a mason jar of something clear with the consistency and taste of lighter fluid. Without exaggeration, you could say I was having a rough night. Then my phone rang, which any idiot would realize only presented the opportunity to make the night much, much worse. And in a monumental display of poor judgment, I answered it.

"Yeah?" I slurred. You know you're blitzed when you slur the monosyllables.

"Jimmy?" Sabrina Law's voice came through the little speaker.

She sounded very far away, and I realized I was holding the phone upside down. I righted the ship, so to speak, and said, "Most days. Jury's still out for tonight, though."

"Are you drunk?" Despite seeing me consume enough beer to float a party barge, Sabrina had never seen me drunk.

"If I'm not, I have wasted a *lot* of liquor. What can I do to you, Detective? Wait. What can I do *for* you? Sorry."

"I need your particular perspective. I'll send a car. Sounds like you're in no condition to drive."

"That's true enough. And besides, I don't have a car here anyway."

"How did you get there?"

"I think I walked. Or maybe I stole a car. Oops. Probably shouldn't say that to an officer of the law. No, now I remember. I mojo'd a hippie into giving me a ride. Then I sent him home. And before you ask, I did not eat the hippie. I hate patchouli."

"I wasn't going to ask. I've got a car on the way."

"How'd you know where to send the car? And where am I, by the way?" I looked around, but for the death of me couldn't remember exactly where I was. I knew I was in a cemetery, but Charlotte's in the buckle of the Bible Belt, and that means a lot of churches. And a lot of churches meant I had about two hundred and forty-seven cemeteries to choose from, and I was pretty wasted. I hate when that happens. But it was reassuring to know that enough booze could still have an effect.

"You're the same place you always go to get drunk. Look behind you." I looked behind me, but all I could see was a tree. "Look down," came the voice in my ear. My eyes landed on a marker, and I remembered everything. The brass plaque read "James Jeffrey Black, August 14, 1973–May 7, 1995, beloved son."

"Crap, Sabrina." I sat down, suddenly sober.

"Sorry, Jimmy."

"How far away is the car?"

"Ten minutes. Get yourself cleaned up and hide the bottles. I don't need to hear about you being tanked when the uniform rolls up. Plus it's disrespectful to leave trash on your grave."

"I'll deal with that. See you in twenty. Wait! Have you called Greg? What have we got?"

"He's on his way here now. It's bad, Jimmy. Real bad."

"Crap," I repeated. Anything that Sabrina considered bad at this point in her association with me was going to be pretty awful. I hung up and started cleaning up the mess from around my feet. I was still a little unsteady, but I was pretty impressed that I only fell off the mausoleum once before the patrol car got there. What had to be a rookie cop got out and started waving his flashlight around the cemetery. He was two rows over from my grave when I stepped out from behind a tree and tapped him on the shoulder.

The kid jumped about ten feet into the air and whirled around as he came down. He tried to draw his pistol, but I had a tight grip on the wrist of his gun hand. "Relax, Junior. It's me."

"Are you Jimmy Black?" the kid asked when he could get his breath back.

"Yeah. Sorry about giving you a scare. But you don't want to be running around graveyards at night waving lights around and yelling.

You never know what kind of attention you're going to draw to yourself." I gave him a little grin and started walking back to the patrol car.

"Yeah, whatever. What am I supposed to be afraid of? Zombies? Or just vampires? Didn't you hear? Vampires are sexy now, and they all sparkle." I wasn't in the mood to correct his misconceptions; I just trailed a hand across my tombstone as I made my way to the passenger seat of his black-and-white.

It was enough that he knew my name. He also probably knew I was a private investigator and worked with the cops sometimes. They don't care how I get results, so they don't need to know I've been dead for better than fifteen years. And they definitely don't need to know about the vampire thing. That would just get too complicated for words.

Chapter 2

THE COP DROVE me into town on Monroe Road with lights flashing. He blew through every stoplight and straightened all the curves, getting me from the corner of Sharon Amity and Monroe to Caswell in no time, then hung a sharp left to bring me into the back of the hospital. He pulled up at the ambulance entrance and hit the door locks, looking at me expectantly.

"You'll have to give me a hint. Do you want me to congratulate you, puke on you, or tell you Richard Petty's got nothing to worry about?" I sat there for a couple seconds, and my liver finally caught up to the rest of me.

"Detective Law asked me to bring you straight to the morgue, sir. She said not to waste any time, and I don't want to piss her off. No offense, sir, but she scares me a little." He ducked his head at this, like he was ashamed to be afraid of Sabrina.

"Don't sweat it, kid. She scares me a little, too." True statement. She was my sparring partner, and if any human was fast enough and strong enough to kill me, it was Detective Sabrina Law. Good thing for me she didn't usually want me dead. Or at least no deader than normal. I slid out of the cop car and closed the door behind me. I stood there for a moment collecting my balance, then made my way into the back entrance of the hospital.

The automatic doors whooshed shut behind me, and the smells and sounds of the hospital battered my senses. There was the overpowering scent of disinfectant, a cloying lemon scent that was supposed to make you think of bright spring sunshine. Probably worked on humans. But underneath the lie was the pungent odor of human sweat, the stink of pain-sweat, the bright spiky tang of fear-sweat, and the underlying musky scent of despair. There was a hint of mold here and there, the bacteria smell that sick people give off no matter how much bleach is used, and the dusky copper scent of old, dried blood. An occasional waft of fresh blood tickled my nose, but it was always tangled with the stark stench of bile and terror.

Then the sounds washed over me, just as disorienting. Underneath the staff chatter and beeping technology, hovering beneath the buzz of machinery and the crackle of the intercoms, there was the frantic squeak of gurney wheels, the clatter of a dropped syringe, the thump of fists on a chest in a steady, if useless, rhythm. I could hear the sprinting boots of EMTs, the serious pace of the doctors, the harried yet assured stride of the nurses. The slop-swish of the janitor's mop two halls over was just as clear to me as the shrill beacon of the heart monitor from the room beside me, and I had to lean against a wall for a moment to beat back the sensory overload.

"Are you okay, sir?" A concerned voice penetrated the haze of scent and sound around me, and I opened my eyes. A young woman, about twenty, wearing a volunteer uniform, looked up at me. Her blue eyes peered at me from beneath a crinkled brow, and I waved her away.

"I'm fine. Just a little bit of a headache. Which way to the morgue?" I knew the way to the morgue like I knew the first seventeen levels of Pac-Man, but I needed to say something to get her to go away. Pretty young girls usually run away at the mention of the morgue—it reminds them that they won't be young and pretty forever. Unless they catch me on a bad day.

"Down this hallway, then left just past the elevators. Do you need me to call someone for you?" She took a step back as she offered to help.

I gave her half a grin, noticing that she didn't volunteer to serve as my escort. "Nah, I'm good now. Just don't really like the way these places smell." Which was kinda true. I don't like the smell of hospitals. Lemons make my nose itch, and it's a sizable nose, so there's a lot to itch.

She smiled and started to back away. "I guess I just don't notice it anymore. Well, if you're okay, I'll get back to my rounds." She pointed at her little cart of books and turned to go.

"Thanks for stopping. I appreciate it." I smiled at her and was a little surprised to find that it was genuine. I really did appreciate her stopping to help, and I *really* needed to get away from her because my vampire metabolism had worked all the alcohol out of my system, and I was completely sober. And really, *really* hungry. My staying would not go well for the pretty young candy striper if I decided to give in to my more puncture-oriented urges. I turned and hurried down the hall to the morgue.

I pushed my way through the metal double doors and saw a motley collection of my complicated associates standing around an autopsy table. Greg Knightwood, my best friend, fellow vampire, roommate, and the other half of Black Knight Investigations, was there in all his black-cloaked, utility-belted glory. At least he was wearing jeans and a sweater. The first time we'd come to the morgue he'd been in spandex.

Sabrina Law stood on the other side of one table, looking stern. I wasn't 100 percent sure if she was pissed at me for getting loaded but sure enough to have bet money that she was. She also didn't like things without rational explanations, and the number of those things had increased dramatically since she'd started associating with me. Her curly dark hair was starting to escape the loose ponytail she had it tied back in, and I refrained from commenting on how adorable it looked. I didn't think she'd kill me for it, but I knew she kept a silver stake in the inside pocket of that particular brown leather jacket, so I picked discretion for a change.

At the head of the room was Bobby Reed, the coroner's assistant, brilliant forensic analyst in his own right, and a vampire's best friend in the city of Charlotte. Bobby ran a black market blood bank for his fine fanged friends, and Greg and I were his oldest, and as far as I knew, only, clients. A former Arena Football quarterback, Bobby was a big handsome black man in his thirties who turned heads when he walked through a room. He'd once told me the reason he liked working with the dead was their disregard of surface details like that. Having been the skinny, awkward guy with a big nose who turned heads in the *opposite* direction when I walked through a room, I couldn't exactly relate.

I shook Bobby's hand and looked over at Sabrina. "What's up?"

"Are you sober enough to be here?" She raised one eyebrow at me. Yep, pissed at me for getting drunk.

I tried to raise one eyebrow right back at her, but I could only raise both of them at once, and it just made me look surprised. I kept trying until I got a hint of a smile out of her, then relaxed a little. "I'm sober. Mostly. Who was that cop you sent over to get me, the littlest Earnhardt?"

"I told him to try and make you puke," she replied with a smirk. "How'd he do?"

"Well, he failed in that assignment, but the adrenaline sure sobered me up. What have we got?" I looked down at the table to stop myself asking any more stupid questions. The shapes under the sheet in front of us were all wrong to be human. The two lumps were too small; they had to be pieces of something and not a body.

Bobby pulled the sheet off the remains, and I looked from him to Sabrina and back again. "Okay, they're bones. I don't get the big deal." I admitted. Lying on the metal table were a pair of human jawbones. Nothing else, just a couple of jawbones. Old jawbones, from the look of them. They were yellowed with age, flaked with dirt, and one of them had a little mold growing along the inside rim. I leaned closer and took a deep sniff, pushing my hyper-sensitive sniffer to the max. I smelled dirt, fresh, loamy earth, and a little bit of dog. There was a hint of something else there, but nothing I recognized. It smelled different, a tangy smell that somehow managed to smell both rotten and alive at the same time.

I stepped back and looked at Sabrina. "Yeah, I don't get it. A couple of jawbones. They look pretty old. Did somebody uncover an old Catawba Indian burial ground or something?"

"Or something." Sabrina said, picking up one of the jawbones. "Both of these mandibles were found this morning by a young man named Harold Vernon. He was playing catch with his dog in the woods behind the Whitewater Center when he discovered the bones." The Whitewater Center is a nature center built with a combination of private and public funds a few years ago. It boasts some of the best man-made kayaking and inner-tubing in the Southeast, along with a mountain bike trail, climbing wall, and all sorts of other sports that people enjoy during the day. Needless to say, I'd never set foot in the place.

"Okay, so we've got some kind of graveyard or dump site. What else did you find?"

"Nothing. That's part of the problem, Jimmy. There were no other bones or remains located within five square miles of the scene."

"You said that was part of the problem. What's the rest of it?"

"This bone." Sabrina waved at me with the jawbone in her hand. "Was matched using dental records to one Kellie Inman, reported missing from her home in Savannah in late 1991. It was thought that she and her boyfriend eloped and ended up here in Charlotte. Now we see that at least half of that is true. She certainly ended here."

"And the other jawbone?" Greg asked, raising his hand like a timid schoolboy. "Is that one her boyfriend?"

"No," Bobby said. He took the jawbone from Sabrina and placed it firmly on the table. "The other remains were identified, also using dental records, as belonging to Teresa Chapin, a bartender at one of the clubs downtown."

"Wait a second," I said. "There weren't any bars downtown in 1991. Not to speak of, anyway."

"That's true," Sabrina said. "But Teresa Chapin didn't disappear in 1991. She was reported missing two weeks ago."

I leaned back in, opening my eyes wide to let in as much light as possible. My senses had returned to normal after the booze and the bone-jarring ride over, so I was finally working on all cylinders. Nothing about the newer bone made sense. It didn't look two weeks old, didn't *smell* two weeks old. If I had to guess, I'd have put that jawbone as coming from a corpse that was a year or so old. Just the discoloration alone made it way too old to have come from anyone who was alive within the last month.

"Something in the report is wrong." I said, standing back up. "This can't be Teresa Chapin's jaw. No way was this jaw attached to a living person two weeks ago."

"That's what all our evidence says, too. We've even drilled a small sample and sent it to the FBI lab for Carbon-14 dating, but those results will take several weeks." Sabrina agreed. "We've sampled the dirt, the bits of tissue that were still attached to the bone, and even a microscopic bit of food that was stuck behind a molar. Everything indicates that this jawbone belongs to someone who was killed roughly ten months ago."

"Okay, then. You've got a forensic mystery. Not my specialty." I mimed dusting off my hands. "Now if you'll excuse me, I need a snack." I reached over toward one of the upper drawers where Bobby kept his blood supply.

"Not so fast, Jimmy." Bobby reached out with a very big hand and slammed the drawer shut. I snatched my fingers back quickly and fondly remembered the good ol' days. When he used to be afraid of vampires.

"What?" I protested. "The solution is obvious. You need a new dental forensic guy. Or the records are wrong. Look, I hate to be the smart one for a change, and trust me, I'm *not* used to the role, but if I'm the only one applying Occam's Razor to this situation, we've got a serious logic deficiency running around."

"Dude, don't use big words. You'll hurt yourself," Greg said from Bobby's desk. He spun around in the chair and waved me over to the monitor. I looked over his shoulder as he pointed. "I thought the same thing, and apparently so did Sabrina before she called us in. But here's how we know the dental records aren't wrong." He pointed to the screen, where an X-ray of a set of teeth was displayed.

"This is a set of Teresa Chapin's dental X-rays. See this area here? That's a crown." He stretched over to the table and pointed to the same spot on the jawbone. "Just like this crown."

"Dude, I'm not saying the X-rays don't match, I'm saying these X-rays don't really belong to Teresa Chapin."

"And I'm saying they do. Because these aren't her last set of dental X-rays. These are her X-rays from her previous dentist. Three years ago." He leaned back in the chair, looking smug. I hate it when he looks all smug at me—it usually means he's right.

"That's a lot of trouble to go to for a bartender," I admitted.

"Yeah, that's what I'm saying. I could see somebody faking *one* set of X-rays. Maybe even two if we're living in an episode of *Dexter* or something. But I've gone back to four different dentists, ever since she got this crown put in, and they all match."

"Which begs the question, why does one woman change dentists the way some people change shoes?" I mused. Greg chuckled and put the jawbone back on the table. I took another look. Everything still said the same thing to me—no way was this woman alive two weeks ago. "All right, I give up. How did a bartender from a meat market nightclub invent time travel? Or was she just the latest Dr. Who companion?"

Sabrina sighed. "I was hoping you'd have a completely outside-the-box idea that turned out to be right or at least worth investigating. Even a broken clock is right twice a day."

I wasn't sure how to take that, and I didn't have a snappy comeback, so I let it go. "So what about Kellie Inman? What's wrong with her jawbone? Is this the part where you tell me she was actually a Civil War veteran masquerading as a Georgia woman in the nineties?"

"No," Bobby replied. "From all we can see, she died in 1991. The age of the bone indicates it has been buried for approximately twenty years. Nothing indicates that it is anything other than the remains of an unfortunate young woman who died two decades ago."

"Okay, so we have one garden-variety cold case murder, and one Syfy-channel murder. Dibs on the Syfy case," I called.

"No. You'll work both, until we know there isn't a connection, and at least one missing persons case as well," Sabrina said, her face going even more grim.

"Who's missing?"

"Teresa Chapin's co-worker, Veronica Moore. She was last seen leaving the bar with Teresa the night she disappeared."

"Two weeks ago," I said. I had the feeling that keeping the timeline straight in my head might be a challenge on this one.

"Exactly. And until today there's been no sign of either of them. No ransom demand, no charges on their credit cards, no access to their email or Facebook pages—nothing."

I looked over at Greg. "You've confirmed this?"

He was already back on Bobby's computer. "Working on that now."

Sabrina looked a little taken aback. "You don't think my guys can do their job?"

"I think they're just fine, babe. But 'just fine' is useless when we've got the All-Star Dork Squad on our side." I waved at Greg's hunched shoulders. "You know as well as I do what he can do with a computer. Can you honestly tell me that you've got anybody on the force with geek-fu like this?"

"Good point. Greg, do you need passwords? I can get those for you." She started to flip through a little notebook, but Greg just waved her off.

"Passwords? We don't need no steenking *passwords!*" He tap-tapped furiously on the keyboard, muttering under his breath about the substandard equipment and how Bobby's machine wasn't fit to play *Minesweeper* on. I ignored him.

"What do we have for suspects?" I asked. "Boyfriends? Girlfriends? Roommates? Parents?"

"Teresa had a boyfriend, and he's been frantic since she disappeared. He calls the station every day right before my shift ends, looking for a progress report. He's clean."

"You're sure?"

"I won't tell you how to eat people and turn into a bat. You don't tell me how to judge a suspect."

"Fair enough, but if you know how to turn into a bat, I'd love to learn that trick." She gave me the look. "Okay, then. Moving on. We don't have any real suspects?"

"Nothing to speak of."

"Then I'm guessing we'll have to get to work? That'll require topping the tank. Bobby, I'm gonna need a couple bags of B-pos. Put it on my tab."

"We're cool. You still have a couple on credit after the nursery thing." A while back a demon had gotten loose in the hospital. Greg and I convinced it to go away. With extreme prejudice. Bobby was appreciative, so he hooked me up with a six-month supply of free blood. That charity was about to run out, though, and I was cool with it. The man had a business to run, after all. I drained two pints of relatively fresh blood and felt much better about life. I dumped them in a hazmat container and looked back at Sabrina.

"Well?"

"Well, what, fangboy?"

"Are we going to see where you found the bones or what?"

Chapter 3

SABRINA AND I turned for the door, and Greg got up to follow. I tried to wave him off, but my partner, never the best at picking up non-verbal cues, was more oblivious than normal.

"Stay here," I whispered. I pitched my voice well below the human range of hearing, but Greg stopped cold and looked at me, brows knit.

"I need to talk to Sabrina. Alone."

"You guys go ahead. I need to work on a couple of things here. On the computer. Without you. While you go to the crime scene. Alone . . . bye." My subtle buddy sat back down at the keyboard and resumed tapping away.

Of course, once I got Sabrina alone in her car I couldn't think of anything to actually say to her, so we rode along without speaking for the first fifteen minutes or so before she broke the silence. "You wanna talk about it?"

"Which part? The getting drunk part, the anniversary of my death part, the Greg hating my guts part, the dead bartender part, or the newly-made girl vamp I'm responsible for might be a bad vampire part?"

"You know, you don't have to be the father figure to Abby. That's what you've got Mike for."

Mike—my best living friend and the only one in my life these days who knew me and Greg from when we were on the other side of the grave. Mike was a Catholic priest and a huge help on some of our earlier jobs.

"Mike's got his own stuff going on right now." Like terminal cancer.

"How's he doing?"

"Not good. I haven't seen him in a couple weeks. He doesn't want us to come by, and I'm thinking that's not a good sign."

"Since when have you let someone else's wishes interfere with what you want to do?"

"Remember that whole 'invitation-only' thing we have to deal with? Well, the front parts of the church don't count, because it's a public building. But Mike's spending most of his time in the residential parts nowadays, and he revoked our invitation. We literally *can't* go see him."

"That sucks."

"Yeah. And without any of the inherent puns I attribute to that word."

"What about the Greg thing?"

"We're getting there. He kicks my ass every few years for turning him into an unholy blood-sucking monster. I drink a lot until he decides he's over being pissed at me for the next few years, and then we play *Halo*. It's a vicious cycle."

"I will never understand men. We're here." I got out of the car and stepped into mud up to my ankle. Since I am not the partner with the fetish for New Rock boots and leather coats (okay, maybe leather coats), my sneaker made a gross sucking sound as I pulled my foot out of the foul-smelling muck.

"That was nasty," I said, trying to pick more solid ground as I made my way around to the front of the car. "I was hoping for a high-class crime scene for once."

We were on the western side of the county, near a string of connected rivers and lakes that form the border of the county. This part of town didn't get much traffic in the best of times, and the middle of the night was no time to try and navigate the mud and the weeds.

"Crime scenes are never classy," Sabrina reminded me. "I ruined one pair of shoes already tonight, so I parked where I didn't have to wade through that crap again. Besides, think of it as your punishment for drinking too much."

"I thought that was the car ride to the morgue with Dale III?"

"I'm a woman. We reserve the right to punish the men in our lives forever for the smallest transgression." She walked off into the woods, following a trail of plywood that someone had helpfully laid down.

I stood there for a minute scraping muck off my shoes and shaking my head at the idea of being the man in someone's life. I'd never been the man in anyone's life, and it made parts of me feel warm and tingly that hadn't felt anything in some number of years. Sabrina had a way of making parts of me feel tingly, but these parts were a little higher up, more in the chest region. Sabrina's flashlight was almost out of sight when I finally shook myself into motion and dragged my butt after her.

I intentionally hung back as we walked through the woods. Even on the plywood runway, I moved silently through the woods and smelled nothing but ordinary North Carolina river smells. We were on the undeveloped side of the river, and the only light for yards in any direction was Sabrina's flashlight and the glow of portable worklights that the CMPD had set up around their crime scene.

Standing close together in the pool of light were two uniforms, one toting a department-issued twelve-gauge, and the other with his service weapon drawn and pointed down the trail at us. They looked a little jumpy, so I faded off into the woods while Sabrina identified herself.

"It's Detective Sabrina Law. Put those things away, boys. It's just me," she said as she walked into the light. I noticed her hand never moved far from the butt of her forty-caliber Smith & Wesson even while she was holstering her flashlight and giving the other cops her most disarming smile/hair-flip combo.

"Detective Law? Nobody told us you were coming back. Lieutenant McDaniel just told us to keep the crime scene secure." The taller of the two stammered a little, but he holstered his gun. The other one shouldered his shotgun, but I stayed out of sight. It's pretty easy to avoid notice when you don't have to breathe. That whole "unnaturally still" thing vampires have going for us makes it easy to duck behind a tree and not draw any attention. It helps that I have a wardrobe mostly limited to black clothing.

"Well, I am back. This is my case, and I get to work it whenever I want to, no matter what McDaniel says. And I brought a consultant, so don't shoot him, either. Mr. Black, you can join us now." I stepped out from behind the tree and into light, giving the two startled cops a wave as I did so.

"Well, Detective. You've successfully dragged me out into a swamp in the middle of the night. What did you expect me to see that couldn't wait until morning?" I took a quick lap around the crime scene, getting the lay of the land and keeping an eye on the patrolmen. I didn't need any witnesses around if I had to play bloodhound.

Sabrina waved one of the uniforms over and said, "Why don't you guys go get a cup of coffee? There's a thermos in my car, and it should still be nice and hot. Give us about fifteen minutes here, and if he finds anything, I'll make sure it gets to McDaniel."

The cop looked at her for a minute, and I could almost see the reasons to object running across his forehead, until Sabrina tapped the gold shield on her belt. The subtle reminder of rank was all he needed, and he waved his buddy over. The two patrolmen clumped through the woods on their way back to Sabrina's car, and I could really get to work.

"Anything?" she asked, moving closer to me.

"Nothing from the ground, but that's a new deodorant you're wearing, isn't it?" She nodded, and I nodded back at her. "Then move back, you're confusing the scene, and trust me, I'm way more interested in smelling you than this mud." I got all the way down on my hands and knees and put my face almost level with the ground to get a good scent. There was Carolina red clay, of course, and the fresh scent of crushed grass. I smelled cigarette smoke, but it was stale, like one or more of the cops today were smokers and the smell was stuck to their pants. There was a rich, damp smell of the river, fresh water teeming with life and fish poop. I moved my head back and forth, trying to catch a scent that was just outside my periphery—there—a hint of decomposition and just the faintest tinge of the living rot smell I picked up in the morgue.

I crawled along in the direction of the stench, not caring about ruining another pair of jeans. The department would reimburse me, and this time I might actually buy new jeans instead of shopping at the all-night thrift store. The scent grew stronger as I neared the water, and I had to get up into a crouch as the wet ground softened further beneath me. I lost it at the edge of the water, but was still smiling when I stood up and turned back to Sabrina.

"Success!" I said.

"Gross," she replied.

I wiped the worst of the muck off my hands and knees, onto my jeans. "Whatever brought the bones here came ashore right there. I can get just a touch of the scent on the wind when I stand here, so I think it came from the island." I pointed out into the darkness where I knew a small island, maybe fifty yards across and a hundred yards long, sat in the middle of the river. "If there are more remains, that's where they'll be."

"We've thought that as well. We should have a warrant tomorrow morning. Anything else?"

"There's something familiar about this smell. I can't place it, but it's like I've smelled it before, or smelled its cousin, or something."

"Smells have cousins?"

"Don't be a smartass. That's my gig."

"Are there any other remains around?"

"None that I could sense. Didn't you cover this part of the world with dogs?"

"Yeah, but I wanted to see if you could find anything they missed."

We started back toward the car. I stopped for a moment and looked across to the island, just a dim outline across fifty feet of river. I tried to imagine what was over there that had left only the jawbone of these two women, twenty years apart. Was it human, magical, or just monster? I turned and followed Sabrina back to the car. I wanted another drink—this one felt like it was going to get worse long before it got better.

Chapter 4

SABRINA DROVE ME back to my place and went inside as I took off my ruined shoes, socks, and jeans. I stood on the porch in just my boxers and a battered Spider-Man T-shirt and just looked around for a minute. "My place" was an old two-story frat house that Greg and I had taken over once we slaughtered the last inhabitants, a coven of collegiate vampires and their "Professor" master, a few months ago. It was a great lair, with two floors aboveground and a full basement that was light-tight and had Fort Knox–level security. I shook my head at the absurdity of living in an undead fraternity house and went inside.

I headed straight for the fridge and grabbed two beers, handed them to Sabrina, and ran upstairs to put on cleaner clothes. As I went down the hall to wash up, I saw the door to Abby's room standing open. The lights were on, but our young vampire coed was obviously not home. "Not home" was fast becoming her favorite place to be, and it had me a little worried. Then my super-hearing picked up Greg trying to coax Sabrina into a marathon video-game session with him, and I pushed Abby out of my mind. A couple of minutes later I was back on the main floor in a clean T-shirt and clean-ish jeans, at least jeans without evident mud- or bloodstains.

I turned to head downstairs when Greg's voice floated up to me. "Dude, you're gonna want another beer. I might have drank yours." I flipped off the air in his general direction and went back to the fridge. A minute later I was loaded down with the remnants of a six-pack of Miller Lite plus two bags of O-positive, and headed down into our new lair. To most observers the place appeared to be a normal two-story house, Craftsman style, with a dining room, kitchen, office, and library on the main floor. Upstairs was laid out like a dorm, with three bedrooms on either side of the hallway, and a big shared bathroom at the end of the hall. Cohabitating with an impressionable girl vampire led to a few embarrassing moments with Abby until I got used to wearing a towel after I showered.

But the real prize of the house was underneath the standard living space. If you moved the right book on one of the library shelves, the whole bookcase swung out, revealing a staircase. Cliché, I know, but the guy who built the place was traditional. I did have to give him props for building an honest-to-God lair at the bottom of those stairs. One of the first things we did was rig the staircase to stay open all the time. My fault, since I could never remember which book was the right one.

The lair is a huge room, about half the size of a basketball court, and when we moved in, there was an air hockey table, pool table, a full bar, and a couple of mattresses that I didn't want to think too much about. We burned the mattresses, moved the pool table into one of the spare bedrooms upstairs, and kept the bar and air hockey table. Vampire air hockey is about ten times faster than the regular game and has at least three times the swearing. Downside is our super-strength means we go through a lot of pucks.

Greg spent a month outfitting the basement into a command center, adding a tabletop touch-screen computer, several huge LCD displays on the walls, comfy seating, and a killer sound system. I was pretty sure he could launch nuclear missiles from down there, but I was a little afraid to ask about it. And let's face it, *Modern Warfare* on a 103-inch LCD display is pretty smokin'. Three months ago I would have just asked him where he got all the money for the toys. But lately Greg was going through a bad patch of hating my guts. I stayed away from anything that might set him off, and I never knew what that was. So, I kept my mouth shut and assumed he found some way to hack ISPs and keep his online poker empire going.

When I got downstairs, Greg was leaning over the computer table, so I put the beer on it. That never failed to get a reaction, except this time it did. He ignored me completely, just grabbed a bag of blood and drained it without looking up. Sabrina and I shared a look, and she gave me an I-have-no-flippin'-idea shrug.

"What's up, bro?" I asked, leaning in to see what he was looking at. On the screen were four pictures. Two I recognized as Teresa Chapin and Kellie Inman, the owners of our jawbones. The others were a decent-looking guy with a slightly dated fashion sense and a brunette hottie who looked about twenty-five.

"I recognize these two, but who's the babe with the eyeliner addiction and the dude trapped in the late eighties?"

"1991," Greg murmured absently.

"Huh?" I said. I say that a lot, I know. But my friends are all confusing. Sometimes I think it might even be on purpose.

"He's trapped in 1991. That's Bruce Marvo, Kellie Inman's boyfriend. He went missing the same time she did. The brunette in the more recent picture is Veronica Moore, Teresa's co-worker that vanished with her. Given what we now know about Teresa and Kellie, I think we have to assume that Bruce and Veronica are also dead. I've been running over their last known activities, trying to find something that sticks out, something that says who took them, but there's nothing."

"Can you define 'nothing'?" I asked.

"Nothing. As in nothing out of the ordinary. The reports from the more recent disappearances are more complete, but even with better files to study there's nothing to indicate anything out of the ordinary. Nobody got grabby at work recently. She's been with the same boyfriend for eight months. They aren't getting too serious. No trouble with anyone at work—nothing to indicate any connections." He pulled a chair over and sat down with a sigh. I tossed him another beer, and he absently nodded his thanks at me. This felt almost normal, like maybe my best friend was going to snap out of it sometime soon and stop hating me. And himself.

"We think this is random? Just two kidnappings twenty years apart? I don't buy it. And something is definitely screwy with the bones. They smell way too old. I'm no bloodhound, but I know dead things, and these things were dead longer than twenty years, not to mention way longer than just a couple weeks. Both girls go missing— Hey, where's Abby?" My train of thought jumped the tracks as I realized that I hadn't seen our newest partner all night.

Greg shot me a grumpy look. "Hunting. Again."

I swear that dude can put more disapproval into two little words than anyone who stands up to pee should be able to convey. Greg did not believe in human hunting and is the next best thing to a vegan vampire. Unless Greg is trapped in another dimension where there are no hospitals or blood banks, he's not going to drink from a living person.

This is yet another bone of contention between us. I prefer my blood fresh, but out of respect to Greg's more delicate sensibilities and a deep-seated desire not to arouse the populace and create vigilantes clamoring to stake me in my sleep, I usually restrain myself. Abby does not. She's a twenty-two-year-old coed with a body like a centerfold and all the entitlement baggage that came with being pretty and young and aware of what that did to men. When she was turned into a vampire a few months ago, she lost her life and her love of chocolate, but kept the entitlement. I didn't always think it was a fair trade.

Abby likes her blood hot and from the tap, and no amount of "discussion" with Greg has managed to change that. Somehow he blames me for her rebellion, like I'm supposed to be anyone's role model. I own the world's largest assortment of comic book T-shirts, and I'm pretty sure that tosses me right out of the running for role model. Role model or not, I still worried.

"Crap. I hope she didn't go bar hopping downtown again."

Greg and I exchanged looks. Ordinary, garden-variety bar fights draw the wrong kind of attention and are bad enough, but bar fights where nobody remembers how they started are worse. Bar fights that spill out into three blocks and spark five cases of spontaneous anemia are downright suspicious. I could tell Greg wasn't happy before he opened his mouth.

"Well, maybe if some folks weren't running off getting hammered at the drop of a hat, she would have better examples in her life."

"Seriously? We're going to have the parenting talk? Now?" My head started to throb at the very idea of having a serious talk about Abby's behavior, so I downed the rest of my beer and cracked another. That earned me another disapproving look from my portly partner. I indicated Sabrina with a gesture and a stare meant to remind him we had other issues at hand. Didn't work.

"We've got to have it sometime, and I know you metabolize beer too fast to get drunk, so it might as well be now."

"I thought we were trying to solve a couple of murders, not worry about what our roommate, who happens to be a grown woman, is doing with her free time?" I could hear my voice getting loud, and I tried to bring it back under control, with little success.

Greg stood up, running his hands through his hair in irritation. "It's about impulse control, Jimmy. She's got to learn to keep herself under control. And if she can't learn that here, where is she going to learn it?"

"If she hadn't learned impulse control by her senior year of college, how has she not ended up on drugs, with every STD in the book, or flunked out of school long before we ever met her?"

"That's different, dude. The rules are different for us. You heard what Tiram said—he thinks none of civilization's rules apply to us. Abby drank the Kool-Aid. She's acting the same way. If we don't get her under control, she's going to end up like him, or worse."

"Worse?"

"Yeah, worse. I don't know how, but worse. I worry, man. And you're better with her than I am. I get all tongue-tied and can't get to the point, and then it all gets awkward and . . ." He sat back down and killed his beer. I handed him another.

I knew the problem. Abby was pretty. Okay, Abby was absolutely smokin' hot, and Greg never had much luck talking to pretty girls. They always treated him like a fat nerd, which he was, and that just made him more self-conscious. Even after we went vampy he didn't suddenly turn into Lestat or one of the other fictional vampire studs. He just became a fat nerd with super-strength, speed, enhanced senses, and serious dietary restrictions. Kinda like being lactose intolerant, but to everything. When you're a guy who likes food, the vamp gig is a bitch.

"I'll talk to her, okay? I'll see if I can get her to chill a little."

"Thanks."

"You two gonna hug it out now, or what?" Sabrina asked from her chair. "Because I can leave."

"Why would you want to do that? Stay. You can be the meat in a nerd sandwich," I said, holding out my arms to her.

"Not right now, nerd-boy. You smell like cheap beer, expensive whiskey, and swamp muck. And that's just to my normal human sniffer. I don't see how Greg stays in the same room with you."

"It's not easy," Greg replied. "You should have smelled his room when we were alive. I made it through that, I can make it through anything."

Except he hadn't lived through that, and it was my fault. I spoke up quickly, more to keep myself from heading down that road than anything else. "Yeah, okay. Point taken," I said. "A shower sounds like a great idea. We've got nothing new here, so I'm gonna go get cleaned up. Wanna wash my back?" I asked Sabrina as I headed for the stairs.

"Maybe next time. But I will go up and catch a few hours' sleep. McDaniel wants me in his office at eight tomorrow . . . I mean this morning . . . before we talk to the families." She followed me upstairs and went into the room she had claimed for her own. I ducked into my room, conveniently right across the hall, wrapped a towel around my waist, and headed down the hall to the shower. I heard a wolf whistle from the crack in Sabrina's door and flipped her off as I passed.

I scrubbed myself all over a few times and finally got most of the smell of the night's festivities off me. Then I just slid down in the shower and let the hot water run over my face for a while as I sat there. It felt good, like the scalding water was peeling layers off my skin. And for every layer it peeled off, some problem went away. My guilt over turning Greg, my issues with Abby, my relationship—if you could call it that—with Sabrina, these new-old dead women, all of it spiraled down the drain and out to sea as I sat there, bare butt sliding along the porcelain.

I don't know how long I sat there, half meditating and half sleeping, but a banging on the door jarred me back to full consciousness. "Jimmy, you still in there?" Sabrina's voice came through the door.

"Yeah, I'm here. Just finishing up. Sorry." I hastily turned off the water, noticing that it had run ice-cold while I was in my daze.

"Well, hurry up, I gotta pee, and I don't want to go all the way downstairs."

"Gimme just a second." I dried off as quickly as I could and wrapped the towel back around my waist. Sabrina stood in the hallway in my Xavier University black T-shirt and nothing else that I could see. That shirt looked a whole lot better on her than it ever had on me. I stepped into the hallway. "All yours," I said.

"'Bout time."

"Hey, that's my T-shirt."

"It was in your dresser, so I guess so. You only keep clean clothes in the dresser, right? I couldn't tell which stacks and piles on the floor were clean, so I took a chance on the dresser."

"Yeah, the stuff in the dresser's clean. And the stacked stuff on the floor is clean. The piled stuff is dirty. It's all organized, I swear."

"If you say so." She slid past me and I saw just a hint of red panties as she slammed the door in my face.

"And I want my T-shirt back! Eventually," I said as I headed down the hall to my room. I put on a clean pair of boxers and crawled into bed, turning off all the lights as I did.

We don't really need to sleep regularly, but it's preferable. We can go for a couple of days at a stretch if we need to, but eventually we crash no matter how much blood we take in. It had been a pretty hectic night, so I was perfectly content to lie down in my own bed, a nice queen-sized frame the former tenants had left. I just flipped the mattress and changed the sheets when we took it over. I wasn't in any hurry to replace the comfy pillowtop, which is why I hadn't run a black light anywhere near the thing. The last residents had been a vampire *fraternity*, after all.

I lay there turning the night over in my head, thinking back to moping over my grave, then trying to figure out what to do about Greg, and worrying about Mike, and wondering how to handle Abby and make sure she didn't get us all staked, and then I shifted over to much more pleasant thoughts of Sabrina in one of my favorite T-shirts and little else. I lied to her—one of the piles was stuff she'd worn that still smelled like her. I hadn't bothered to wash that stuff. I liked having her scent in the room even if she wasn't. And thinking like that took me down a whole different road, pondering our relationship and where we were going.

I mean, why would she want to be with a dorky dead guy who looks a decade or so her junior? And what would I do if we did really turn into something? I was having enough trouble dealing with Mike's mortality, and close friend or not, I'd never been in love with him. And was I falling in love with Sabrina? I didn't know what that was supposed to feel like for living people, much less corpses. A disarmingly witty corpse, but still no one that you could take home to mother.

I spent the better part of an hour driving myself crazy thinking until my door opened. I had just enough time to see a curvy female form in the doorway before something black and soft landed on my face. It smelled faintly of lavender and my laundry detergent as I pulled it off my face. "Close your eyes and roll over, fangboy."

I did as she asked, and I felt the bed shift as Sabrina slid into bed behind me. She wrapped her arms around me and nuzzled up against my neck. I could feel every inch of her pressed against my back, from the smooth muscles of her thighs to the soft swells of her breasts. I froze for a minute, not really knowing how to react. This was something new for us, but I liked it a lot. She kissed me softly on the side of the neck and whispered, "It's okay to breathe, I won't run away."

"I don't have to breathe," I replied, and felt her stiffen behind me.

Sometimes Sabrina forgets the finer points of dating a vampire. Like the whole part about me being dead. I rolled over and took her in my arms, pulling her face to my chest and kissing her forehead. "Thanks," I whispered.

"For what?"

"Reminding me what it feels like to be alive." I kissed her forehead again and held her as we drifted off to sleep.

Chapter 5

I DON'T KNOW how long we were asleep, but I was snatched out of a pleasant dream involving a pier at Myrtle Beach that I vaguely remember from my teens by the sound of tires squealing into our driveway. I jumped out of bed, startling Sabrina awake, and I was already out the door before she could have realized I'd moved. I ran down the stairs, taking them three at a time and, at the door, almost bowled right into Greg, who had come up the stairs from the basement almost as fast.

"What's the deal?" I asked, jerking open the door to the coat closet and reaching inside for my twelve-gauge.

Greg didn't stop as he ran past me into the kitchen. He yanked the dishwasher open and ducked his head inside. I cocked my head to one side as he came back with a pair of 9mm Glock 17s.

"What?" he asked. "We don't eat off dishes. We drink blood out of bags and beer from the bottle. Might as well use the thing for a gun rack."

I had no time and no argument, so I just took up a position in the hallway facing the door. The sun was up, but I was far enough back that direct rays wouldn't hit me. All I had to worry about was a little discomfort from the brightness. Greg stationed himself to one side of the door where he'd be out of my field of fire but have a clean line on anything that could survive the double-ought buckshot loaded in my Mossberg. The first round was a beanbag round, just in case. But everything after that was a custom mix of silver and iron shot, designed to cut bad guys, dead or alive, in half at close range. I heard a third pistol cock and looked up to see a long expanse of leg stretching down the stairs. I followed the leg up to where Sabrina had her service weapon, a forty-caliber Smith & Wesson semiautomatic, at the ready.

Whoever was outside cleared the front porch steps in a single bound and threw open the door, bursting inside with inhuman speed. All we could see was a black-clad form, but it was an instantly recognizable form.

"Abby!" I yelped. "What the hell are you doing? The sun's up! Are you friggin' nuts?" I pushed past our new arrival to slam the door closed and drew the heavy curtain back over the window as Abby Lahey jumped from one foot to the other in the small foyer.

'OwowowowowowOOOOWWWWW!" Abby yelled, plucking at her clothes like she was burning, which she probably was. She was clad head-to-toe in a clingy black material, like spandex, complete with a tight black ski mask and dark ski goggles. She started shedding clothes like mad, flinging fabric right and left until suddenly there was a gorgeous twenty-something blonde vampiress in our foyer wearing nothing but panties, a bra, and what looked like first-degree burns over the rest of her very curvy body.

"Shit that hurts!" Abby swore, pulling at her bra and underpants.

"Jimmy, give her your T-shirt," Sabrina shouted down to me, and I obeyed without thinking. My T-shirt would hang down almost to Abby's knees, but I peeled it off and threw it on over her head. Then Abby performed that magical contortionist's trick that women do where they take their bra off without taking off their shirt. She skinned out of her panties, and sighed, her discomfort obviously reduced by having less clothing touching her body.

Greg scampered into the kitchen to put his pistols away, and came back with two bags of blood from the fridge. "Here, this will help with the burns," he said, handing the blood to Abby. She greedily drank one of them down in an instant, then took almost a whole five seconds to drink the other one. She let out another deep sigh and started to relax. As the new blood hit her system, we could almost watch it supercharge her healing. The lobster skin tone she was sporting faded to a pale pink within a couple of minutes, then almost all the way to her natural color in a few more.

By the time Sabrina and I had gone upstairs, dressed, and come back down to the den, Abby was back to her normal super-pale complexion and had stopped swearing like a sailor. She'd even managed to put her underpants back on, or at least they weren't lying in the foyer anymore, and from the less-than-ladylike way she was sitting curled up in an armchair, she was apparently wearing something under my T-shirt. If all the women in the house were going to keep wearing my shirts, I was going to have to do laundry more often.

"Would you like to explain what all that was about, now that bursting into flames is no longer imminent?" I asked, sitting on the couch. Sabrina curled up beside me, and I put my arm around her shoulders. Her hair smelled *good*, but I tried not to get distracted or dwell too much on how easily we had settled against each other. As if we were good at this relationship business.

"I thought if I wore non-porous synthetic materials that I might be okay with limited exposure to the sun. So I tried it."

"Where did you get that idea?" I continued. She didn't answer. I opened my mouth to press her, then caught her glance and turned my attention to my partner. Greg was making a valiant effort at sinking through his chair into the floor, but that's a lot of mass to sink, and we don't have that power, so he wasn't getting anywhere. "Knightwood? What the hell did you do?"

"I didn't do anything, bro! I promise! I might have mentioned a theory to Abby, but that's really all it is—a theory. We're nowhere close to human trials yet."

"Human trials aren't the issue. Humans don't get flash-fried when they try to get a little tan. I'm more concerned with this *vampire* trial." I glared at both of them.

"Greg didn't have anything to do with this! I decided that it sounded like a good idea, so I gave it a shot! Don't yell at him for what I did! And, anyway, what gives you the right to yell at anybody? You're not my dad, so don't try to act like it." She got right up in my face and shoved me backward.

I decided to try a little diplomacy for a change. Diplomacy wasn't my strong suit, but I didn't feel like repairing the walls if Abby and I really decided to argue vamp-style. I spread my hands and put on my best "calm face." "Abby, I don't want to yell at anybody, but I don't want you getting hurt. If you guys had just asked, I could have told you that this was what would happen. I tried it already."

"Yeah?" Greg asked.

"Yeah, in 1998. It might work with a hazmat suit, or even with leather, I haven't tried that. But even synthetic materials like spandex have to breathe. And they're not treated to repel UV rays. Plus we don't even know *why* sunlight hurts us. For all we know it could be some magical thing, and no matter what we do, we get crisped if we go outside during daylight hours. All I know is that the effect lessens over time, so after a decade or so you can get from the car to the house without dying. But in the first few years, everything you remember about Count Chocula is pretty much gospel."

"Why couldn't we just sparkle like the cool kids out West?" Abby moped, flopping down in her armchair and doing unsettling things with the hem of my T-shirt, which made only the most meager attempt at covering her long legs.

"Because we're real, and we're not that pretty," I said with a grin.

"Speak for yourself, beanstalk. I'm a total babe." I couldn't disagree with her there. She was absolutely worthy of being a basic-cable vampire, even if Greg and I looked more like walk-ons.

"So . . . where you been?" I asked innocently, not really ready to start another fight but knowing that a discussion was needed. Sabrina, helpful as ever, made some noise about showering and working and got out of the line of fire as quickly as possible. Greg didn't even speak, just bolted for the stairs, leaving me alone with Abby for our little "chat."

She looked at the pair of them leaving then sighed and leaned back in her chair. "Where's the camera crew?"

"Huh?"

"If this is an intervention, shouldn't there be somebody taping it for later broadcast? I mean, this oughta be a ratings blockbuster— Vampire Intervention—When Bloodsuckers Go Bad or some crap like that. Go ahead, tell me how bad I am for eating takeout all the time. Tell me how it opens us up for exposure and makes everything more dangerous for everybody. Tell me how we're the top of the food chain, but with great power comes great responsibility. Or are you going to quote Batman instead of Spider-Man this time?"

"Well, if you know everything I'm going to say, why should I bother?" I asked calmly. Maybe if I kept cool, this wouldn't turn into another yelling match. We'd had those already, and nothing had changed. I figured giving the reasoned approach a shot might not be terrible.

"I don't know, Jimmy. Why should you bother? What does it matter that I hunt? It's what we're supposed to do! We drink blood. Humans make blood. Obviously they exist to feed us, right? And I know what I'm doing." She started to tick off points on her fingers. "I never drink from the same human twice. I never hunt in the same place twice in a week. I never go to the same place looking the same. I always mojo the snack into going home and sleeping it off. I always make them think they hooked up with a chick at the bar who looks nothing like me. Come on man, I'm careful."

"Careful isn't what it's all about, Abby. I mean, look, I'm not the poster boy for abstinence here. I enjoy the occasional Meal on Wheels too, but *every* night is too risky. That's why we cut our blood deal with

Bobby. It's why Greg is doing IT work for the Master of the City to get access to his blood wine cellar. So we don't have to be out there every single night. Every time we take a victim, it exponentially increases the chance of someone catching on to us. So we have to be judicious about things, and only eat takeout when we have to."

"But it's so *good*." She writhed a little her chair, and the hem of the T-shirt inched up to show off even more distracting young leg.

Worse, I had no argument for her.

"I know. You're right. It's way better straight from the tap. Just like draft beer is better than bottled beer. And steak is better than hamburger. But we have to suck it up and eat hot dogs sometimes so we can afford to eat steak for special occasions. You get it?"

"No. That's a stupid analogy. We're rich. Or at least we can get all the money we want by mojo'ing a bank teller. So we don't have to eat hot dogs. Come on, Mr. Apex Predator. Mr. Top of the Food Chain. Give me one good reason why I shouldn't go out and hunt every night whenever I get hungry."

"Because I said so, that's why." As soon as the words came out of my mouth, my eyes went wide. I felt like the stupidest asshat in the world, and the look on Abby's face told me she agreed.

She let out a peal of laughter and then flipped me off. Then she leaned forward and said, "Look, Jimmy. I like hanging with you and Greg. I really do. And I appreciate the whole keeping me from dying a couple times thing. But let's be clear here—I am not your bitch. I am not your little sister, your daughter, your protégé, or any damn thing else. *And* if I want to go out and be the Big Bad and drink from the puny mortals, I will. *And* if you try to stop me, we'll throw down. Are we clear?"

There was a cold look in her blue eyes. I knew she was serious. I didn't have much in the way of an answer.

"So if you want me to leave, I'll pack my shit and be gone come nightfall. Or if you want me to stay, I'll be happy to hang around and play Scooby Gang with you and Sabrina and Greg. I like you guys, I really do. But this is who I am now. This is who you helped make me. And that's just the deal. So can you live with it, or do I leave?"

I thought for a long moment, then looked her in the eyes. "You're discreet?"

"Like a ninja."

"You're careful."

"Like a bomb tech."

"You really want to stay and help us fight the bad guys?"

"Yeah, it's fun."

"Then we'd like for you to stay." She squealed a little and clapped her hands, looking even younger than she really was. I held up one finger. "But I do have one request."

"Lay it on me."

"Can you at least try to be a little more subtle, sensitive even? It really bugs Greg, so just . . . don't flaunt the hunting thing, okay?"

"I'm a hot blonde, Jimmy. Subtle ain't exactly something we're taught. Subtle is for brunettes and girls who wait in line at clubs. But I'll try to be sensitive to Greg's point of view."

"Thanks. I'm gonna get a little more sleep. I think we're gonna have a busy couple nights. The Scooby Gang may have caught another case." I got up and started for the stairs.

"Hey, Jimmy?" I stopped and turned to look at her.

"Yeah, Abby?"

"Thanks. I don't want to leave. I really like it here."

"We like you, too."

As I went upstairs I couldn't help but think we weren't finished having this conversation.

Chapter 6

I MADE IT AS far as the first floor, but got detoured on my way back to bed by the smell of bacon cooking. Since there was only one person in the house still capable of digesting solid food, I figured that must mean that Sabrina was up. I'm pretty smart that way. I padded into the kitchen on my tiptoes, hoping to get a good yelp out of her as I snuck up on her, but all I got was a swat on the ass with a spatula when she turned out to be hiding behind the door.

"You sneak like a spastic hippopotamus," she said, dumping the spatula in the sink and grabbing her plate. Sabrina was dressed for work in slacks, her boots from the night before, a maroon scoop-neck blouse, and a jacket that I knew was covering a shoulder holster. Her hair was pulled back, and I guessed she had taken a shower while I was having my little "discussion" with Abby. I had a brief, fleeting dream of Sabrina finally taking me up on my long-standing offer to wash her back, and I cursed myself for missing what might have been the perfect opportunity. She looked at me, and it was like she could read my thoughts, because she gave me a little wink that made my heart feel like it was actually pumping blood again.

We sat across from each other at the small kitchen table. Sabrina tucked into what looked like a delicious helping of bacon and eggs, then slathered butter on a couple of pieces of toast, just to add insult to injury. I lived vicariously through her stomach and drank blood from a bag. I'd tried to come up with ways to flavor blood, but it never worked. Mixing it with various beverages produced fairly disastrous results, and no matter how hard I tried, I could never get the bacon seasoning to come together right. So I smelled the bacon, and drank my O-negative.

Finally, she broke the silence. "How did your little chat go?"

"About like you'd expect."

"Sorry to hear that."

"Yeah, me too. But she agreed to not be a complete bitch about it in front of Greg, and I agreed not to be a complete tool about it with her, so I think that counts as compromise."

"Did you break any furniture reaching this compromise?"

"No, and there was surprisingly little profanity and yelling."

"Good God, Jimmy, I think you might be growing up."

"Well, it's certainly taken me long enough." Despite my youthful good looks, I'm almost forty. I'll always look twenty-two, because that's how old I was when I was turned, but I don't trust Greg not to throw me a fortieth birthday party anyway.

Sabrina stood up, scraped the crusts into the garbage, and put her dishes in the sink. "I'll get those tonight, don't worry about washing up after me." I laughed, and she looked at me for a second, then laughed herself. "Oh yeah, forgot who I was talking to. Don't let Greg worry about washing up after me."

"He won't. He's been using the dishwasher as a gun cabinet. Don't ask."

She started to say something, then just shook her head, and I walked her to the front door. This was one of the new things in our "relationship," the whole saying good-bye in the morning thing. I wasn't very good at this part, so it usually consisted of me stammering and looking at my feet a lot until Sabrina left. This morning felt different, somehow, though. So I just pulled her close to me for a minute, letting her warmth soak into me through my T-shirt, then I stepped back.

"See you tonight."

"Okay. See you tonight." Then she tilted her head up, and I kissed her good-bye, like it was the most natural thing in the world. And maybe for some guys it would be, but I'm not that kind of vampire. She slipped out the door, careful not to open it too wide and torch me, and I stood in the foyer, smelling her on my clothes.

Until a sound like a herd of thundering rhinoceroses came barreling down the stairs. I got out of the way before Greg crashed us both through a wall, and put out a hand to steady the rushing ball of pudgy detective. "Where's the fire, partner?"

"I remembered the smell!"

"What smell?"

"The funky smell on the jawbone, dude. You remember how it was kinda rotten, and kinda damp, and kinda dead, and kinda not, and all gross?"

All thoughts of the really nice kiss I'd just experienced went swirling around the toilet drain of my memory as the scent of the morgue came back to me. "Yeah, I remember it," I said sourly.

"I remembered where I smelled it before!"

"You wanna share that with the rest of the class, genius?" I was *so* not thrilled with this abrupt shift from happy boyfriend kissing a hot girl to detective talking about gross stuff.

"Troll." Greg beamed at me like the first time he beat Zelda. The second the word crossed his lips, I was bombarded by a ton of sense memory. Green monsters with battle-axes, evil faeries shooting me, cage fighting for ridiculous sums of money, meeting my first dragon, getting beaten to a pulp several times . . . he was right. It smelled like troll.

"You're a genius, bro. Now where does that put us?"

"Well, I guess we're looking for a troll." The air went out of Greg like I'd popped a balloon giraffe at a six-year-old's birthday party. I put my hands on his shoulders, turned him around, and pointed him down the stairs toward the basement.

"Now, go do your internet magic, Jedi master, and go find us a troll." I gave him a little shove, and he started toward the stairs. I followed him down and threw myself into a comfy chair while he settled in behind his desk to get sleuthing.

"What are you going to do?" he asked, looking over to where I was curled around the Xbox controller.

"I'm going to do what I do best during the daylight hours, of course."

"Play video games, scratch yourself in inappropriate places, and drink beer?"

"I might not drink much beer today, but yes to the rest of it." I fired up *Arkham City* and commenced to kicking butt Batman-style. We spent most of the day that way, playing video games and researching trolls on the internet, until sunset when we could really start to work. Abby joined us about mid-afternoon, and we worked out an uneasy truce between her and Greg where I pretended to have never spoken about her hunting, and she pretended not to have any issues with either of us.

Chapter 7

I WAS DRESSED to go out when Sabrina came over after work. "Dressed to go out" for me meant I had a black sweater pulled over my latest *Sandman* T-shirt and a black jacket to hide my shoulder holster. I had my Ruger LCP in an ankle holster on my right leg, a Glock 17 under my left arm, and knives tucked into several places around my waist, wrists, and ankles. I decided to leave the sword at home, at least for tonight, but I was loaded for anything short of the zombie apocalypse nonetheless. Come to think of it, we'd dealt with at least one zombie apocalypse with a lot less firepower.

Sabrina pulled back after giving me hug hello, confusion wrinkling her forehead. "What's with the artillery? Do you have a lead I don't know about?"

"Maybe. Did you get anything at work today?"

"No. We had four sets of parents to meet with, one from each of the women we have remains for, and the worst ones were the parents of the ones we haven't found remains for yet. They still have hope, even Bruce Marvo's parents, who know in their hearts that he's dead, but they can't let him go."

I thought back to Greg's baby sister, and how much it hurt him to cut himself out of her life, and winced a little. I held out my arms to Sabrina again, and she stepped in to me. I hugged her tight and stroked her head for a minute, then she backed off and looked me in the eyes. "So what's the plan? You must have someplace specific to go, or you wouldn't be packing all this armament."

"Can't slip anything past you, babe. You ever thought about police work as a career choice?" She laughed, which was one of the hallmarks of our relationship. I tried to keep her laughing. If not with me, I'd settle for at me.

"We gotta go to the Angel."

Sabrina pulled back, her nose wrinkled. "Are you kidding me? You know I hate that place. And that woman."

"Yeah, but Greg remembered the smell, and she's the only one in town that can give us a lead."

"What's the smell?"

"Troll."

"Crap."

"No, troll. They smell really similar, but there's a slight difference. And there's only one person in Charlotte that keeps trolls around."

"Only because you killed the evil faerie prince that ran the cage-fighting outfit."

"He needed killin'. So you wanna wear that or you wanna change?"

"What? You don't think this is appropriate?" She had on the slacks, jacket, and blouse from this morning, and she looked great. But she might be a little overdressed for where we were headed.

"I just thought you might want to change is all. It's kind of a girl thing, isn't it? Three or four outfits per day?"

"Bite me, fangboy. The last place I want to go tonight is a strip club run by an immortal criminal godmother, so I'm sure as hell not going to change to fit in."

I held up my hands in surrender and grabbed Abby's keys off the table in the foyer. "We're outta here," I yelled up the stairs.

"Wait for us!" came Abby's shout back, and I felt a headache coming on. Greg was not my idea of the perfect companion for a gentlemen's club, no matter how poorly named the establishment. My worst fears were abated somewhat when he came downstairs in a black polo shirt, black leather jacket, and blue jeans. He managed to look almost like a normal pudgy twenty-something, except for the four-inch platform boots he was sporting. They had more chrome on the toes than my last car had on the bumper, and there were purple flames dancing around the toes.

"Nice boots," I said, covering my mouth with one hand so he wouldn't see the grin.

Greg, of course, is immune to my sarcasm after all these years, so he just glanced down and grinned. "These old things? Thanks. I've had them for uh . . . weeks and weeks." I knew he was lying, of course. His clothes had gone up in the same fire that destroyed all our belongings a few months ago. That's when we took over the frat house. I was about to crack on him more when I caught sight of Abby walking down the stairs.

I stopped in mid-snark with my jaw hanging open as she came into view one leggy step at a time. Abby was rocking the stripper heels, a pair of four-inch Lucite jobs that made her look even taller than normal. The view was impossibly improved by the skin-tight mini dress she had on. The mini was no more than three or four napkins sewn together in strategic spots. "Damn, Abby," I whispered. "You know we're going there to investigate, not find a job, right?"

She just walked past me, reached out with one hand and slowly closed Greg's mouth for him. She leaned in and gave him a little kiss on the cheek, reaching out for her keys as she did so. "Careful, Greggy. You'll catch flies." She sidled past us to the door and opened it, turning to look back at where Greg and I stood frozen by the stairs. "Coming boys?" I gave myself a shake, earning a glare from Sabrina, and followed the girls out to the car.

I didn't even have any witty comments for the ride over to Lilith's place. I'm a big enough vampire to admit to a little touch of nerves. Lilith scared the crap out of me. She was older than anyone I'd ever heard of, going all the way back to Adam, or so she said. I didn't know what kind of power she was packing, but she's the kind of woman used to getting her way, and when she didn't, we weren't on the best of terms. I thought we were in her good graces at the moment, but it's always hard to tell with her. She's immortal, gorgeous, and has her fingers in pretty much every criminal enterprise in several states. Plus she has troll bodyguards, and trolls are just *nasty*.

One of the human valets opened the door to the Escalade as Abby rolled to a stop under the portico. She hopped out, blew him a little kiss, and asked him to keep the car close. He stammered some type of agreement and almost tripped over himself looking at her ass. Abby just laughed, a little silver trill that had Sabrina and me sharing a nervous glance.

"She's way too good at that for comfort," I muttered, taking Sabrina's arm as we walked to the door.

"She's blonde, built like a centerfold, and twenty-two. What do you expect?"

"Point to you, but I don't have to like it."

"Actually, Jimmy, you do. You're not her dad, her uncle, or even her big brother. You're just one of her roommates, and she's going to use sex as a weapon just like you use mojo. We all have our little gifts. Hers just happen to come in a D-cup." I gave her a sharp look as she outlined all of Abby's arguments from earlier in the day with half the words and none of the yelling. I was about to mutter something about hating smart women when I ran into the palm of one of the bouncers.

I had to look up into his dark glasses, which doesn't happen to me often. He was about the size of a Porta-Jon, with hands the rough size and shape of shovels. One of those shovels was pressed firmly against my chest. I looked down, then at him, then back at his hand in a polite, non-verbal invitation to get his paws off me.

"I gotta frisk you, pal. Sorry, but it's the rules."

"Since when?" I'd never been frisked when Phil, the former proprietor, ran the place.

"Since a couple guys from out of town started some trouble. Now there's a strict no-weapons policy."

He seemed pleasant enough, so I decided against kicking him around the parking lot to show off my manliness for my girlfriend. I locked gazes with him and spoke very clearly. "You checked me thoroughly. None of us are carrying any weapons. We're all clear."

He repeated my words exactly, if his tone was a little wooden. His partner looked from me to him and back again, then I repeated the process, mojo'ing him into thinking we'd all been frisked. I even let them think they copped a feel on Abby. Might as well give the guys a little thrill if I'm going to muck around in their heads, right?

The Fallen Angel was one of the higher-end strip clubs in town. Unfortunately, our work had led Greg and me into all of them at one point or another. Some were charming in their utter failure to make the grade as a "club." Those joints were really more like biker bars that happened to have naked women dancing around poles watched by a lower class of bad guys than the sophisticated criminal element found in the true "clubs." The true test of a strip club versus joint was not so much who was on their poles, but who stared at their poles.

I liked those classless joints—they appealed to the badass rocker hiding deep inside my geeky exterior. Okay, that rocker hides underneath several layers of my geeky interior, too, but that's beside the point. The joints were barely legitimized brothels who'd pulled a liquor license to keep up appearances. But the Angel was a tall step up from those joints, as topless bars went. At any given time you could find some of Charlotte's top athletes in private booths, see business deals getting done over a lap dance, and penicillin could easily take care of any diseases you'd contract from a visit to the buffet.

You could also find a good sampling of Charlotte's supernatural population, which wasn't always helpful to our cause. Our last visit forced a spontaneous renovation of the interior. A gargoyle took offense at a vampire walking through the door of his favorite strip club. We might have destroyed a great deal of furniture.

Lilith made more than cosmetic changes to the place during the subsequent remodeling. Changes definitely for the better. The sound wasn't as loud, the lighting was a bit brighter, and none of the girls were under the influence of anything stronger than coffee. At least not that I could tell.

The four of us clustered uncomfortably by the bar as I tried to get the bartender's attention. No easy feat when there's a topless woman dancing on the bar in question. Between heels that could crush a skull and legs that looked like they could probably do the same, the barkeep wasn't paying any attention to my waving twenty-dollar bill. The dancer, however, was on my photo of Andrew Jackson like a shark on fresh tuna, and before I could even open my mouth to ask about Lilith, my twenty bucks was gone and a stripper was kissing me on the cheek and whispering sweet nothings in my ear.

I pulled back, trying to escape the grasp of a stripper on a money-hunt and the wrath of Sabrina. I looked frantically around for reinforcements, which I did not find. My ever-faithful partner was entranced by the redhead on stage, or at least doing a good job of pretending to be so. Abby hid her giggles behind a hand and made no attempt to help. Sabrina finally pried the girl off my neck with the most effective mood-killer I've ever seen—her police badge.

The stripper skidded backward, dropping to her butt on the bar, and scurrying to the floor before running off. The bartender glared over at Sabrina, and she nodded down at the badge.

"Where's Lilith?" she asked over the music and the commotion coming from the kitchen.

I had just enough time to figure out that my night was going to suck before a troll came barreling out the swinging doors leading to the kitchen. He was glamoured to look like a block-headed human with shoulders the width of a Buick and no neck, but I could smell him from twenty yards away, despite his being covered in stripper perfume. Without stopping, the troll blew through two tables of businessmen and one cluster of NFL linemen on his way to the door. I jumped after him. No way was I losing a potential lead in two murders smelling suspiciously of troll involvement. Abby and Greg followed, but even at vamp-speed we weren't going to be able to catch the troll before he made the parking lot.

"Help me! They're with the IRS!" the troll yelled as he passed the doormen. The bouncers obviously had deep-seated tax issues they wanted to discuss, because they immediately turned to block our path.

"Take care of these two. I'll go after the troll!" I yelled. I never slowed down as I reached the bouncers, just dove right over them and rolled to my feet a few yards past the confused men. They turned around to find Greg and Abby standing in their faces, fangs on display. I heard a whispered "holy shit" from one of the doormen, and knew he was only a few seconds from Dreamland. At least I hoped he was. I needed Greg and Abby pronto because I had no particular desire to face the troll alone. I tried to keep the troll in sight without actually engaging him until they could catch up.

Unfortunately, the troll must have realized the odds had improved in his favor about the same time I did, because he came to a full stop and turned to face me. Trolls are everything you've ever thought they should be—better than eight feet tall, kinda greenish-yellow skin that smells like six-month old pumpkin, and patches of hair longer than my thumb growing out of various moles scattered all over their faces. Not attractive creatures, I promise.

A gap-toothed grin split the troll's hideous face, and he held out both hands to me in a "come and get it" motion. I didn't want to. Really, I didn't. I know exactly what a six-month-old pumpkin smells like, and I don't want to get that close to anything smelling that bad again. Not that I had much choice. I was barreling through the parking lot at better than twenty miles per hour, far too fast to stop. So I went and got it. Right in the face I got it.

"It" was the troll's fist, of course. A fist about the size of a Thanksgiving turkey covered my entire face and delivered an impact that felt like running into a brick wall. A brick wall that stunk worse than my middle-school gym shorts. I wish I had bounced off the fist. That would have hurt way less. But no. My feet and body kept running, right past and under the troll's outstretched arm, so that I flopped flat on my back in the parking lot like a cartoon character and bounced the back of my head off the asphalt. Repeatedly. If I'd been capable of getting a concussion, I would have had three right there. Even with my vamp immunity to the normal bumps and bruises of life, I still saw little stars and bats tweeting around my head for a second before one encyclopedia-sized foot came crashing down onto my chest, driving the breath out of me and cracking at least six ribs.

The breath wasn't the problem; I don't need to breathe. But broken ribs *hurt*. And with no breath, I couldn't even swear at him. The troll reached down and picked me up by my throat, again keeping me from the sweet healing magic of profanity. I gathered my wits as best I could and shook one of my knives free, dropping it into my palm and stabbing the troll through the wrist as he reared back to punch me in the face. He opened his hand and sent me crashing back to the ground.

The troll yanked my knife from his arm and flung the blade aside, stepping back like he was going to kick my head somewhere into the next time zone. I rolled out of the way and drew my Glock as I came to my feet. I was shaky, but the full load of blood I'd drunk over the course of the day was already knitting my ribs back together. I drew a bead on the troll's forehead and said those words that most people with a gun actually don't mean. "I don't want to shoot you." I meant it, however. This guy was our only lead in at least two murders, so I didn't want to shoot him. In the head, at least. Truth be told, I really did want to shoot him a little bit, but Sabrina's been working with me on this crap she likes to call "impulse control."

"Bullets won't kill me, vampire. Ogg is strongest one there is!"

"Pretty sure that's the Hulk's line, buddy. And these are silver bullets. Does that make any difference?"

"No. Silver not hurt Ogg. Only cold iron."

"Good to know," I said as I pulled a fresh clip out of my shoulder holster and swapped it for the one in the pistol. "These are cold iron rounds. Now would you like to sit down and talk this out like civilized monsters?"

"Crap. Ogg hate vampires." He turned and walked slowly to a Hummer parked a few spots away. He dropped the tailgate on the Hummer and sat. The back end of the vehicle sank about six inches, then held.

"Nice ride," I remarked. I sat on the trunk of a Lexus parked nearby.

"Thanks. That's Ginger's car you're on. She won't like that."

"I won't tell her if you don't."

"Okay." When he wasn't trying to stomp me into a bloody smear in the parking lot, Ogg seemed like a decent enough troll. Maybe when this was all over we could hang out. I shook myself. I gotta stop looking for friendship in topless bars—it never ends well and is frequently very expensive.

"All right, Ogg. Why did you run when you saw us?"

"Last time you come around, big fight. Didn't go so good for gargoyle. Before that, another fight. Lots of trolls end up dead. Ogg didn't like odds."

Smarter than the average troll, I mused. "Good point. Well, we're not here to kill anybody this time. Well, not specifically."

"That's good to hear, little vampire."

Crap. I turned to see Lilith standing behind me, holding Greg and Abby by their elbows. They weren't struggling, but the look in Abby's eyes would have turned Lilith to ash if vampires had those kinds of powers. And if magic still worked on Lilith, which I wasn't at all sure about. The one thing I was sure about was that she didn't look happy.

"Ogg is much more than a troll. He's a valuable employee, and I would hate to think how much I would hurt you if you killed him."

"Hi, Lilith."

"Hello, James. Shall we go inside and discuss this like civilized beings, or do I need to call out reinforcements? Your friends here have already destroyed my front door, my awning, and three patrons' vehicles."

I raised an eyebrow at Greg, and he shrugged. "Sorry, dude. Those door guys weren't quite as human as I thought they were. So things got a little breaky."

"Are they alive?" I asked.

"They're alive," Abby spat. "But only because your partner has a bleeding heart. If he hadn't stopped me, those morons would have been the ones with the bleeding hearts."

Lilith laughed, a light, cheerful peal that nonetheless resonated with something in my gut and made me shiver. "I like this one, James. Can I borrow her sometime?"

"Keep away from the jailbait, Lil. I don't want you to have to kick my ass over it," I responded.

I slid off the trunk of the Lexus with a wince as the last broken rib poked me somewhere uncomfortable. I pulled up my shirt and saw it poking out under the skin of my abdomen. I gave it a sharp shove to snap it back into place. Then I leaned my head on the trunk of the car and pounded it with my fists for a couple of minutes while I whimpered every curse word I'd ever known and a few that I'd never tried before. When I stood up, there were a series of round, baseball-sized dents in the trunk of the Lexus.

Ogg looked at the car, then back at me. "Ginger is not going to be happy."

"Tell her it was a freak hailstorm," I muttered, stalking off toward the demolished entrance of the club. It looked like a grenade had gone off up there. Mangled metal and shattered glass littered the whole area. A pair of six-foot-tall planters lay on their sides with bouncers stuffed into them headfirst. One bouncer kicked feebly at me as I walked by, so I pulled him out of the huge concrete flowerpot. The other guy was out cold, so I figured it was better to just leave him there.

Sabrina was waiting for me inside what was left of the doorway, now just a gaping void surrounded by cinderblock and electrical wires. "Never a dull moment with you, Jimmy. I gotta give you that one."

"This wasn't my fault. I was busy getting my face kicked in by an elephant." I took her arm as I walked past, and headed right back to the bar. I ordered three doubles of Patrón and a beer chaser, and had two of the tequila shots burning their way down my throat by the time Lilith and the others made it inside.

Chapter 8

LILITH SLID IN next to me at the bar and downed my last tequila shot. I glared at her, reaching in my pocket for cash, but she shook her head at me and nodded at the bartender. Since I got the shots for free, I figured I wouldn't whine too much.

"Would you like to move this discussion to my office, James, or am I mistaken? Was your blonde friend only here for amateur night?" Lilith purred the questions in my direction, but didn't wait for an answer. We followed her down a hallway past the VIP rooms into her well-appointed office. Lilith had taken out the pole and small stage that Phil had in one corner of the office. She'd replaced it with a conference table and half a dozen high-backed leather chairs. I pulled a chair out from one end for Sabrina and took a seat near her with my back firmly pointed at a wall.

Abby and Greg sat, then Ogg tried to wedge himself into one of the remaining chairs. After a couple of unsuccessful attempts, he dragged a granite end table over and crouched more than sat on it. The troll loomed over the entire table, looking mildly ridiculous, but every time I glanced in his direction my ribs reminded me that he was anything but funny.

"Can I offer any of you a drink?" Lilith inquired from the head of the table. Ever the perfect hostess, she pressed a button on the wall and a leggy blonde came in to take drink orders. Sabrina and Greg passed, I requested a beer, and Abby asked for a bag of B-positive. The blonde returned with my Miller Lite, a huge mug of something foul-smelling for Ogg, and a glass of amber liquid I presumed to be scotch for Lilith. Then she sank to her knees in front of Abby and pulled her hair to one side. Abby looked around the table for a second, then shrugged and drank deeply from the girl. I smelled the fresh blood as soon as her teeth made contact, and took a deep swallow of my beer to keep my hunger in check. It's hard to drink beer when your fangs involuntarily extend. I managed not to spill anything on my shirt. Barely.

Abby pulled away from the girl's neck and looked at me with one eyebrow raised. I declined with a shake of my head, and she whispered her thanks to the girl who'd just offered herself up as a snack. The girl stood on shaky legs and left the room, hopefully to go lie down and maybe have a cookie or something. I looked at Lilith, and she returned my stare with one even blanker. We sat in silence for several long minutes before Ogg raised his hand.

"Yes, Ogg?" Lilith sighed.

"Ogg gotta pee."

I burst out laughing, which made Greg and Abby laugh, which made Lilith chuckle, which made Sabrina elbow me in my broken ribs, which made me collapse face-first onto the polished oak table, which made Ogg look even more confused.

Sabrina was the first to regain control of herself, probably because she never truly lost control. "Ogg, you can't leave this room until you answer my questions."

"Which means you shouldn't pee, either," Lilith hastily added. She looked at Sabrina and shrugged. "Troll urine is harder to get out of a carpet than blood, and there's no ScotchGard-ing that crap."

Sabrina's shoulders sagged as she saw yet another interrogation veering into territory never mentioned in the police academy, but she took a deep breath, set her shoulders, and soldiered on. "Ogg, what do you know about the death of Teresa Chapin?"

"Nothing," the troll replied.

"What about the disappearance of Veronica Moore?"

"What about it?" came the sullen reply.

"Where were you on the night of March 17th?"

"Here."

"Can anyone verify your whereabouts?" Sabrina was up now, prowling the room like a mountain lion, all lean muscle and danger.

"What's a *whereabout*?" The troll's head was on a swivel trying to keep Sabrina in his sight.

Lilith cut in. "I can verify that Ogg was here all night. Saint Patrick's Day is one of our busiest nights, and Ogg is one of my best bouncers. I'd never give him that night off."

"Sorry, Lilith, but you're not the most trustworthy alibi. Is there any proof that what you say is true?" Sabrina turned her attention to Lilith, and I reminded myself to be somewhere else whenever these two finally threw down. Lilith sat at the head of the table, all calm reserve and inscrutability. Sabrina stalked the room like a predator. It was a classic spider versus scorpion matchup, and I wasn't really sure who was who.

"I'm pleased you hold such a mediocre opinion of me, Detective. Of course there is video of the evening's activities. Would you like the entire club, or just the VIP rooms?" Lilith gave Sabrina a nasty smile that implied all sorts of naughtiness.

"I'm not interested in voyeurism, just proof that Ogg was on the premises all night."

I raised my hand and said, "If I could get a copy of those VIP-room tapes, it would be great."

Sabrina said, "Crap."

I could almost see the wheels turning in her head. Ogg was our best lead, but not only did he have an airtight alibi, I actually believed it.

Greg raised his hand, and Sabrina nodded to him. "Not to be stupid or anything . . ."

"Not that you've ever let that stop you." I couldn't resist.

He went on after taking a moment to pause and flip me off. "But isn't there a different question we're all forgetting to ask?"

"Yes. Feel free." Sabrina made a confident "go ahead" gesture with one hand as if she was two steps ahead and already knew what Greg would ask.

"Ogg," Gregg started. "Why did you have human jawbones in your possession?"

"Ogg bought them," the troll replied.

The non-trolls at the table exchanged confused looks. The troll's answer, while probably completely honest, didn't clear anything up. Greg followed up with the next logical question. "Why did you buy jawbones?"

"Ogg wanted teeth." An apt statement, since getting any information out of the troll was like pulling teeth. I gave Greg my best "let me hit him" look, but he just waved me off.

"Why did you want teeth, Ogg?"

"OggMarie make necklaces and earrings out of teeth. Sell for big money. Ogg trying to save up for place in the suburbs to make OggMarie happy, so we pinching pennies. Pennies scream if you pinch hard enough." The troll actually chuckled at that. I got just a hint that there was something buried deep behind that stupid demeanor. But just a hint, then he was back to being stupid.

I sat back down at the table and put my head in my hands. "So we've got a crafty yet fiscally conservative upwardly mobile henpecked troll buying human jawbones to make girl-tooth necklaces. Somebody please explain to me how this is a better use of my time than me being drunk in a graveyard?"

"At least you're not littering," Abby said, reaching over to give me a pat on the shoulders.

Sabrina continued pacing, more a frantic stomping around now than the measured stalking she'd been doing. "So now what? We know Ogg didn't kill these women, so who did?"

She turned to the troll. "And more importantly, Ogg, where did you buy the jawbones?"

"At the Goblin Market."

Sabrina froze in mid-step and turned to look at the troll. Lilith leaned forward as if to slap the green-skinned goliath upside the head, and Abby, Greg, and I just looked at each other in confusion.

Sabrina spoke first. "What is the Goblin Market, Ogg?"

"Shut up, Ogg. One word and you're fired, and you know what OggMarie will do to you if you lose another job. This interview is over, and I'd like for all of you to leave." Lilith stood and pointed at the door. Nobody moved. She repeated the gesture, with similar effect.

I stood up and put a hand on Ogg's shoulder. The troll was just sitting there, staring up at Lilith in terror at the mention of his wife. "Don't worry, big fella. She didn't mean it. Did you, Lilith? Ogg's not really going to be terminated for cooperating with the lawful authorities, is he?" I put as much weight into my words as I could, but it's hard to intimidate a woman who remembers Moses before he had a beard.

"Cooperating with the lawful authorities is listed in my employee handbook as a termination-level offense, Black. But no, I won't fire Ogg. But you all have to leave, now. No one here will tell you anything about the Goblin Market. We've already said too much."

"But you haven't told us anything!" I protested.

"That's the point. And that's all I will tell you. Now get out of my club." She pointed toward the door again, and this time I felt a little push behind my eyes. Suddenly the desire to get out of that room and not come back for a long, long time was almost overwhelming. I looked around for Greg, to see if he felt it too, but he and Abby were struggling to get through the door at the same time, a fight that was going very poorly for Abby. I gave my head a sharp shake, but the feeling didn't slacken. Greg had finally pushed his way past Abby and through the door, freeing up that logjam. Abby was hard on his heels. Sabrina was almost at the door with them, and it took everything I could muster to grab hold of the table with one hand and draw my Glock with the other.

"Lilith, don't make me shoot you," I said through gritted teeth. She glared at me, but said nothing. I leveled the gun at her left leg and squeezed the trigger. Lilith moved faster than any living creature I'd ever seen, and faster than more than a few dead ones as well. She snatched the bullet out of the air and flung it back at me hard enough to put a hole in my leather jacket. I poked a finger into the hole to make sure she hadn't managed to actually hurt me, but the crumpled bullet just fell to the carpet, all its energy apparently expended.

I was kinda glad I hadn't actually shot Lilith, and even more glad that my attempt to break her compulsion had worked. Greg and Abby were standing just outside the office door looking at one another, probably wondering how they'd gotten there. Sabrina had stopped just inside the room.

I just stood there staring at the immortal woman and said, "This is my favorite coat, you know."

"And this is one of my favorite legs."

"Then we understand each other. Now will you stop screwing around in our heads and let us get the information we need, or will I have to go through a whole clip?"

"Sit down." She waved me to the table and retook her seat. I did the same, leaving my pistol on the table. Lilith raised an eyebrow at that, and I gave her a little shrug. If she was going to play mind games, I figured I needed to keep my artillery handy. I had no illusions about actually being able to hurt her, but the experiment of a moment ago proved distraction was good enough to screw up her mojo. I'd take it. The others took their places around the table, sharing worried glances. When everyone was settled, I turned back to the troll, who had never moved.

"Ogg, tell us about the Goblin Market."

He shook his enormous head, and I repeated the request. He shook his head even more forcefully, and a few long strands of troll-slobber escaped from his bottom lip. I picked up the Glock and pointed it at his kneecap. "Ogg, tell us about Goblin Market or I'm going to start shooting you. These bullets are cold iron bullets, so they've got a better chance of killing you than anything else I can think of. But even if they don't, they're still bullets, so they're going to hurt like hell. And I have a lot of bullets. So either start talking, or I'm going to have to recarpet Lilith's whole office."

Ogg looked at me with a furrowed brow, then grinned and said "Oh! Ogg get it! You have to do new carpet because Ogg bleed all over the old carpet." His smile disappeared, and a coldness flashed across his face that sent a shiver down my spine. "Ogg not like that idea."

"Then tell me about Goblin Market."

"Uh-uh. First rule of Goblin Market is no talk about Goblin Market."

Another facepalm moment and I had only met this guy tonight. Usually it takes weeks for someone to become this irritating. Ogg was verging on world-record status here. "Ogg, that's *Fight Club*. And it's a movie. It's not a real thing."

"Actually, it was a book first, by Chuck Palahniuk," Greg chimed in.

"I know that!" I said, motioning for him to be quiet.

"No, you didn't. I know better. And really, Jimmy, it's not like you're a big reader."

"I read!" I protested. My partner is admittedly the smart one, but I'm not a total Neanderthal.

"What was the last thing you read?"

"*Transmetropolitan.*"

"What was the last thing you read that wasn't a comic book?"

"Shut up." I turned back to Ogg. "Now, about Goblin Market."

"What about it?" the troll replied. I still wanted to shoot him, just a little, but I thought Sabrina might object. Or worse, that Lilith might.

"What is it?" I asked with a deep sigh. I braced myself for some kind of half-assed non-response, but Ogg surprised me.

"It's where you buy stuff. From the goblins."

"What kind of stuff?" Sabrina asked.

Lilith finally contributed to the conversation. "Anything you want. Jawbones for necklaces, extra years to live, baby's breath, stardust. Whatever you want, you can get it at the Goblin Market. You need a love potion? Goblin Market. You want a cloak which will let you walk between raindrops? Goblin Market. You want a lampshade made of human skin? Goblin Market."

"But cheaper on eBay," Ogg added.

"So this is where you bought the jawbones?" Sabrina continued.

"Yeah. I got a guy. He save them for Ogg."

"Saves them from what?" I had a feeling I didn't want to know, but I asked anyway.

"From man-brain stew. He buy heads from some other dude, makes yummy stew, but no meat on a jawbone, so he save them for Ogg."

Sabrina looked horrified; Greg looked grossed out. Lilith looked smug, but Lilith always looked smug, so I had no idea if it had anything to do with Ogg's revelation or if it was just her face. Abby looked fascinated, and I felt a little queasy, but also just a little bit hungry. And that made me *even more* grossed out. I leaned in to Ogg. "You're going to take us to see this brain stew guy. We need to talk to his supplier."

The troll shook his head. "Uh-uh. Ogg can't go back to Goblin Market. And wouldn't take humans if he could. Bad for humans there. Lots of things there don't like humans."

"In case you missed it, I'm not exactly human anymore, Ogg."

"Don't matter. These things hate vampires more than normal humans. They call you wingless bats." Ogg's shoulders shook a little at that, like he was holding back a big laugh. I was less amused.

I reached over and grabbed Ogg's chin, getting a fistful of slimy flesh and troll spittle. "Ogg, let me be very clear. You will take us back there. You will take us to the guy who gives you your jawbones. Or I will put so many bullets through your head that your face looks like moldy Swiss cheese."

Ogg looked me straight in the eye, all hint of goofy troll guard gone. In his eyes I saw the monster all the faerie tales talked about, vicious, intelligent, and absolutely not interested in taking orders from a skinny vampire with a big nose. When he opened his mouth, it was like I was hearing to a whole different monster.

"Take your hand off me vampire, if you want to keep it. I've had enough of your stupid questions, enough of your condescension, and enough of this ridiculous charade Lilith calls a 'job.' Lilith, I quit. I'm going home. Vampire, if you value what passes for a life for your miserable carcass, you will stay far away from the Goblin Market."

Ogg took my wrist firmly in one hand and removed my hand from his face. I thrashed the best I could, but I couldn't even think about breaking his grip. The troll stood up, released me, and stepped to the center of the office. He made a few strange gestures with his hands, and a glowing yellow circle appeared out of thin air. Ogg turned back to Lilith, gave her a very formal bow, and stepped to the circle. As he was about to step through, he paused and looked back at me.

"Remember what I said, vampire. The Goblin Market is no place for you or your people. Ignore this warning at your peril." Then he stepped through the glowing circle and disappeared. I got up to run through the circle after him, but crashed into the iron bar of Lilith's outstretched arm. She clotheslined me like vintage Hulk Hogan, and for the second time tonight my feet kept going while my shoulders and head stopped cold. I flopped to the carpet on my back and the air *whooshed* out of me in an explosion of profanity.

"What the hell did you do that for?" I demanded once I'd regained both oxygen and my feet.

"If you're going to get yourself killed chasing after him, I don't want it coming back on me. Ogg was a very good servant, and now I have to find a replacement. I will not have you starting an inter-dimensional war in my office on top of that. You have inconvenienced me quite enough for one night. Now get the hell out of my office."

I thought about pushing it, but took a good look at the fire in Lilith's eyes and decided that I may have pushed enough things for one night. I got up with all the dignity I could muster, which wasn't very much, and headed for the door. Greg and Sabrina were right on my heels, but Abby hung back. I looked at her, and she waved a hand for me to go on without her.

"I've got a couple of things I wanted to talk with Lilith about. I'll meet you guys out front." I didn't move for a minute, not liking anything about those two getting chummy, but Abby waved a hand at me, and I turned around, muttering about snotty kids these days. Sabrina laughed and grabbed my arm as we made our way past rooms with loud music and even louder guttural noises coming from them. The club was much busier than it had been when we first arrived, and I had to push my way past several dancers and a couple of drunken patrons on my to the door.

One of the drunker guys took exception to me blocking his view of the stage, and decided to get in my face. He reeked of sweat, stripper perfume, and stale Mexican food, and that's what I could smell from three feet away. When he got up close and started poking me in the chest and slurring things about my manners, I was done. I grabbed his wrist and squeezed, hard. The snapping of a couple of bones brought the slovenly asshat to instant sobriety, and I pulled him even closer. I looked deep into his eyes, and spoke with all the power of my mojo behind me.

"You can only be aroused by fetish porn of women over the age of seventy dressed up in animal costumes. This fascination with furry GILFs will continue for seven days from right now. You will find nothing appealing about any woman who isn't old enough to drink Ensure for every meal until the week is up. Now get out of my way and learn some manners." I shoved him back into his chair and made it the rest of the way to the door without incident.

"Man, that was harsh," Greg said as he joined me at the door.

"Grandmas need love, too."

"Yeah. But that wasn't a punishment for him, it was a punishment for *them*. Now the town's going to be full of old ladies getting perved on."

"Only for a week. Just be glad I didn't take away his attraction to women altogether."

"Can we do that? Make somebody switch teams like that?"

"Of course not, bro. Being gay is a choice, remember? Don't you watch Fox News?" Greg stared at me for a minute, then we both cracked up.

Sabrina walked up just then, her sidearm in her hand. "Jesus! I thought I was going to have to shoot my way through there. I haven't been groped that much since I wandered into a mosh pit in college."

"Glad somebody got lucky tonight," I grumbled. I waved the valet over and mojo'd him into getting Abby's car without the ticket. I wanted to hit the road, and if the blonde bimboshell was going to get all cozy with an immortal pseudo-succubus, she might have to find another ride home unless she surfaced pronto. I didn't have to feel badly for stranding her. Abby sauntered out well before the Escalade made its way around.

"What was all that about?" I asked.

"None of your business," was the flat reply.

"I think it might be, Abby. Lilith is dangerous, way more than you know."

"I don't think you know anything about her, and you don't know much more about me. So why don't you just crawl back inside a bottle and leave me alone." I jerked my head back like I'd been slapped. That one actually stung a little. I got in the backseat of the Escalade without saying another word, just trying to figure out what I'd done to get Abby so upset.

Chapter 9

IT WAS A QUIET ride back to our place, but when she pulled up in front of the house, Abby didn't turn the engine off. "Everybody out," she declared, putting the SUV in reverse and holding it in place with the brake.

"Where are you going?" Greg asked.

"Don't worry, Greggy, I'll be home before dawn this time. I promise. But I've got a couple of errands to run, so I'll see you later, okay?" She was at least still being nice to Greg.

I tried to let it slide, but it's not in my nature, so of course I opened my mouth before I had any idea what I was going to say. "Errands for Lilith?"

"Errands. If I want you to know more, I'll tell you. Now are you getting out or do you want to ride along and watch?" I opened the back door and stepped out to stand by Greg and Sabrina. We stood in our front yard and watched Abby slam the Escalade into gear and peel out onto the highway, slinging a little gravel in my direction as she did so.

I watched her go, feeling uncomfortably like the parent who just let his prom queen daughter go to her first rock concert unescorted. After a few seconds of brooding, I yanked my mind back to the problem at hand, namely this mysterious Goblin Market and somebody selling human jawbones there. I walked up the steps to the house, in past Greg, and headed down the stairs to the den. Sabrina was already there, leaning over the tabletop computer thingy and working her Google-fu. I grabbed a beer and gestured with it at her, but she waved me off. Silly sense of duty and propriety.

I was just about to pop the top on my beer when Sabrina's cell rang. I looked at my phone, saw it was after nine, and set the beer down. Greg stopped halfway down the stairs and we blatantly eavesdropped on her conversation, which consisted of a lot her saying "yes, sir" and "uh-huh." She finished with an "I'll be right there," and clicked off. She looked up at us and said, "Did you two get all that?"

I ticked off the high points on my fingers. "Missing couple. Abandoned car in mall parking lot up by the lake. Baby in the backseat. Responsible parents otherwise, so it looks like it's one of ours."

"That's the gist of it. Let's go."

"Got any idea where?"

"Yeah, we're going back to where the bones were found. If this is a fresh kidnapping, that's where he's going." She pulled her jacket back on and headed up the stairs.

"Or it." I added, following her.

"Huh?"

"That's my line. Or *it*. Whatever we're after probably isn't human. And it probably isn't on our side of the river, either. So you call ahead for a boat, and I'll get some reinforcements." I started punching numbers into my phone as we headed down the porch steps to Sabrina's car.

"Should I call Abby?" Greg asked.

"No," I said. "She wants to go off and do her own thing, we should let her. She made it abundantly frickin' clear that she had plans for the night that didn't include us, so we'll fill her in when we see her again." I slid into the passenger seat and dialed my oldest living friend, something I hadn't done often enough lately.

Father Mike Maloney answered on the third ring, sleep coating his voice and making him sound way older than his almost forty years. "Hello?" It sounded so un-Mike-like that I actually checked the number on the screen before I spoke again.

"Dad? That you?"

"James? How are you, my son?" He sounded better, at least until he pulled the phone away from his mouth to cough. There was a nasty rattle going on there, the kind you read about people having. People that are dying. I pushed those thoughts aside and forced a cheer into my voice that never made it onto my face.

"I'm good, Dad, how are you? The drugs working okay? Sounds like you got into the medicinal weed again."

"I'm much better, thank you. The chemotherapy is doing wonders to shrink what's left of the cancer cells, so they tell me. The drugs are ... difficult, but I'm managing. They do make me very tired, though." This was bad. This was the guy who less than a year ago had literally stood with me and Greg against a demon, and now he was tired before Leno came on? Crap and double-crap.

Mike had been diagnosed with cancer of the esophagus a couple months ago, right about the time everything in our lives turned upside down. Since finding out our best friend was maybe terminally ill, Greg and I had acquired a roommate who drank more blood than both of us put together, had our house burned down, gone to Faerieland, and almost gotten killed a couple of times. I still found time in there to feel bad about not visiting Mike more.

"Glad to hear that, old buddy." I put a little extra teasing stress on the "old" part. Mike, Greg, and I were all the same age and had been best friends since middle school. Mike was the only one who looked his age, but if his voice was any indication, he might be looking a lot older than he really was nowadays. "Mike, we need help. If you're not able to come out, that's cool, but we really need you to drum up a little support, and the support we need kinda hates me."

"You mean Anna. What can I do?" I could hear him pulling on pants in the background.

"I need you to get Anna to meet us out by the rafting center. I'll text you the address. Tell her she's gonna want pants for this one. And boots that she doesn't mind throwing away at the end of the night." Anna was a witch friend of Mike's from a comparative theology quilting bee or something. She hated my guts, and suffered Greg only slightly better. But she was a real witch, with plenty of juice backing her up and a full coven, so she was useful.

We blew through town with Sabrina's dash light going, making it up to the crime scene in half the normal time. A familiar dark sedan pulled up a few minutes later, and Sabrina waved them through the police tape.

I stomped over to Mike's car. "You shouldn't be here. You're too sick."

"That's what I told him. But for some reason he's very loyal to you two abominations," Anna said, stepping out into the mud. Anna was dressed in jeans with fishing boots on, a good choice by my best guess.

Mike got out of the car in his priest uniform, except he'd added a set of ridiculous-looking but very practical hip waders. That wasn't the problem; it was everything else about how Mike looked. To put it bluntly, he looked like crap. His hair was gone, and Mike was not a guy who could pull off a bald look.

Worse than the hair was the way his skin hung off his face. Mike had been pudgy all through school and adulthood, and the scholarly life of a priest had blown pudgy up a little, to say the least. Now his usually round face was stretched, with jowls and deep wrinkles around his eyes. His skin had a peculiar yellow cast to it, too, like jaundice but not quite. But it was the smell that brought tears to my eyes and made me quickly turn my head to look out over the river. I could hear from the sharp intake of breath beside me that Greg was right behind me and smelled it too. I gave Mike a hug and held on tightly for a minute, then felt Greg's pudgy arms reach around both of us in a kind of group hug that would have normally made me a little uncomfortable, but right then felt like the only thing we could do. I felt the hitch in Greg's breathing as he hugged me, and I pushed them away. If he broke down right now there was no way I was going to hold myself together.

I pulled back, keeping one hand on Mike's shoulder, and repeated, "You shouldn't be here. This could get serious, and you're sick."

"Yeah, you look terrible, Mike. What do the doctors say?" Greg asked from beside me.

Mike looked at me for a long minute before answering, and we both knew the score. "I'm doing as well as can be expected, Gregory. Now what's going on out here that you've got to drag me away from *American Idol* to consort with heathens like this fine young lass." He always leaned a little heavier on his hint of a brogue when Anna was around. I thought, not for the first time, that she might be the one to make him regret his vows.

"Well, since you're here . . . We've got a problem, Dad. Anna, thanks for coming. We really need some help on this one." I reached out a hand, and she shook it limply. Anna made no secret of the fact that she wished I would take a long walk into a beautiful sunrise, but I needed her expertise, so I didn't bite her. It didn't stop me from wondering if witch tasted like other humans, or if it was true what they say, that witch tastes like chicken.

"Always happy to help the police, Black." I noticed that she never said she was happy to help me, but I let it slide.

"Fine, whatever. There were some remains discovered near here, and we have reason to believe that the murders took place on that island over there." I pointed across the river to a small wooded island formed when the river split for about a quarter mile. It was maybe the size of a football field, but no more.

"And what are we supposed to do about that?" Anna asked. She stood with her arms crossed and her chin out. I knew from past experience that nothing about dealing with her was going to be easy, so

I took a deep breath and spit it out.

"What do you know about something called the Goblin Market?" I jerked a thumb back over my shoulder.

Anna went white. And I'm not talking just a little blanch, I'm talking she was suddenly paler than me, and I haven't seen the sun in this millennium.

Slowly, I continued, "Because we think the Market is over there, and we think it's the reason at least two women are dead and another couple is missing."

She looked around like the bogeyman himself was going to jump out at her from the tree line, and she skittered back from the water's edge so fast she lost a boot and went tumbling backward. Lucky for her, I was paying attention, because I vamped out and caught her before she did herself any permanent harm. She didn't even get her foot muddy, because I had her standing upright again before anyone else noticed what had happened.

"Are you okay?" I asked. She looked up at me with big eyes and nodded. I stepped back slowly, keeping an eye on her to make sure she wasn't going to do anything else crazy, like try to move. "What's wrong?"

"The Goblin Market is over there?" she whispered. She took an involuntary step back and almost lost her balance. She caught herself and stood stock-still, staring across the water like she was expecting Jason, Freddy, and the Loch Ness Monster to come out of the darkness and eat us all.

I nodded. "That's our best guess, anyway. A pair of human jawbones were found out here, and the guy who bought them told us he got them at the Goblin Market. That seems like the most likely place."

"Then we have to get the hell out of here, now!" Anna hissed. She kept looking around like the ground was going to boil over with rats, spiders, and snakes at any moment. I'd seen Anna exorcise spirits from a dozen zombies in one night, but I'd never seen her spooked like this.

"We can't leave until we get into the Market and rescue the missing couple," Sabrina said from behind me. I nodded and crossed my arms.

Anna shook her head again. "Maybe you can't leave, but I'm out of here. I'm just a witch, I can't deal with the kind of things that go to a Goblin Market."

I held out both hands to her. "And we don't want you to. We

don't want you to deal with anything. I wouldn't ask you to fight our battles for us, Anna."

"Then what do you want me to do?"

"We just need you to open the door for us," I said, trying to use my best "everything's okay" voice on the terrified witch. I was starting to think that maybe this shopping trip was going to take the top spot on my list of Really Bad Ideas.

Chapter 10

"NO WAY." ANNA had regained her balance by now and was standing firm. "No way in heaven, hell, or any other dimension am I opening up a portal to Faerie for you to use to go to the Goblin Market."

"Is it that dangerous?" Mike asked.

"Michael, the Goblin Market is the most wondrous and deadly place you could ever imagine. It's the beautiful snake that has venom that could kill you ten times in a second. It's the lovely orchid that gives off a scent that makes people drop dead from just one whiff. It's . . ."

"We get it." Sabrina cut her off. Anna opened her mouth to protest, but Sabrina held up a hand. "We get it, Anna. And we don't care. We have to go. Lives may be at stake."

"Oh, they are, Detective. What you don't understand is that the lives at stake are yours." Anna was as scared as I'd ever seen her, but her pale face took on a greenish cast as Sabrina whipped out her cell phone and held it in front of the witch.

Sabrina opened the photo app and slid her finger across the screen as she spoke. "This is the car that David and Elizabeth Carmichael were snatched out of this afternoon. This is Andrew, their eight-month-old son who was left in the backseat. This baby had his parents snatched out of his life right in front of him and was left in a parking garage for hours without food, water, or changing. And his parents might still be alive somewhere on that island. You are the only person we know that can get us there and get this baby's parents back alive. Now suck it up, witch, and open the goddamn portal!" I looked at Sabrina, shocked. There were tears standing in her eyes. I resolved to push a little further on this subject later. Much later. When she was unarmed.

Anna took a deep breath and nodded. I said, "Does that mean you'll do it?"

"Yes, I'll do it. I hate it, but I'll do it."

I thought about saying something stupid to lessen the tension, but decided that Anna would probably just turn me into a frog. "Now, what's the plan? Do we need candles, because I'm all out. And a little skittish around fire. You know, the whole combustible vampire thing and all."

"Shut up, Black," Anna said with a laugh. "You're a moron, but at least you're amusing. First we need to get to the island."

"I have a boat," Sabrina said, waving a uniformed officer over. He spoke into a radio and a few minutes later a pontoon boat pulled up just offshore. "We'll have to get a little wet."

I looked at Anna and Mike in their hip waders and wished, not for the first time, that I could have been born smart instead of just pretty. They trudged through the mud and the shallow water and clambered up the aluminum ladder off the side of the boat. Sabrina looked down at her hiking boots and wrinkled her nose. "Look at it this way," I offered. "Now you have an excuse to go shoe shopping. And you're a chick. That's like an excuse to breathe to you, right?"

"Contrary to popular belief, Jimmy, not every woman loves shopping for shoes. Although I've never met one that doesn't. And I could use a new pair of boots." I laughed and scooped her up into my arms, then took two running steps and leapt out over the water onto the deck of the boat. Sabrina looked up at me and gasped.

"I'm impressed," she said when I set her down.

"So am I. I usually miss the boat on the first try." I reached out to help Greg over the railing as he fell just a couple of feet short on his long jump attempt and ended up crumpling the rail and almost going backward into the water. I grabbed the front of his shirt and pulled him the rest of the way over, then got out of the way as the uniform climbed up the ladder and moved to the cockpit. I looked under cushions and in the fish well, but came up empty.

"I don't think you'll need a life vest, Jimmy. It's a pretty short trip," Sabrina teased.

"I don't need a life vest because I've been dead since you were in middle school. I'm looking for the beer," I shot back.

"Why would there be beer on a police boat?" Mike asked.

"Look at this thing, Dad. It's not a police boat, it's a friggin' party barge! There's gotta be a six-pack on here somewhere." I got the laugh I wanted out of Anna and Mike, then went to sit next to the witch. She didn't stand up and move to the other side of the boat immediately, so I knew she was more nervous about what was to come than she was dedicated to pointing out how little use she had for me.

"Come on, Anna. It can't be that bad. I've dealt with dangerous stuff before. I mean, can it be worse than going into a dragon's lair and the dragon sneaking up on you?"

"Yes."

"Worse than getting shot in the heart by an evil faerie and then getting put into a cage fight with trolls?"

"By a mile."

"Worse than fighting an archdemon who wants to bring about Hell on earth?"

"No, I'll give you that one. But you had an angel for backup that time."

"And this time I've got you. I know you're scared, but it'll be okay. I promise." I reached out and patted her on the knee.

She grabbed my hand like it was something dead, which technically it was, and smelly, which it was not, and moved it off her leg. "That would be great if I had any faith in you, Jimmy. But you're an idiot. Just try not to get Mike killed. It would really mess up my karma if I had to curse you." I had a feeling she wasn't talking about turning me into a toad or anything nearly that gentle, so I got up and walked to the other side of the boat myself.

"That went well," Greg said as I leaned on the railing next to him and Sabrina.

"Bite me."

"No thanks." The boat ran aground with a gentle thump, and I grabbed Sabrina and hopped over to solid ground again. This time when Greg overbalanced I just let him land on his ass in the mud. Served him right for making fun of me. I did at least put out a hand to help him up. The cop driver lugged a couple of cases of battery-operated crime scene lights to the edge of the boat, and I hopped back over to give him a hand. He showed me how to set them up and get the area at least partially illuminated while the others made their way ashore. Greg and I didn't need the light, and I was pretty sure Anna could make plenty of light on her own, but I decided I might as well let the poor guy feel useful. He was about to get a serious introduction to the man behind the curtain, so I let him think the world was normal for a few more minutes.

Anna walked slowly away from the boat. Her head was back, long hair streaming behind her. She had her eyes closed and her hands reaching out in front of her and to the sides, feeling her way like a blind person, only somehow different. It was like whatever she was feeling for wasn't in our world, but another one. I felt magic tickle my skin and the hair on my arms stand up. I knew there had to be some serious hoodoo floating around this place if it triggered what little sensitivity I had. I looked around, and the cop who drove the boat was the only one who looked unaffected. Greg was shaking his head like a Labrador that got a noseful of pepper. Mike was off to one side of Anna about twenty feet away, leaning heavily against a tree. He was glowing a little, bathed in a pleasant white light that was sharp and somehow warm at the same time. Sabrina wasn't suffering any obvious physical effects, but the cross she wore under her T-shirt had started to glow a bright green, maybe somehow attuned to the faerie magic. I'd seen holy objects glow white or red around demons, but never green.

I stepped up behind Anna, my Glock in hand like I thought it would do any good against anything magical. I had three magazines for each gun with me: one loaded with normal hollowpoints, one carrying silver-jacketed rounds dipped in holy water, and one packed with cold iron rounds. Despite my bravado with Ogg, I'd never fired the cold iron rounds, not even at the range, so I was a little nervous about them. I'd had these specially crafted by a guy I found online who claimed he could even make bullets out of wood. That idea made me a little nervous, so I paid him for the cold iron rounds and then paid him that much again to take the wooden bullets off his website. After I bought a case, that is. I didn't know if they'd work like a stake through the heart, but figured it was worth a try. He agreed to stop selling wooden bullets for a small fee, roughly the gross domestic product of Belize. I paid him. I put it on a credit card, figuring there was a good chance I'd outlive the bank it was issued by. And I was only *slightly* exaggerating.

"Here," Anna said, stopping abruptly in front of me.

I stopped myself before I ran into her, figuring since she already didn't like me I shouldn't dump her in the mud. "What do we do?" I asked.

"You get back. Mike, I need you." Mike pushed himself off the trunk of the tree and shambled over. He walked like a man in his seventies, not almost forty. But he hopped to when Anna spoke, and as he reached her side he pulled out a pair of holy symbols from under his priest's collar. One was the crucifix that I'd watched his mother give him the day he was confirmed. I remembered that like it was yesterday, because it was one of the only times I went to Mike's church. I was raised Protestant, so the Catholic Church was full of mystery to me. I thought it was cool, all full of incense and chanting in a forgotten language. Mike was confirmed, and then his mom gave us five bucks each to get banana splits at the old Dairy Queen on Central Avenue. Those were the best banana splits in the world. Now, seeing that crucifix around Mike's neck, I could smell his mom's Aqua Net hair spray again, feel myself sweating through my dress shirt in the back of his dad's gigantic Caprice Classic, and taste the extra cherries I wheedled out of the DQ guy.

The other symbol was unfamiliar but glowed the same color as Mike and his crucifix, so I figured God was okay with the dual identity thing. It was silver, a circular design with Celtic knotwork all over it, and a sense of great age about it. By the way Mike handled it and how Anna looked sideways at him, I knew this was a holy symbol, but not necessarily something that was specifically Catholic. I stepped back again, not because I'd been told, but to get close enough to a tree that I had some cover in case things went bad. Because things always go bad after the holy symbols come out.

Chapter 11

ANNA HELD HER arms out to the side and started chanting. Mike stood right behind her and started a chant of his own. This one I recognized. While Anna was chanting who knows what in whatever witchy mother tongue she spoke, Mike recited the Lord's Prayer in Latin. Anna's hands started to glow a bright yellow. Mike's white glow moved from all around him to center on his hands. All the while they kept chanting, and glowing, and chanting, and glowing, until finally their hands blazed like tiny stars, and I had to holster my pistol to cover my eyes. I heard the uniform muttering under his breath and realized that he and Sabrina were praying, too.

The chanting stopped abruptly, and Anna spoke in a strained voice. "The portal is open. We should go through quickly. I don't know how long I can hold it."

I brought my hand away from my eyes and saw, sure enough, a glowing portal hanging in the air right in front of where Mike and Anna were standing. On the other side of that portal was a very big, very mean-looking troll with a battle-axe longer than I was tall. The troll took one giant step through the portal and raised his axe to chop Anna in half. I dove for her, knocking both her and Mike to the ground, out of the path of the axe. We hit the ground in a tumble of arms, legs, and irritated witch as the axe slammed into the turf right behind my back foot. The portal winked out of existence with a loud "pop," and the troll turned back to bellow at the empty air.

"Great. Two troll fights in one night. I love my life," I muttered as I tried to get myself untangled from Anna and Mike and get to my feet before I was cut in half by the pissed-off, and now stranded, troll.

I got lucky for once. The troll had swung so hard trying to chop us in half that he had a hard time digging his axe out of the sucking mud. I was on my feet, drawing the Glock before he had dislodged his weapon, and Greg had him flanked on the other side. Sabrina and the boat-driving uniform took the other compass points, and the troll growled at us.

"Don't do anything stupid," I said. "I don't really want to kill you."

"Too bad, human. I really want to kill you!" He bellowed, yanking his axe free of the mud and charging me. I got off a couple of rounds before he reached me, then dove off to the side away from where Mike and Anna were still trying to get to their feet. Sabrina and the patrolman emptied their magazines into the troll, but it only seemed to irritate him. He swung back around with the axe, and I rolled aside again. This time he took out two small saplings and almost decapitated Sabrina, who dove out of the way at the last minute.

I'd fought trolls before, hand to hand even, but this guy was the Hulk Hogan of trolls, if there was such a thing. I don't mean he wore a yellow wife-beater and had a funky mustache. He was big, bad, and tough as hell. I fired off a couple more rounds, this time aiming at a knee in hopes that his joints were weaker than the rest of him. The round just clanked home with a sound like shooting steel plates. My bullets found their mark just fine, the only problem was the mark was pretty much impenetrable. The shots to the knee did cause the troll to stumble, which gave me enough time to clear out of his immediate strike zone.

I looked back at the uniform and waved him over. "Get Anna and Mike out of here. They don't stand a chance against this thing."

"And you do?" he asked, eyes wide. I felt the air moving behind my head and dove forward, taking the cop down with me. The axe whistled through the air where I'd just been standing and the troll let out another howl of frustration as the force of the axe swing spun him.

"Do you stand a chance?" he repeated.

"Probably not. But do it anyway. Greg, you got any bright ideas?"

"Cold iron?"

"Yeah, that's about what I thought."

The troll had turned his attention to where Mike and Anna were trying to take cover in a stand of trees. He was working his way through the trees with a savagery that would have made Paul Bunyan proud.

"Hey, green teeth!" I yelled. "What did those trees ever do to you?" I stood about thirty feet from the troll when he turned and charged me again, but this time I stood my ground as long as I could. My Glock barked sharply, and three bright yellow holes appeared in the troll's chest. The creature stopped dead and stood straight up, looking down at his chest.

He poked one of the holes with a giant finger, looked back at me, and screwed his face up into something I almost recognized as pain. The troll stood there for a second, said "Ouch," and fell over backward.

"Nice shooting," Greg said, stepping up beside me.

"Not really. I was aiming for his head. These cold iron bullets tumble worse than silver. Makes them drop six inches over ten yards."

"That sucks for accuracy, but you got him." He held out a fist, and I bumped knuckles with him.

I walked over to Mike and Anna, who were making their way out of the woods. "You guys okay?"

"We're fine, Black. But there's no way in hell I'm opening that portal again." Anna snarled.

"We need to get over there. And besides, this dude, if he was the guard, is dead. And none of us even got a scratch on us. If he was an innocent bystander, what are the chances we'd open on another one."

"Uh, Jimmy?" Sabrina said from behind me. "You might want to rethink your optimism."

I turned around to see the eight-foot troll standing behind me with a very angry look on its face. Admittedly, I think every expression on a troll's face looks angry, but since he had the whole nostril-flaring, spit-flinging, eye-bulging thing going on, I'm pretty sure I was right about his feelings. Especially considering the number of times I'd shot him.

"Ouch," the troll said slowly, pushing at the wounds in his chest. After a few seconds of mashing around in there, three misshapen chunks of iron popped out of his chest and landed with a splat in the mud. The troll looked up at me and grinned. I knew my night was about to take another turn for the worse.

"Run," I whispered to Mike and Anna. "Get to the boat and get the hell out of here. Get Sabrina and that cop, too. Drag them off if you have to. Spell them. Whatever. There really need to not be any humans here in about eight seconds. I can't look out for any of you while I try to take this thing out."

I heard them take off and heard Greg's forty-five spit four quick thunderclaps into the night. The troll lurched forward, propelled by the force of the bullets, then spun around, lashing out with his axe. Greg got an arm up to block the axe handle, or the swing would have taken his head. As it was I heard the crunch as both bones in his right arm broke and saw Greg go flying several feet before he hit the ground with a wet thud. I saw Anna and Mike splash toward the boat while Sabrina and the uniform laid down cover fire. The troll didn't even take notice of their slugs hitting his broad back. He'd already turned his attention back to me. Just what I needed—a partner with a compound fracture and seven hundred pounds of pissed-off faerietale creature hell-bent on ruining my manicure. If I got manicures, which I don't. But you get the idea.

"Troll, I told you not to do anything stupid. And there you had to go and hurt my friend. Now why don't you open that portal back up and get your slimy green ass back to Faerieland, where you belong?"

I saw the pontoon boat pull away from shore while the troll was staring at me. Mission number one accomplished—get the humans to relative safety. Now for mission number two—make sure the vampires don't get smeared to toothpaste by the Big Bad. Greg staggered to his feet behind the troll, but I waved him off. His arm was hanging limp at his side. I could see he was going to be no help.

I whispered, "Get to the trees and drink something. Even a squirrel will help."

He nodded once and slid off into the woods where he wouldn't be a distraction. My attention returned to the troll as he threw his axe to one side and pulled a pair of long knives from his back. Not a sheath on his back—the sheath *was* his back. No wonder Greg's bullets didn't do any harm—they hit the troll in his swords. Crap, crap, and double-crap.

"Come on now, Greenie, we don't want to kill anybody," I said, completely ignoring the fact that I was holding a pistol with now twelve rounds of cold iron ammunition and he had a pair of knives that were each longer than my forearms. He started to twirl his blades faster, making a whooshing sound that quickly grew into almost the whirr of helicopter blades. Only sharper, and with points on the ends. And coated with troll blood, which undoubtedly had some things growing in it that I couldn't spell on my best day. This was probably going to hurt a lot.

He suddenly lunged forward with a double thrust, and I had to jump back to keep from becoming a vamp-kebob. Just like the bouncer at the club earlier, he'd been playing dumb and slow, because now instead of a lumbering brute with a battle-axe, I faced a giant ballet dancer-cum-ninja with a pair of razor-sharp blades and mad close-combat skills. He followed his lunge with a slash to the sky, and I was forced to jump backward, twisting my ankle as I landed awkwardly. He slashed at my midsection, and I leapt into a backflip. I came down heavy on my left leg with a curse, and rolled to the side as both swords slashed down at my head. I moved fast, but the troll had developed super-speed that would make the Flash hang up his winged baseball cap if he saw it. The beast planted both swords in the turf and used them as a pivot, lashing out at me with both feet and connecting like the world's smelliest wrecking ball.

Both size-thirty-three feet slammed into my chest, and I felt a couple of things pop. I tumbled ass over teakettle through the underbrush and slammed into a tree. I lay there for a couple of seconds looking at the pretty birdies circling my head until I remembered that there was a monster trying to kill me. By that time the troll was back on his feet, swords in hand, and headed my way. I scrambled to my feet and looked around for an exit strategy. Or an air strike. Or a small thermonuclear device. Or the 101st Airborne. Any of those three might stand a snowball's chance of slowing this beast down, but I sure didn't. All I saw was a bunch of trees, mud, and a giant green monster that wanted to dissect me, then kill me. He reached me the same time I realized there was nowhere to run, and he came at me with a furious combination of slashes, thrusts, and cuts that would have turned me into sushi if I'd still been standing where he expected me to be.

Instead, I was looking down on him from a tree branch twenty feet straight up. It took Greenie a few seconds to realize I was gone, and by the time he looked up, I was on my way back down. I hit the ground five feet behind the troll, dropped to one knee, and emptied my magazine into the back of his kneecaps. The cold iron ripped into his flesh and spewed troll bone chips and yellow blood all over the trees. I danced back out of the way as the troll toppled over backward, writhing in pain as he grabbed at his knees. I looked down at the monster as he lay on his back and flailed at me with one sword like a really ugly, dangerous turtle.

"I guess there's no chance you'll just magic open a portal and leave me alone, is there?" I knew the answer before I even asked the question, but I figured I had to give him a chance.

The troll rolled over and started crawling toward me on his

shattered knees, using one sword as a crutch and flailing at me with the other. "I will crush your skull and pick my teeth with your spine, little Sanguine."

"That's what I figured." I reached down into my ankle holster and pulled my back-up gun. I swapped out magazines and put six cold iron rounds in his face. He toppled over into the mud and lay still. I picked up one of his swords with both hands and cut off his head with one clean stroke. I danced back and fell on my ass in the mud trying to avoid the spurt of blood from his neck, getting myself probably dirtier in the process than if I'd just let him bleed on me.

I heard a weak chuckle from behind and looked around. Greg was leaning against a nearby tree, his Colt 1911 in his hand. "I'm glad you carry a spare pistol. I'm not sure I could hit the broad side of a barn right now." He looked like crap, but he'd splinted his arm, so that was good. We heal really fast, and if he hadn't gotten the bones straight, we'd have to re-break it later. And that would suck.

"I don't need you to hit a barn, bro, I just need you to call Sabrina to come back and pick us up. I think we might have to call this a night. We've only got a couple of hours left 'til sunrise, and now we're both beat to hell."

"Yeah, I can't fight anything else tonight—I can barely stand."

"And for me, well, it's a good thing I only have to breathe to speak, because I think I've got a bunch of broken ribs. Maybe a punctured lung. So can you make the call?"

"Yeah, no problem. But why don't you call? I'm sure she's at the top of your speed dial."

I didn't answer, just held up my shattered cell phone for him to see. I'd landed on it at least a couple of times during the fight, and it was long gone. A few minutes later Sabrina got back with the party barge, and we headed back to our place. We were all congregating on the porch watching Greg dig his keys out of his pocket with the opposite hand when I noticed the uniform had followed us.

"Uh, look dude, I'm sorry about this, but . . ."

He held up a hand and cut me off. "I know the deal, Mr. Black. I know what you guys are. I know that we're dealing with something out of the ordinary, and I want to help."

"Officer . . ."

"Nester. Michael Nester." He stuck out his hand, and I shook it. He extended his hand to Greg, who gestured apologetically at his dangling arm and finally wrestled the door open.

"Officer Nester, I'm not sure what you think you saw, but I assure you . . ."

He cut me off again. "I know. I know. These are not the vampires you are looking for, or whatever. Look, Mr. Black. I've known about you and your partner for months now, ever since Detective Law started working with you. And I haven't outed you yet. I've actually run interference for Detective Law a few times with the lieutenant, although she didn't really know about it. My point is, I want to help. I had a sister that disappeared when we were young. She was in high school, I was in like fifth grade. I think she might have been one of the ones taken to this Goblin Market. The timing fits with the 1991 kidnappings. You can trust me, and I want to help, so please, don't do the mind-wipe thing. Let me help you."

I looked back and forth from Greg to Sabrina, but they were no help. Greg was subtly shaking his head while Sabrina was nodding hers. This one was all on me. Finally, I sighed and said, "Whatever, just don't get dead. If I'm going to take in strays, I guess taking in armed strays is better than blonde strays with big boobs."

"Says who?" Greg said as he finally got the door open. We all spilled into the foyer and split up. Sabrina headed upstairs for dry clothes, Greg and I made a beeline for the beer and blood in the fridge, and Mike and Anna headed downstairs. I grabbed a couple of pints of blood and a six-pack of Miller Lite and headed for the downstairs war room, then noticed Officer Nester standing nervously on the porch.

"Come on in, Officer. We're the ones that have to have an invitation, not you." He gave me one of those startled looks that people give me when I remind them that I'm an undead creature of the night, then followed it up with the nervous "I hope he's not about to bite me" chuckle that I've grown accustomed to from my human acquaintances.

Nester followed me down the stairs and grabbed a seat with his back to a wall. *Smart guy, guarding your back in a roomful of predators.* Or maybe he just knew that Greg liked to sneak up on the new mortals. My chubby partner clumped down the stairs after us, a straw in his blood bag like it was a juice box. He sucked the sides flat on a pint of blood before he made it to the basement, and pitched the empty into a trash can with a contented sigh. He'd regained what color he normally had, and the swelling in his arm was almost gone already. I gave him a quick look and thought that with another pint he'd probably be close to normal strength, if not quite fully loaded.

I was a little the worse for wear, too, and it was going to take at least two pints to get me back to fighting trim. The first bag pretty much took care of my broken ribs, but I needed every drop of the second bag to make the bruises, scrapes, and pulled ligaments go away. I thought about a third, but we were running through the rations pretty fast, so I grabbed a beer instead.

Greg was already at the computer table, with Sabrina leaning over it with him. I walked over to the couch where Anna and Mike were sitting. Mike had heated up this morning's coffee, and like a good Irish priest, he'd put a little something extra in it. I could smell the whiskey mixed with the rich coffee scent, but under all that I smelled Anna's fear. Fear so thick I could have broken a piece of it right out of the air and eaten it. I knew I wasn't getting her to open that portal again. But I had to try.

Chapter 12

"DON'T EVEN START, Black. I'm not doing it," Anna said the moment I sat down across from her.

"I know. It's too much for you. I should never have asked." I sat there for a second drinking my beer, hoping my reverse psychology would work.

"That's not going to work, Black. I know I *can* open the gateway between worlds. I just won't."

"I know. I just wanted to give you an out in case your conscience was bothering you."

"And why would my conscience bother me?"

"Because of the baby. You remember the kid in Sabrina's picture? The little boy who won't have any parents if we don't get through the portal to rescue them? I thought that might prey on you just a little. But, hey, good on you if that doesn't bug you. I mean, it's one thing for it not to bother me, but I'm a soulless undead monster. I figured being all attuned to the positive forces in the universe and stuff that you might be more sensitive than me. Glad to see I was wrong. More power to you."

"It kills me that I can't help that little kid."

"Won't."

"What?"

"You can, you already said that. You just won't. So don't sit there and give yourself an out. If you're going to insist on treating me like a monster every chance you get, you've got to own your own fangs and claws, too, sister. I'm fine being a monster, just don't pretend I'm the only one in the room without a soul." We stared at each other for a long couple of minutes without speaking. Mike drew a breath once like he wanted to speak, but I gave him a look that shut him up.

Anna looked up at me, her eyes rimmed with red. "I can't, Jimmy. I'm so sorry, but I can't do that again. When that troll came through the last time, I felt such an imbalance in the energy of our world . . . I just can't risk that happening again. If something even worse were to come through, or something that you couldn't deal with . . . I just don't know what I would do or what would happen to me. I'm sorry, I really am."

"Oh, shut up," a harsh female voice snapped. "You sniveling little witch. Open the portal, don't open the portal, but quit your whining. You make my teeth hurt."

I turned and drew my Glock in as smooth a motion as I could manage after the night I'd had, which wasn't saying much. Lilith stood at the bottom of the stairs, Abby right behind her looking smug. I relaxed a little when I saw who it was and returned my gun to the shoulder holster. Lilith walked over to me and perched on the arm of the sofa, patting me on the head as she walked by.

"Nice moves, little vampire. I think if you were in top form you might even have been able to shoot once before I ripped your head off. Now bring me a scotch," the immortal succubus said with a wave of her hand. I was halfway across the room before I realized I was being ordered around in my own house. Then I remembered exactly how much Lilith scared the crap out of me, and I went on to the bar and made her drink.

I brought Lilith's drink to her and asked, "What are you doing here, Lilith? I thought you were pissed at us?"

"I am. Ogg was an excellent employee. But your young friend here is very persuasive, so I reconsidered my position and decided to open a portal to Faerie for you." I stared at Abby for a minute, then crooked a finger at her. She was grinning like a Cheshire cat as I grabbed her by the arm and yanked her over to a corner of the room where the others hopefully wouldn't hear.

"What the hell are you doing?" I hissed at her. I tried to pitch my voice below the range of human hearing, but I was pretty pissed, so I might have failed.

"What do you mean? I'm helping. You made it clear I need to pull my own weight around here and be a team player. You need to get to Faerie. I made a deal with Lilith to get you there. What's the big deal?"

"What did you have to promise her?"

"Why does it matter? It's not a big deal, Jimmy. Chill out. And let go of my arm before I break your ribs again." She glared at me, and her blue eyes were cold. I was suddenly a little bit worried about taking her on. Abby was crazy strong for a young vamp, maybe even stronger than me.

I leaned in even closer and whispered, "It matters because she learned to lie from Lucifer himself, Abby. Lilith is a top-rate power, the kind that was around before people understood fire. She thinks in centuries, not weeks, and she could kill all of us without even batting an eye. So I'm a little worried about anything you might have promised her."

"Thanks, *Dad*, but you don't need to worry. I've got it handled, and she's going to open the gate for you. Now let go of me and be grateful for a change." She shrugged out of my grasp, and we walked back over to the sofas.

I turned to the immortal mistress of Charlotte's criminal underworld. "Thank you, Lilith. I appreciate your willingness to assist us."

"Think nothing of it, James. I like your little friend Abby. I think we're going to get along famously." She smiled at Abby, and I got a sudden chill.

"Let's do this, then," I said. "Hey guys, get over here. Greg, you all healed up?"

"Yeah, I'm fine." He didn't look fine, but I had to take him at his word.

"Well, let's go." I stepped to the middle of the room and looked around. Anna and Mike were still on the couch, obviously going nowhere.

As the others moved, Lilith held up a hand and people froze. Maybe if I live to be a bajillion I'll have that effect on people, but I doubt it. "No one goes on this little jaunt but Black and the fat one." Lilith stood silent for a few minutes while Sabrina and Abby voiced their disagreement with her plan, but eventually the ladies quieted down, and Lilith continued, "I wasn't opening the floor for debate. I was telling you what was going to happen. I can only open a small portal to the lands of the Fae, and I can only hold it open for a very short time. Only two may pass." She looked over at me and Greg. "Try not to screw things up too badly. I'd hate to have to live through another Ice Age because you two morons pissed off Queen Mab."

"No problem, Lil. I'll be on my best behavior," I said.

"That's what I'm afraid of." Lilith waved her hands and a glowing yellow circle opened up in the middle of our den. Greg and I looked at one another, shrugged, and stepped through the door to Faerieland. Again. Hopefully, this time we wouldn't come back sparkly.

Chapter 13

WE STEPPED INTO an open space the width of at least four football fields, with dark forest at our backs, facing what I assumed was the Goblin Market. What looked like wild-growth thornbushes and hedge surrounded the whole complex. There was no gap to be seen anywhere. Nothing had ever grown that dense and that uniformly compact in the history of the world. Of course, we weren't in the world anymore, so all the rules might be out the window. One rule that had already been tossed was the whole "vampires burn in sunlight" thing. Just like our last trip to Faerie, it was apparently the middle of the afternoon, yet Greg and I stood in the bright pink sunlight without any ill effects.

Yeah, I said pink sunlight. Milandra, the Queen of the Faeries, was a total girly-girl, with the love for all things pink and purple that came with it. So the sky was pink, with big puffy lavender clouds. The grass was green, and yellow, and electric blue, and every once in a while a patch of rainbow clover would pop up. All in all, it was like walking through a box of Lucky Charms. The hedge was green and brown with inch-long thorns that looked razor-sharp. The edge of the forest was about twenty feet from the hedge, which ran in both directions for several hundred yards. If this thing was anywhere near as long as it was wide, finding anyone inside was going to be very difficult. Once we got through the hedge, that was.

"Well, boy wonder, you got any ideas how to get inside?" I asked Greg.

"Well, we could try to go through, which is probably a bad idea."

I looked at those thorns and agreed. "We could try to go over, but I've got a feeling that would not produce positive results, or we could walk in one direction until we find a door."

"Or we could wait right here until somebody comes along and follow them inside," Greg said, pointing to a dirt path coming out of the woods right behind us. The path was faint, but I could see the track two wagon wheels had cut through the dirt recently enough that rain and wind hadn't erased the evidence.

"We don't know how long that will take."

"We don't know how time moves in Faerie, either. It might already be next week for all we know."

"Good point." I agreed. "Well, we have to do something, may as well try Plan A."

I took a moment to make a mental note of the time and date for my diary, thinking this was probably going to turn out worse than most of my bad decisions. Then I looked at the hedge, took a deep breath more for effect than anything else, and made a running leap at the thorn wall. It only looked ten or twelve feet high, and I should have been able to clear it easily. And I did. Clear twelve feet, that is. Unfortunately, that height wasn't enough once the wall reacted to the intrusion. The wall inexplicably grew taller, grabbed me with its thorns, and bodyslammed me to the turf. All the air went out of my lungs in a pained *whoof*, and my injured ribs pitched a fit that could only be matched by a junior–high school girl with a zit on her nose on school picture day. I lay there on the ground for several moments, looking up at the purple clouds and thinking how much they all looked like My Little Ponies.

"You okay?" Greg asked. He leaned over me and shook his head. "Man, you gotta at least yell out 'Hey Y'all! Watch this!' whenever you're going to do something remarkably stupid. Otherwise, why did we bother going to Clemson?"

I flipped him the bird, then held up a hand for him to pull me to my feet. I dusted myself off and kicked a little dirt into the Jimmy-shaped impression in the ground, then flipped off the wall for good measure. The whole hedge shook, as if it was alive somehow and laughing at me. Obviously, the hedge was female, based on its reaction to me.

"Okay, now what? And whatever it is, you're trying it first," I said to Greg while I limped around and popped various shoulders, ribs, and other body parts back into place.

"I think we just go inside."

"I just tried that. But feel free to try it your own self."

"No, I mean I think we just walk toward the hedge and expect it to open for us. After all, we're magical creatures, too. There's no reason the Market wouldn't see us as customers, and it stands to reason that the hedge wasn't created to keep real customers out, just the suspicious ones trying to break in."

I shot him a dirty look and said, "Fine, but you're going first."

Greg walked up to the hedge like he belonged there, and damn if he wasn't right. The vines and bushes parted for him, and he walked right through. I followed close behind him, and the wall of thorns stayed open for me to pass through, although it did seem to intentionally reach out and snag my arm if I slowed down too much. We walked through what felt like ten feet of hedge, but I suspected a trick of the magical wards. Finally, we emerged on the other side, and I stopped cold with my mouth hanging open.

The Goblin Market looked like a cross between old Las Vegas and a psychotic farmer's market. There were neon signs blinking everywhere, flashing brightly even in the blinding sunlight. The sky wasn't pink anymore, just a vast expanse of blue with a huge yellow sun beating down. It was crazy hot, like Egypt in July hot, but I didn't break a sweat. I was pretty sure my sweat glands were dead, but if anything would test them, it was this place. Sand blew everywhere. We saw rows and rows of tents, tables, and booths covered in unidentified foods, animals, weapons, clothing, and a few things I couldn't even imagine the purpose of. The aisles, if you could call them that, were just packed down lanes of sand between the booths. And everywhere creatures yelled for attention and money. The signs flashed, the barkers bellowed, and dozens of types of mysterious animals cried out.

My super-sniffer was assaulted with a plethora of smells like I'd never experienced, and the sensory overload of sight, sound, and smell almost brought me to my knees. Layers upon layers of scents filled the air: fae, troll, vampire, human, and other creatures I didn't recognize. Perfumes and spices wafted from the booths and tables, and there were food smells like I'd never imagined. It was kinda like a cross between a cooking show and a haunted house. I couldn't figure out where to look, so I just stood there, turning around in circles and getting jostled from all sides.

Throngs of beings crammed the aisles—human, faerie, ogre, and other things I'd never seen before. A man walked proudly through the Market wearing scimitars crossed on his back. At least he looked like a man from the neck down. He had the head of a Bengal tiger, complete with fangs. I discovered the fangs when I got in his way and he snarled at me. I stumbled back and bumped into an ogre browsing food at another booth. He shoved me absently away, which sent me almost sprawling into the dirt. Greg caught me and pulled me off to the side out of the way of traffic. We stood in front of a stall selling trinkets, pretending not to freak out while I quietly freaked out.

"Dude, we are so not in Kansas anymore," he said, trying to be subtle while still looking in every direction at once.

"Yeah, no kidding."

"And you'd better keep that to yourselves if you ever want to see Kansas again." A voice came from beside my left elbow. I looked down and saw a four-foot-tall lizard standing there. He looked like a chameleon, except for being four feet tall, standing on two legs, wearing a tailcoat, and talking.

I try to be open-minded, especially when I'm in Faerieland, but I'll admit the talking lizard made me jump a little bit. And maybe yelp a tiny bit. Or maybe I jumped about eight feet in the air and screamed like a little girl. One of those.

"Why do we need to keep our origins a secret?" Greg asked. I hate the fact that he takes things in stride better than me. And he's smarter than me. I take solace in the fact that I have a girlfriend, unlike certain male vampires that live in confiscated fraternity houses in North Carolina.

"Oh, no one cares that you're from the mundane world, my dear Sanguine. Everyone can see that within a breath of laying eyes on you. But you don't want the vendors to find out this is your first Market. They'll fleece you terribly if they catch on, and you won't have a gem left to your name before you even find what you're looking for."

"Oh, we're not here shopping," I said.

The lizard held up a hand. "I never mentioned shopping, sir. I said before you find what you're looking for. And everyone is looking for something, now aren't they? So what, dear vampires, are you looking for?"

Greg punched me before I could answer. "I think, my unnamed friend, the question is what are *you* looking for."

"Not to mention who are you?" I chimed in. Greg shot me one of his "let me deal with this" looks, and I stepped back, digging for sunglasses in my jacket pocket. After our last trip to Faerieland, I went out and bought a pair. Wearing the glasses wasn't just about looking like a badass, they were also a necessity. My eyes hadn't been exposed to sunlight in fifteen years, I *needed* a pair of shades. Cool was just a bonus.

"I am Martifluousyntherianthemum Gregorovichinglingaringding-dingdong, but you may call me Marty. I wish to assist you for no reason other than the goodness of my cold-blooded little heart. And because this is my uncle's stall, and if I give you information hopefully you will leave quickly and allow the real customers access."

I could understand that motive—greed, and said so. The lizard nodded and went on. "You are obviously from the world of Man, so you are likely unfamiliar with the rules of common courtesy in the Market. I can help you learn these rules so you are less likely to be killed."

"For what price?" I growled.

"Simple. When you leave Faerie, take me with you."

"What?" Greg and I said in unison.

"Seriously, dude, how many lizards do you see around here, talking or otherwise? I need to get some action, and it's not happening in Faerie. Besides, there might be a few entities in the Market that aren't very interested in my well-being at the moment. Or, to be more precise, they are very interested in my well-being, that is to say, in the less well and perhaps ending of my being."

I took a minute to try and parse the sentence, then realized that he said somebody wanted to kick his ass.

"I am not pimping out a lizard. That's . . . ," Greg spluttered. I elbowed him and pushed in front of him to shake Marty's hand.

"If you swear not to eat or harm humans, that's just fine, Marty. When we leave, we'll take you with us. But you're not living with us. We're vampires, not an animal shelter. You're out on your own as soon as you get through the portal, deal?"

"Deal. I wouldn't live with vampires anyway. You'd only cramp my style."

I took a look around to see if anyone thought it was strange that I was talking to a waist-high lizard in a tux jacket, but none of the passersby had even given us a second glance. "So, Marty. If you wanted to buy a jawbone in this Market, where would you go?"

"What type of jawbone are you looking for?"

"Human."

"*Hmmmm* . . . there are only a couple of stalls in the Market that sell human bits, and they're quite expensive. Wouldn't you be better off getting a jawbone yourself? After all, there are plenty of humans where you come from."

"We're not looking for a jawbone, Marty," Greg said, looking around nervously.

"Well, if you're not looking for a jawbone, why are you asking me where to buy one? Is this a test? Oh, I do love examinations! Let me see, you want to know if I'm truly worthy of your time and trust, so you're asking for a purveyor of parts just to see if I truly know the lay of the land. Very wise, good sirs, very wise."

"Yeah, it woulda been, if I'd thought of that," I said, putting a hand on the excited lizard's shoulder. He'd started thwacking me with his tail at the first mention of a test, and I needed to calm him down before he did one of us serious injury. I hadn't seen anybody that excited about taking a test since Greg got his first trigonometry exam. My partner was captain of the high school math team. Seriously, his nerd-fu is off the charts.

I patted Marty on the shoulder and leaned down so we were at least eye-to-collarbone. "Marty, we're not looking for a jawbone, but we're looking for someone who sells jawbones. Someone has been kidnapping humans from our world, and we need to find out who and then we need to stop them."

"Oh! Then you want *fresh* jawbones! Well, that's a whole different color unicorn, as the saying goes. There are lots of places to get garden-variety old, stale jawbones, but if you want fresh jawbones, there are only two places to look. We are looking for human jawbones, right?"

"Yes," I confirmed. Again.

"Well, then, I suppose we should start with Doctor Orbly. He is likely to have harvested a human or two for his experiments, so we'll start there." Marty darted out into the throng of people with an agility you wouldn't expect from a lizard in formal wear. Greg and I turned to follow, and Greg stepped right into the path of a giant *something*. The something couldn't stop in time, and it smacked into Greg with a wet thwack like a cooked ham hitting a tile floor on the way to the Thanksgiving table.

Greg staggered back a couple of steps and looked up at a huge, shaggy beast with a protruding lower jaw and curved fangs sticking out between its lips. The thing grunted and took one step back, then stepped forward and glared down at my partner. "Get out of the way, bloodsucker!" It stuck out a huge paw to backhand Greg into the middle of next week, but I caught its wrist before he picked up much momentum.

"I don't think so, pal," I said, looking up at the thing. "My friend is sorry for getting in your way, but that's no reason to go hitting people."

"I feel like hitting someone! That's all the reason I need." And it drew back a fist and threw a haymaker at my face. I stepped sideways, stuck out a foot, and gave the monster a little shove in the small of the back as it barreled past. It landed face-first in the dusty walkway, rolled over and did a perfect kip-up to a ready position—then stopped cold as it saw my Glock six inches from its face.

"We're leaving. You're not going to try to jump us from behind. You're not going to challenge us at all. You're going to go on your merry way, and so will we. And if I ever see you again, I'm going to shoot you in the face."

"You dare break peace-bond in the Market? You're crazier than a werejaguar in a catnip field!" It turned and ran, and I holstered my weapon. I turned to see where Marty had gone, and found myself face-to-face with four very angry-looking faeries holding swords. One had his blade at Greg's throat, and the other three were pointing weapons at me. I knew from past experience that I wasn't going to be able to shoot all three of them before they killed me, so I just put up my hands.

"Um . . . Hi?" I said.

One of the faeries stepped forward and beat his right fist against his chest. He was a little taller than the others, gorgeous, with cheekbones you could slit your wrists on, a dimpled chin, and curly blond hair. Blue pupil-less eyes glittered at me like giant sapphires, and I felt my heart race. Then I remembered everyone's warnings about the beauty of the Fae, and all the warnings not to fall in love with one. Then I remembered that I like chicks, and managed to curb my baser instincts. His armor had a couple extra stripes on the shoulders that the other guys didn't have, so I assumed he was the sergeant or ranking fae. "By the orders of the Ancient Ones, no weapons are to be drawn in the Market on penalty of death. One infraction is allowed without punishment. What is your name, offender?"

"Jimmy Black," I said, thinking that maybe he'd heard of me and might cut me some slack. We'd done a couple of favors for the Queen of Faerie a while back, including setting things up for her to live happily ever after with her beloved dragon.

Apparently the faeries aren't networked, because the sarge just looked me up and down and said, "You may go, but know this, Sanguine. You draw steel in the Market only on pain of death. We do not tolerate violence within these walls."

As usual, my mouth started to operate without any involvement from my brain. "So if I need to kill someone, drag them outside the fence, is that the deal?"

The faerie stared at me for a second, then burst out laughing. "Indeed, Sir Sanguine. If you must kill someone, please remove them from the Market first." He stuck out a hand, and I reflexively grasped his.

"I am glad to see that we understand each other. Now, please move along. There is much to be done, and I must return my men to their work." The faerie gave my hand a firm shake and led his troops on through the Market.

I stared at their backs, jaw hanging open. Apparently, I had narrowly avoided starting a huge inter-dimensional incident. For a change. Greg stepped up beside me, eyes wide, and Marty crawled out from under a nearby fruit stand, brushing dust off his waistcoat as he did so.

"Dear sir, I apologize most sincerely for not informing you of the penalties for drawing a weapon in the Market. Had I any inkling you were so unfamiliar with local custom, I never would have let you wander about with your hands unbound." The little lizard's tail was twitching again, but this time just the tip and much more slowly.

I took this to mean some type of embarrassment, so I patted him on the top of his head. "Don't sweat it, Marty. I'm used to stepping on my own junk in new places. It's what makes being me so exciting."

"And what makes being your friend so terrifying," Greg muttered.

I shot him a look and turned back to the somewhat mollified lizard. "Now Marty, you were talking about going to see a doctor about human jawbones?"

Marty jumped, his tail twitching faster than ever. "Yes, yes, yes! We must go see Doctor Orbly! If there is one creature in the Market likely to have fresh jawbones for sale, it will be the doctor."

I danced back to save my ankles from a thrashing and asked, "What exactly does he do with the jawbones, Marty?"

"Or the rest of the people?" Greg added.

"I'm sure I have no idea. But the doctor is a wise man, very wise, and he does great things. Very great things. We should go to him at once." Marty started off down an aisle in a bizarre hopping stride. Apparently lizards were never intended to walk on two legs, or wear tuxedos, so the strain of doing both at the same time was making Marty walk like an old cartoon character. Of course, half the things around us looked like they were imagined by George Lucas and the other half looked like Jim Henson creations. I never thought I'd find a place that made Greg look normal, but this was it. This and anime conventions. I smothered a laugh and started after our little green guide.

"What?" Greg asked as he fell into step beside me.

"Just thinking that if he breaks out a ukelele and starts singing 'Rainbow Connection,' I'm gonna lose it."

"Pay attention. I don't think I trust our guide."

"Why not? He's just looking to get a little tail. I figure that's the oldest motivation in the world, so I can kinda buy it."

Greg gave me his patented "my partner is a moron" look. "Isn't it a little too convenient that he happened along right as we showed up? Don't you think he might be the Goblin Market's equivalent of the guy waiting at the bus station for the cute girl from Kansas to land in LA?"

"And we're the cute girls?"

He nodded.

"Man, your imagery sucks. But I get it. He's probably working an angle. And not just one that gets him a nice square of swamp in Human-Land. I'll keep an eye on him. But for now, he knows people, and we don't. So if he can get us around in here without drawing Milandra's attention, that would be a pile of awesome."

"Why don't you want Milandra to know we're here? She could help us."

"Yes, but help from monarchs isn't usually stealthy, at least from what I've read in the funny books. And I don't think we have time to go to seventeen state dinners before our kidnap victims are rendered down to their component parts. Nor do we have time for a quest. We have a need for speed, and dealing with the court politics in Faerieland is not likely to get us out of here quickly."

"Well, when you put it that way, it all makes sense. Now where did the lizard go?"

I looked around and saw our little guide about a hundred yards in front of us. Marty was moving fast, and his head was barely visible in the distance, so I stretched my legs to catch up. I rounded a corner and found the lizard leaning up against a pole, one foot on the ground, one foot on the pole, filing his nails with an insolent posture that came straight out of an old James Dean movie. He even had the collar of his tailcoat popped. "'Bout time you got here," he sneered.

"What's gotten into you?" I glared at the snotty little lizard.

He immediately dropped the bad-lizard pose and fell back into what I had come to think of as "Normal Marty," where normal could be applied to a talking lizard. "I am sorry, oh Sir Sanguine. This is not the bestest area of the Market, and it may perhaps behoove one to appear to be more dangerous than one is. Unless one is, in fact, dangerous, as you are, sir."

As usual, it took me a second to untangle his sentence, but no time at all to recognize the thugness in the four guys that had come out of the alley behind him. I backed up into the main thoroughfare to give myself a little room to move, and took a look at our new friends. All four of them were mostly humanoid, but with pig heads and long, curved tusks jutting out from their lower jaws. They were garbed in what looked like scrapyard armor, with bits of chain mail showing between layers of hardened leather and what looked like pots and pans hammered flat and fastened on as breastplates.

The leader was the biggest guy in front, rocking a bright red Mohawk and steel points capping his tusks. He had fists the size of Christmas hams and huge, knobby knuckles that sprouted tufts of black hair from the backs of his hands.

"Martifluousyntherianthemum Gregorovichinglingaringdingding-dong, how good to see you." He had a surprisingly mellifluous voice for somebody that looked like a cross between *Star Wars* and *Mad Max*.

"K'thoth, fancy meeting you here!" Marty bowed so deeply that his head almost scraped the dirt, then scuttled around behind me. I looked down at the lizard, who looked back up at me with huge eyes.

"Help me," Marty whispered. I patted him on the head and hoped he was more reassured than I was.

"Our boss wants a word with you, Martifluousyntherianthemum," the one I now knew as K'thoth said. He still had that super-pleasant tone to his voice that just screamed imminent bloodshed.

"I'm sorry," Marty said from behind me. "I'm on very important business right now. As soon as I complete this quest, I will seek out Lord Buterin Great-Teeth and settle our accounts. I swear upon my tail."

"I think that's *my* tail, Gregorovichinglingaringdingdingdong. If I recall correctly, and I always do, you wagered that tail on a mundane sporting event several moons ago." I had to look way up past K'thoth's head to see where this new, high-pitched voice came from.

There was a squirrel with a red Mohawk of his own standing on K'thoth's head. The squirrel wore a leather jacket and a sword, but before I could draw any Reepicheep comparisons, I looked down at

Marty, who had gone so pale as to be nearly transparent. He was scared shitless of this squirrel.

"Lord Buterin Great-Teeth, I presume?" I asked the squirrel.

"Yes. And what is your business with this welcher?"

"He is our guide through the Market. We are on very important business, and Marty is essential to that. I'm sure he can settle any debt he owes you as soon as our work here is done."

"Unfortunately, that's not an option. Too many people are aware of Martifluousyntherianthemum Gregorovichinglingaringdingding-dong's debt to me and his reluctance to pay it in a timely fashion. If this is allowed to continue, I risk a decline in my ability to collect other debts. I'm sure you see the problem with that."

"I do, and I understand that this puts you in a very difficult position. But we cannot be delayed in our mission, and finding another guide would delay us greatly." Crap, now I was starting to sound like these guys.

"I don't care. K'thoth, bring me the lizard's hide for a new jacket," the squirrel said, then scampered down K'thoth's back and vanished into the throngs of the Market.

"Hey guys. Nobody wants any trouble here, do we?" I asked, both hands in the air. Marty nodded so hard I thought his head-ridge was going to flop off. Greg took up a position to my left and a few feet away, close enough to cover my weak side but out of the way enough that I could move freely.

"Seems like you've got trouble, Sanguine. Either give us the lizard, or we kill you too. Come to think of it, some fresh Sanguine blood would be excellent for my stew tonight." K'thoth licked along the edge of a huge cleaver he'd pulled from his waist.

"Now boys, I'm sure you know the rules against weapons at the Market," I said, looking around at the array of kitchen implements the hoodlums were polishing.

K'thoth grinned back at me. "What weapons? We just got our cooking tools. Ain't no rule about using our cooking tools, is there? And if you just happen to fall down on my cleaver, well, that's just bad luck, ain't it?" He laughed, and his friends followed suit. Everybody wants to laugh with you when you're the guy holding all the blades.

I whirled my head from side to side, looking for a handy alley to run down or a stall to hide in, or a friendly guard who'd come running at a scream for help, but there was nothing. The few stalls near us had hastily shut their tent flaps and covered their wares when the upcoming scrap became obvious.

"I think I get it," I said, drawing the KA-BAR knife from my belt. "And since I carry this knife to open boxes, it's not a weapon right? If you happen to impale your piggy little eyeball on my boxcutter, then that's just a freak accident." I heard the hiss of metal on leather behind me as Greg drew a pair of knives from his utility belt.

I smiled my most feral grin at K'thoth and stepped forward, feeling my fangs extend into view. I took a couple more steps forward and said, "Who's gonna be Daddy's appetizer?"

K'thoth lashed out with his cleaver, but his armor and general bulk slowed him down too much to ever get a clean shot at me. I sidestepped his clumsy slash and jabbed him in the armpit with my KA-BAR. A kick to one knee and another to his head left him sprawled in the dirt, out of the fight for the moment.

Greg charged a huge orc-thing with a warhammer, bowling his opponent over into the middle of the street. A few quick slashes of his "cooking knives," and the odds were much more even. The last two thugs looked at us, then the blood on our blades, and beat feet. I knelt beside K'thoth's head and grabbed his Mohawk. I put my blade near the base of the crimson ridge of hair and quickly chopped off the decorative hair. I grabbed a fistful of bright red hair from the ground and shoved it under his nose. "You tell the squirrel that Marty is under our protection, and if he ever hassles our friend again, I won't stop cutting with hair." The beaten K'thoth nodded, and I stood up. I let out a long breath and put my knife away.

Greg grinned at me and did the same, then looked around. "Marty? Where are you, buddy?"

The lizard came crawling out from under a nearby tent flap and brushed the dirt from his lapels. "Well done, sirs. I had no doubt that you would handle that situation with aplomb and dignity, and you did not disappoint."

"And just in case, you hid like a scared little girl?" I asked.

"I was preparing to leap out to your defense from an ambush position, of course!" Marty's tail twitched and his head-ridge flushed a pale pink.

I patted him on the shoulder. "Of course. That makes perfect sense. Good thinking, Marty. Now, we were going to see this Doctor Orbly?"

"Yes, yes, yes! He is right here, of course!" The lizard turned and waved grandly at the tent he'd been hiding in. I looked closer, still seeing nothing but a nondescript canvas front to a tent stall that looked for all the world like it was closed for the night. Marty reached out and knocked on a tent pole.

"What?" came a craggy voice from within.

"It is I, Marty. I return, bringing guests from another realm." The lizard pronounced, his little chest puffed out so far I began to wonder about the structural integrity of his cummerbund.

"So what?" the voice from inside shouted back. "I don't want any!"

Marty sagged a little, then stood up straight and rapped on the tent pole again. "Great Doctor, you agreed to give audience to my esteemed clients, the Sanguine from the mundane realm. I demand you grant us entry!" I looked down at Marty, who stood ramrod-straight, his head-ridge stiff and pulsing a faint reddish color.

"Oh," came the voice, much more pleasant this time. "Why didn't you say you'd brought the vampires for supper, Marty? Please come in!" The tent flap pulled back and I ducked inside, Greg right behind me. I had just enough time to think, *What was that bit about dinner?* And then we were inside.

Chapter 14

I LOOKED AROUND, feeling like I'd stepped into a *Doctor Who* episode. The tent was much larger than it looked from outside. What looked like a ten-foot-square tent on its best day opened up inside to at least twice that size, with a hallway leading off to the side of the room. There was a small sitting area to the left, and that's where I first spotted our host. He was a wizened little guy, kinda like Yoda without the green face paint. He had big, floppy ears that sat near the top of his head and bent over in front like a dog. His face probably started off as human, but it was the oldest human face I'd ever seen. At least the oldest-looking human face. Wrinkles deep enough to grow potatoes crisscrossed his forehead, and he had the reddish bulbous nose of an Irish town drunk. His huge pink lips flapped a little in the breeze as we opened the tent, and his eyes were set deep under his shriveled brow.

There were cushions on the floor, and I sat on one across from our host. The corner opposite us had a small chair and a desk piled high with books, scrolls, and scraps of parchment. The other entire side of the tent was taken up by a low table scattered with herbs, vegetables, clumps of meat that I tried not to think too much about, and a few flies and bugs crawling along. I gagged a little at the rancid stench rolling off the table, but even the rot of the meat dimmed in comparison to the thick smell of blood, old and new.

The table had blood soaked so deeply into the wood that it was almost black in the dim light. The center of the room was dominated by a giant cookpot, with a vent hood rigged along the center tent pole to take most of the smoke out of the tent. It couldn't clear everything out, so layers of smoke stratified the room in a pale bluish haze. The doctor had obviously been cooking, and it smelled *amazing*. Hints of pepper, curry, saffron, and thyme danced around the lightest dash of garlic and something I didn't recognized combined to make my stomach growl and my mouth water. Then I remembered what we were there for and my gorge threatened to rise. I pushed that thought to the back of my mind and waved for Greg to come sit by me.

"Doctor Orbly, I presume?" I said as I sat cross-legged on a cushion. Greg twisted himself around and landed with a small thump on the floor beside me. He heaved himself off the dirt and onto a cushion, and I turned my attention back to our host's answer. Marty picked a huge cushion in a corner of the tent, turned around three times in a circle, plopped down, and promptly went to sleep.

"I am Orbly. I am indeed. And what can I do for you young gentlemen?" His voice had an odd sing-song cadence to it that put me at ease almost against my better judgment.

"We're looking for someone selling human jawbones to a troll."

"And why would that be a problem? I understand that as cousins to humans you may find the practice distasteful, but I assure you that jawbones are not on the prohibited trafficking list. As a matter of fact, humans have no body parts that are forbidden to be transported between worlds. They are almost unique among semi-sentient species in that regard."

"I understand that." I didn't understand a word of what he was saying, but figured everything would go better if I pretended to. "But these jawbones are attached to the rest of the living human when they leave our world, and they come back into our plane by themselves. We need to know what is happening to the humans between the time they leave the mundane world and the time they come back as only jawbones."

"Well now, why didn't you say so?" He leaned back on his cushion and let out a thready cackle. "That's a much easier question, after all. They're eaten."

"Eaten?" Usually whenever somebody that isn't me mentions eating people, it means that I'm going to get clocked on the head and wake up somewhere unpleasant, so I stood up abruptly, looking around for the threat, but we were still the only things in the tent.

"Why yes, the rest of the human was obviously used for stew. There are several places here that serve it, but only one chef knows the best recipe. He claims that it has been handed down through generations of his family."

I sat back down, still keeping alert for large creatures with blunt instruments. "I'm sorry, I don't think I understand. You're saying they eat people?"

"Humans, not real people. We'd never eat a faerie, or a nixie, or a unicorn. We only dine on the unintelligent species that serve no other use than to nourish the higher life forms." The little guy reached over and sipped something from a cup. I gaped at him, and he offered a cup to me. "Tea?"

It was hard to argue with him, especially since I'd been preaching "top of the food chain" to Greg for a couple decades now, but the callous way he talked about humans didn't sit well with me. "I'll pass, thanks. I don't drink with cannibals."

His eyes went cold, and his ears stood erect on top of his head. "Not a cannibal, little Sanguine. Far from cannibal. Yes, I eat human. I eat many unintelligent species. Fish, human, cow, fowl. But I am no more human than you are, no matter how much we may appear to be. And what do you eat now? Humans. All enlightened species dine on the ones below them, it is the way of the universe."

I started to say something, but Greg put a hand on my arm. "Of course, Doctor. It is the way of the predator, after all."

"Exactly. I see you are much more evolved than your skinny friend."

"I've been saying that for years. Now, if we wanted to try this stew, where would we go?" I shot Greg a look, but he tightened his grip on my forearm, and I shut up. I might have whimpered a little, but I didn't speak. He had a helluva grip.

The little doctor's ears twitched as he thought about the best deli for human stew in the Goblin Market. I shook my head at my life. After a few seconds, he nodded and said, "You must go to the source. Your first taste of human stew should not be repackaged by some peddler, but straight from the chef himself. Marty, you know where the chef's tent is?"

Marty's head snapped up far too quickly for anyone who was actually sleeping, so I had no doubt the little lizard had been listening to everything. He said, "Yes, Doctor, I know it. It is near the center of the Market, the cook tent with dozens and dozens of tables, all full of goblins and trolls and orcs munching on nummy nummy human stew! Makes me hungry just remembering how to get there!" He rolled over on his back and patted his belly in a little rhythm.

"Thank you, Doctor. We appreciate all your help." Greg started to stand, but the little doctor whipped out an arm and yanked him back to his cushion faster than I could see. Greg glanced over at me and made a calming gesture. Didn't work.

"Is there a problem, Doctor?" I asked quietly, reaching slowly for my KA-BAR.

"No problem, only the small matter of payment. I have performed a service, I deserve recompense. Would you not agree?"

"Of course," I said. "What can we do for you in return for your valuable information?"

"I require a trinket from the mundane world. Give me something spectacular, something amazing, something I have never seen before! Produce magic for me, Sanguine!" He gestured wildly with both scrawny arms and almost fell backward off his cushion in his excitement.

I looked at Greg. He looked back at me and shrugged. "Magic is your field," I said.

"I've got my watch," Greg offered.

"Try it."

He turned to the doctor, his watch held out in his hand. "Take this magical timepiece from the world of man, Doctor. It indicates the hour and minute through precise movement of the magical mouse's hands under the glass." He pointed to the yellow hands ticking across the face of the watch. The doctor peered closely at the watch for a few seconds, then clapped his hands and fastened it around his own wrist.

"It is brilliant! This is truly an extraordinary gift, Sanguine. I wish you much success in your journeys." The doctor stood up from his cushion, although even standing he was only about three feet tall from ear tip to toe. Greg and I stood up and got out of the tent before we became beholden to the strange little creature for more than a watch.

Chapter 15

WE EMERGED BLINKING into the harsh sunlight of the marketplace. "Okay, Marty," I asked, "take us to the chef's tent. He's got some explaining to do."

The little lizard blinked up at me. "But you don't mean to attack the *chef*, do you? That would bring down the rage of the entire Market upon your heads, not to mention what it would do to the supply of decent stew."

"Marty, he's chopping up people and putting them into the stew. We can't let that happen. There are people in danger, right now, and we need to help them." I bent down and looked our guide right in his wrinkly green face. I wasn't trying to mojo him, just impress upon him the urgency of the situation.

"But why?"

"Why what?"

"Why must you aid these humans? They are not your kin. They are obviously poor warriors, if they were captured by the chef, so what possible use could they have in your world?"

I looked up at Greg. He gave me a "you're on your own" gesture and began studying the wares at a nearby stall. I racked my brain for a minute, but nothing in my experience had prepared me to debate comparative morality with a four-foot-tall lizard. I shook my head once, and then had an idea. "It's our job, Marty. We are tasked with defending the weaker humans from creatures more powerful than them. We're kinda like guardians, protectors of the innocent, that kind of thing."

"Like the Sanguine of the stories protected the Faerie Kings and Queens in ancient times? It's a quest? I'm important in a quest?" Marty asked.

I had absolutely no idea what he was talking about, but figured if it got me a couple steps closer to the chef's stew tent, it couldn't hurt. I nodded. "Exactly like that. We are carrying on the duties of our ancestors, only in the mundane world instead of here in Faerie."

"Oh, that makes sense then. Follow me." And again we were off, Greg and I dancing around pedestrians and annoying shopkeepers while trying to keep Marty's little plumed head in sight. He juked, bobbed, and weaved his way through an ever-thickening crowd until finally he came to a dead halt on the edges of a huge clump of people and things.

"Here we are!" trumpeted the little lizard. "This is the end of the line."

"End of the line for what?" Greg asked.

"This is the line to get the chef's stew, of course. We really should have gotten in line when you first entered the Market to get the first servings. You wasted an awful lot of time dilly-dallying around with Doctor Orbly if all you really wanted was some stew."

I ignored our guide's revisionist history and looked around. There were hundreds of faeries, ogres, trolls, humans, and some races I didn't recognize gathered around in a loose line. Every few seconds the line shuffled forward a few steps, bringing the mob closer to a huge tent some thirty yards away. The thoroughfare had been widened here to accommodate the traffic, and knockoff food vendors had set up shop along the route. Every few feet were sad-looking little tents with signs hanging out front proclaiming their stew to be "Just as good at half the price!" or "Lower in Fat and Gristle than the Chef's!" or even one that seemed to choose truth in advertising over any hope of making actual sales. On a crude hand-lettered sign were the words, "The Meat's not too rotten. And you're hungry!"

I pulled Greg out of line and off down a side alley. I looked around to make sure no one could overhear us and said, "We don't need to be in the serving line, we need to get around to the back where they cook up the stew."

"Yeah, we need to see if the Carmichaels are still alive, or if they were today's lunch course," my partner replied.

"I'm not even letting myself think about that," I replied. "Until we get some proof, we're here for rescue, not revenge."

"Okay, Pollyanna, whatever you say." The look on Greg's face definitely said that he didn't expect to find the Carmichaels alive, and I knew he was probably right. But I had to try. I had a lot to make up for before I'd be worth somebody like Sabrina, and saving the Carmichaels would be a step in the right direction.

"What do I need to do, oh great and powerful defenders of the innocent?" Marty asked.

I looked down at him and said, "When we get into the back of the tent, we need you to cause a distraction. Run into the front, where everybody's crowded around, and scream that you saw a rat or something."

"Why would I scream about a rat? Everyone knows that rat adds flavor, and they're cheaper than oregano." The lizard looked confused.

"Then think of something that would be disgusting to find in your stew, and scream that you found it." Greg explained calmly.

"Oh. Okay, I'll yell about potatoes or something. Yuk!" He screwed up his face and made his eyeballs bulge on command. There's something to be said for getting your assistants from another species—they have the most unique talents that you'd never, ever think of.

Greg, Marty, and I meandered through the maze of tents and vendor stalls until we had the rear of the cooking tent in sight. It was a massive thing, easily big enough to hold a hundred cots in rows. There were more than twice that many beings lined up through the tent now, all waiting for their chance at a nummy lunch. And we were about to wreck that chance. This rescue mission's crew could easily turn out to need a rescue mission of our own if we weren't careful.

Greg leaned over to me and whispered, "This is the part where you share your brilliant plan, right? Please tell me you have a plan. Better yet, please tell me you have a plan that is not just 'punch things until we get to where we need to be.'"

"My plan is a little more complex than that, but not much. Follow my lead." I squared my shoulders, rolled my neck, and started confidently toward the tent.

Greg grabbed my arm before I had made it three steps. "Please tell me you aren't stupid enough to be trying the health inspector gag. You have to know there are no health inspectors in Faerieland."

I stopped and looked at him. "Then what's your plan, Mr. Smart Guy?"

A facepalm later and Greg pulled me back into our side alley. "Were you really going to do the health inspector thing?"

"Nah. I had faith in you stopping me before I got too far."

"So you don't have a plan?" Greg asked.

"Since you don't seem to consider punching things until I get what I want a plan, then no."

"Okay, gimme a minute and lemme see what I can come up with."

Greg closed his eyes to think, and I shuddered at what might be going on behind his chubby little eyelids. After a moment his eyes flashed open and he grinned at me.

"You know if I pull this gimmick off you can never make fun of my utility belt again," Greg said.

"Let's not get ahead of ourselves, Chubby-Wan Kenobi. I might give you a week, but you'd have to get crowned King of the Faeries to get me to lay off your utility belt *forever*. What's the plan?"

"Not so much a plan as an item. This." He pulled a black cylinder off his belt and held it up with a grin. "We cut open the back of the tent, then toss this in and sneak inside in all the confusion."

"What magical item is this, Sir Sanguine?" Marty asked, his browridge vibrating in excitement.

"This is called a flash-bang, Marty. It makes a lot of noise, a bright light, and a little smoke to disorient enemies. I carry a couple of them in my utility belt for quick escapes."

"Or the opposite, in this case," I added. "Okay, Marty. Run around the front of the tent and start raising hell. We'll wait until everybody's looking at you, then try Greg's little firecracker here." Marty nodded and darted around the tent out of sight. A few seconds later we heard a commotion coming from inside the tent. I nodded at Greg and slashed a two-foot hole in the back of the tent with my KA-BAR. Greg tossed in the flash-bang, then turned away with his hands over his ears and eyes squeezed shut. I did the same, but even with my hands over my ears the noise was tooth-rattling. I shook my head to clear the cobwebs, and widened my cut in the tent into something Greg could fit through.

I ducked into the tent and blinked my eyes furiously against the smoke. I had cut the hole right into the area beside the serving line, so the space was crammed with beings of all shapes and sizes. Something big slammed into me and knocked me back a step, and I almost crashed to the floor.

Greg caught me and kept me upright. "Now you won't give me anymore crap about my night-vision goggles, will you?"

"I sure as hell will. You look like the Steampunk Marshmallow Man. Which way to the kitchen?"

He pointed off to the left, and I dove into the crowd, pushing and dodging my way across the tent. I vaulted the serving table and landed on a quivering goblin taking refuge from the stampede. I regained my footing and forged ahead into the kitchen. The "kitchen" was another, smaller tent butted up against the main serving tent. A lone goblin stood stirring a pot of stew and generally ignoring the fracas in the main tent.

The goblin looked up at us as we barged into the kitchen and stepped back, holding the huge ladle up like a sword. The goblin was about four feet tall, with deep green skin, three fingers and a thumb on each hand, and double rows of pointed teeth. This particular goblin was spectacularly obese, almost bigger in circumference than it was tall. Rolls and rolls of green flesh hung down over its waist, and huge turkey-necks of flesh hung from its arms. I couldn't really tell if it was male or female, and didn't have any interest in asking.

On a second table, a few feet behind the goblin, was a mound of human body parts, all cut apart and chopped into bite-sized chunks. I recognized a couple of thighs, a forearm, and what looked like it might have been a pair of buttocks but had now been reduced jiggly half-moons of flesh lying on the cutting board. The goblin grabbed a giant cleaver and brandished it at us, flashing all sixty-something of its teeth.

"What do you want? You're not here to eat, and if you think you're going to steal my recipe, you've got another think coming!"

"You must be the chef," I said, stepping closer. "We're looking for the most recent humans you kidnapped."

"And they'd better be unharmed, or you might end up in your own stew." Greg stepped up beside me and glowered at the goblin.

"You'd make a couple of good pots yourself, fatty." The chef shot back, waving the cleaver at Greg. "Who do you think you are, coming in here making threats? I run a respectable business here. I don't kidnap nobody!"

"So people just randomly show up at your doorstep and say 'Eat me!'" Greg said. I was getting confused by his attitude. I was always the "bad cop," now he was stepping on my shtick. I gave him an elbow, but he ignored me.

"I buy my meats from a legitimate vendor. Here's the paperwork! They're already dead when they get here, I swear it!" He reached over to another small table and grabbed a clipboard. He waved the clipboard in Greg's face and got more and more agitated. "I run a respectable business here, and all I ever get is Sanguine giving me shit! That ain't right! You eat people too, you just don't bother to cook them first! Now get out of my kitchen!" He took a step forward and brandished the ladle at us. After a second he realized what he was doing and swapped the ladle for the cleaver.

I stepped between Greg and the goblin before my partner got anything useful chopped off and said, "Look, chef. I apologize for the disturbance, but we really need to find these humans before they're chopped up and delivered to you. So can I see that clipboard for a minute?" I took it from the chef and read the address written there. "Where is this? In the Market?"

"Of course it's in the Market, you moron! What are you, a mundane?" A light flickered in the chef's eyes, and a slow grin spread across his face. "You *are* mundanes, aren't you?" Greg and I nodded.

"*Hmmm*, mundanes. And Sanguine, to boot." The chef mused softly, scratching his chins. "Mundanes so far from home, lost in another dimension, wandering through the dangerous Goblin Market with no rights, no protection from any of the beasties that live there, whatever shall they do?"

"That's starting to sound like a threat, Chubby, and I don't like threats." I put my hand on the butt of my Glock to drive the point home, but the fat little goblin just kept grinning at me with those pointy teeth. "What are you smiling at, Lard-ass? There are two of us and only one of you, and in case you hadn't noticed, we're a little bigger . . ." I yanked the emergency brake on that train of thought when I saw the goblin's smile grow even wider. "There are a lot of your little buddies behind us, aren't there?"

The chef nodded, then bellowed, "Get them! But I want them alive!"

I turned and saw half a dozen goblins massed behind us with various clubs, meat tenderizers, and cleavers at the ready. At the chef's command, they all surged forward at once, threatening to overwhelm us with sheer numbers in the first few seconds of the fight. Fortunately, Greg is crazy strong, and I'm a lot faster than I look, so we were able to block and parry long enough to get ourselves set shoulder to shoulder and start to fight back. I drew my Glock and fired two rounds into the forehead of the nearest goblin, then stared as the rubbery green flesh just collapsed in on itself and quickly spit the bullet right back out. The goblin I'd shot shook his head, wiped a trickle of yellowish blood out of his eyes, and swung his club at my knees again.

I jumped over his club and came down with my KA-BAR in hand. That put me a lot closer to the goblins than I wanted, but whatever magic they had going that made them bulletproof didn't extend to a slashed throat. The first one dropped, and I turned to see if Greg needed my help. He had two goblins on him, both with clubs, and he was using one goblin to block the other one's attacks. Obviously, these guys didn't fight beside each other very often, because they kept getting in each other's way. I turned back to face another oncoming beastie when I felt the air moving behind my head. A giant flash of light and pain exploded in my skull, and everything went black.

Chapter 16

I CAME TO WITH a raging headache, a throbbing ache in my wrists, needles of ice all up and down my arms, and what felt like hot pokers being jabbed into my shoulders. And *then* I realized the screaming pain in my left bicep. I shook my head to clear it, and a wave of nausea bubbled up from around my toes and swept over me like a tsunami. I choked down the bile and blinked my crusty eyes open. I was chained to a big X of timbers in another tent. My arms were supporting most of my weight, which explained the pain in my shoulders. I got my feet under me and tried to turn my head far enough to the side to see what was holding me. I turned to the right and saw exactly what I expected to see—sturdy rope with a thin silver chain twined around it, effectively sapping all my strength. I looked over to the left, expecting to see the same thing there, and had to fight the vomit down again when I got a good look at my arm.

The little bastards had cut my arm off! Not really, my arm was still there, but the bicep muscle was gone! My arm had been butchered while it was still attached, and I could see all the way to the bone. And bone was about all that was left. My bicep, tricep, and forearm muscles had been stripped away as clean as you please, leaving white bone and a few fibrous ligaments holding the pieces together. I tried to scream, but all that came out was a reedy croak.

"Good morning, sunshine. Glad you could join us." Greg's voice came from behind me. My head snapped up at the sound, and I returned to trying not to vomit.

"Don't puke," he warned. "They're not much for cleaning us up around here, unless we barf on a piece they want to cook."

"What the hell happened? What are they doing to us? They cut my friggin' arm off!" I could hear my voice going up into squeaky thirteen-year-old-boy territory, but I couldn't help it.

Greg's voice came back to me, and the calm in his voice helped me keep myself together. "Chill, bro. They didn't cut your arm off, they just cut all the meat off your arm. There's a difference."

"Yeah? You wanna point out exactly what that difference might be?"

"You won't like it."

"I'm tied to a cross with silver chains and my arm's been chopped up like sushi. I don't think I like much right now." I shook my head again and spat out a mouthful of bile.

"The meat will grow back once we feed. If they'd just cut off the arm, it wouldn't." All of a sudden, I got it. All the pieces fit, from the chef yelling that he wanted us alive, to cutting out the muscle and not the ligaments.

I took a ragged breath and hissed to Greg. "We totally just became the lunch special, didn't we?"

"And probably dinner, and I'd even bet we're part of the Goblin Breakfast Burrito, too."

"Of course. Since our muscle tissue grows back, they don't have to buy fresh, or even rotten meat anymore. They just cut us up carefully and we're a renewable resource."

"Reduce, reuse, recycle," I muttered.

"Don't forget regenerate. You gotta respect a goblin who runs a green kitchen, and keeps his overhead low to boot," Greg added.

"You got a plan yet?" I asked.

"Not a clue. You?"

"I just figured out that I was an entrée. Gimme a couple seconds." Of course that's when the grinning green lardball of a chef decided to waddle back in, grinning with all sixty-some teeth.

"How are my prizes doing today? I brought you some din-din!" He held up a bucket, tipping it forward to show the blood within. He jammed a straw between my lips and held the bucket up to my face. I tried to turn my face to the side but he grabbed my chin with his fleshy mitt and held my face to the bucket. I smelled the rich metallic scent of the blood and started to drink. I could feel the strength flowing into me from the rich liquid until the silver sapped it right out of me, leaving me helpless again. I drank and drank, the lukewarm blood coursing down my throat and flowing into all my muscles, rebuilding the destroyed arms and regenerating the missing flesh. I finally let go of the straw and looked over at my arm, watching in horror as the muscles spun out of my arm like threads, twining around themselves, fastening to the tattered ligaments and bones, regrowing the skin, and then inflating it like a balloon.

"We'll regenerate faster if you bring us something better than pig's blood, you know," I said when I was able to tear my eyes away from the disgusting sight of my arm growing back.

The chef was holding the bucket up to Greg's face now, and my partner was trying to drink enough to grow back his right calf muscle. "I don't think so, fangboy. I don't want you getting back any more strength than my little silver bands can keep under control. Abdullah, get over here!" Chef yelled over his shoulder, and a lean goblin with a narrow face and slightly paler green skin darted into the tent. This new goblin wore a belt with a startling array of knives dangling from it, everything from tiny scalpels and art knives to a Bowie knife almost the length of his arm.

Abdullah stopped in front of me and drew a pair of knives from his belt. In one hand he held a wicked short blade that curved back to a vicious-looking point. In the other he held what looked like a fillet knife that my dad used to clean fish with. He grinned at me, showing all his teeth at once and said, "This might hurt. A lot. But only if I do it right." Then he sliced across my regrown bicep with the short knife, making two quick deep cuts across the arm. Once he'd slashed me to the bone at the elbow and inside my shoulder joint, he switched hands and used the thin knife to make long cuts lengthwise, sliding the blade right along the bone and sending a screech of blade on bone through my ears and every nerve ending in my body.

I managed to keep from screaming until the fillet knife went in, and managed to remain conscious for almost the entire butchering procedure. I only passed out when he took the bicep muscle, held it up in front of my face and gave the raw edge of the muscle a long lick. His beady eyes fluttered shut, and he gave a contented sigh. That's when I passed out.

I came to sometime later, and looked over at my arm, at the ligament and bone it had become again. A few tendrils of muscle fiber tried valiantly to reattach to something. This time I felt a screaming pain in my right arm, too. Without looking, I knew I'd been filleted on both arms this time.

"Greg, you there?" I whispered.

"Barely," his voice wasn't a whisper, but it sounded like he was using every bit of strength just to speak.

"What did they cut off you?"

"They peeled both arms, cut off both calves and one quad."

"That's the big muscle in the leg, right?" I asked.

"Yeah. They nicked an artery in my leg and had to stop. Apparently our circulatory systems still work, which came as a surprise to me and our captors."

"Why wouldn't they work? We still survive on blood, right?"

"Jimmy, you do know there's a difference between drinking blood and a transfusion, right?"

"Oh, yeah. I guess it's magic, then."

"Yep, we're made by elves, just like the cookies." Greg giggled a little, and I could tell he was goofier than normal because of the pain.

"So . . ." I started. "About that plan for escape?"

"I was hoping you had one."

"Nah man, that's your gig. Remember? I get us into stupid situations, and you get us out of them. Well, I did my part. Now it's time for you to step up. Use that overstuffed head of yours for something other than a hat rack and get us out of here. You think it up. I git 'r done."

"Sorry, pal. I got nothing." Greg fell silent, and after a few seconds I could hear him snore lightly. I've never understood how in the hell a guy who doesn't breathe can snore, but that falls into the category of "things I'll worry about when I'm not in imminent danger of death." I tested my bonds again, but I was tied tight. No matter what Abdullah cut off my forearm, he always left enough meat on my wrists to keep me bound. Then I had an idea. It sounded terrible even in my head, but I was out of options.

I took a deep breath and shoved my arm forward as hard as I could, into the rope holding me upright. The bonds cut into my wrist at first, but enough blood had soaked into the rope to give it a little stretch, and after just a few seconds I'd shoved my forearm through the loops, which now hung loosely against the bloody bones of my lower arm. I had just a little extra room to maneuver, so I twisted, tugged, and generally tried to contort my way out of the bonds without giving the silver chain too much contact with my exposed bones and flesh. Everywhere it touched it burned like lemon juice on a paper cut—only a thousandfold. I pulled and twisted and yanked and stretched and cursed and wept for several long minutes before I realized I was getting nowhere and sagged against the rope, held fast by expert goblin knots and my own stupidity.

I hung there, defeated, for what seemed like an eternity until the chef came back into the tent. He took a look at my forearm and said, "That must have hurt."

"Like a sonofabitch," I replied. Chef motioned at the goblins behind him, and a pair of lackeys came forward. One held a stake over my heart with a mallet while the other untied my wrist and rebound me to the cross.

Chef came over to me with the bucket I tried to resist, but a nod from the chef to the goblin with the stake set the little bastard to scraping along the bones in my arm with his knife. After about three seconds of that blinding agony I resigned myself to drinking, and reached out with my tongue for the straw. Chef grinned as he watched my flesh regenerate, then moved around behind me to feed Greg.

I decided to give my stellar negotiating skills one more shot. "You know we weren't alone when we came in here. Our friends will be here for us any minute now."

Chef laughed, a deep belly laugh that made me feel really bad about the prospects of my rescue. "You mean the lizard? The lizard is well known to us. He's a decent purchase most days, but he doesn't stay bought. You paid him in promises, I paid him in three bowls of stew and an all-you-can-eat voucher for his next visit. That little bastard was so stuffed when he left that his belly hung lower than his feet. He had to lift his gut with his forelegs to walk out of my tent! So I don't think you'll be getting any rescue from him. No, Sanguine, you're here until I decide that free vampire isn't tasty any longer. And I love the taste of free."

"At least tell us where you were getting the humans from. We came here trying to rescue them. It's not like we wanted to disrupt your business, we just wanted to—"

"You just wanted to steal away the main ingredient for my stew!" Chef came around to face me again. "For that I should gnaw hunks out of your buttocks and make you sit in a salt bath! I should drain you dry and feed you vampire blood! I should peel every inch of skin from your body and paint you with acid! Then I should regenerate you and do it all over again! This is my livelihood, bloodfiend, and I deserve to make a living just like every other goblin in the Market!"

"But these are *people*, Chef! Just like you and me! Well, maybe not *just* like you and me, but people regardless! And you're killing them and chopping them up for soup stock. How is that right?"

"I'm not killing anyone, moron. I buy my meat fresh, but not *that* fresh. This isn't a slaughterhouse, you know."

"Coulda fooled me," Greg said from behind me.

"Shut up! What kind of monster do you take me for, Sanguine? I told you, I get the human meat in on a daily delivery from my supplier, and it's dead when it gets here. Well, mostly dead, anyway."

"What do you mean, mostly dead?"

Chef opened his mouth to answer, then all hell broke loose.

Chapter 17

I'M NOT RIGHT often, and usually it happens by accident. Like now. In my bluff to the chef, I'd inadvertently told him a truth. Our friends really were on the way to rescue us, but it wasn't Marty. Or at least, it wasn't *just* Marty. He darted into the tent, jumped up and down with his head-ridge twitching for a second then ducked back out. I heard him shout something unintelligible, and fervently hoped that it was a call to the cavalry. It was.

Sabrina, her cousin Stephen, Anna, and Abby burst into the back of the tent guns blazing. Or actually, swords and hands blazing mostly. Stephen held my sword, the one I'd borrowed from Milandra the last time we were in Faerieland, and it was glowing bright blue. Apparently my sword liked goblins about as much as I did. Anna's hands were glowing with a pale yellow light, and there was a similar golden aura coming from her eyes. Given her dislike for me, I wasn't sure having her super-powered was a good thing, but I knew that Sabrina holding a Mossberg Persuader twelve-gauge shotgun was a *very* good thing. I'd helped her spec out the mixed silver and cold iron shot she loaded that puppy with, and I knew that if goblins weren't acquainted with the concept of a "boom stick," they were about to get an introduction.

Chef and his bodyguards spread out to try to flank the attackers, but the first one to step forward got blown to chunks by Sabrina's Mossberg. Little bits of goblin spattered across my face, and I knew I was never getting that smell out of my hair.

Sabrina racked another shell and said, "If the rest of you want to stay in one piece you'll lie facedown on the ground and behave while we rescue our friends."

Chef and his minions dropped to the deck, and Abby came over to cut us loose. I was able to stand, but Greg sagged against her and she had to half carry him back to where Sabrina kept her gun trained on the chef.

"You're making a huge mistake, human," Chef said from his place on the floor.

I stepped on the back of his head as I walked past and said, "Wouldn't be the first time, Greenie. And we came out of those scrapes just fine, too."

"I'm afraid that won't be the case this time, Sir Sanguine. You have been found in violation of the peace of the Market for a second time. The penalty for this, as was explained to you upon your first infraction, is death. Kill them all." The new voice came from the same faerie guard that I'd met earlier. The good humor he'd shown then was gone, and he had more friends. There were at least half a dozen faeries with him, all armed with swords and long daggers. They spread out to block any exit and advanced on us slowly, swords drawn.

"Wait a minute, I'm unarmed. And my friends should only get a warning. They haven't gotten a warning," I protested. The faeries stopped, looking at one another. Apparently most people didn't try to talk their way out of a fight here. Honestly, it wasn't my favorite tactic either, but I didn't think I had much of a chance to kill all of them and still rescue the Carmichaels from whoever or whatever had them.

"But you have been warned, and now you are once again in the center of a disturbance in the Market. I am within the bounds of my authority to order you all executed to avoid further nuisance. I so order." The faeries started in again, renewed in their resolve to make little vampire bits all over the floor.

"You don't want to do this, pal. We're friends of Queen Milandra." The faeries froze again as I stretched the truth just a little. Technically, we'd done her one big favor, and then started a small war in her throne room, but everything turned out all right in the end, and there were hugs when we left. Really, there were. Anyway, it worked. At least for a minute. I saw several of the faeries look back at their captain, or sergeant, or whatever with concerned glances. Milandra was known to change the color of the sky to match her dresses, and they looked a little concerned that her capriciousness might be turned on them if they chopped up her friends.

"We conveyed your likeness to Her Majesty after our first encounter with you, Sanguine. She informed us that you were to be left alone and extended all courtesies unless you or your associates violated one of the more serious laws of the Market. Killing goblins is in violation of exactly thirteen serious laws of the Market. And the Market is not under the jurisdiction of the Queen. So I'm afraid your precious lizard-loving queen can do nothing for you now." Great, all the guards in Faerie and we run into the one that hates Milandra's sometimes-dragon husband.

I stepped forward to where the guard captain stood and pitched my voice low so no one else could hear us. "Look, we know you don't really want a big fight on your hands. We don't want a big fight, either. I'm tired, and my buddy here is still trying to regrow his legs. So why don't you just step aside and let us go, and you'll never have to worry about us again."

"If I stand aside you will leave the Market, never to return?" he asked.

"As soon as we find the chef's supplier and rescue the humans he's kidnapped, yes."

"That is unsatisfactory. You have violated the laws of the Market. You must now face the consequences." He drew his sword and came at me, and he was *fast*, faster than a vampire fast. The only thing that saved me was an inherent distrust of everyone, so I was already diving backward when he started to reach for his weapon. I hit the deck, and his blade whistled through the air where my neck had been.

Then the fight was on. Stephen leapt into the fray and took on the captain, twirling my sword with an inhuman grace. Stephen wasn't human, but a faerie swapped in infancy with a human child. His swordwork was pretty spectacular, but the guard captain was a real soldier, with possibly centuries of experience. Stephen put up a good defense, but the soldier quickly proved that he was the better warrior. He deflected a flurry of attacks from Stephen and dove in for a thrust that would have gutted the young faerie if I hadn't managed to regain my footing just in time to kick the captain in his knee. He howled and went down, and I turned my attention to the rest of the fray.

Abby was standing over Greg's prone form, taking on two guards with nothing more than her bare hands and what looked like a soup ladle. She was doing a good job of holding them off, but I could see her breathe a sigh of relief when Stephen stepped up and ran one of the guards through. Abby quickly stepped inside the stroke of the second guard and sank her teeth into his neck. A bit old-fashioned, maybe, but damned effective.

Sabrina had three guards pinned down behind an overturned table with her Mossberg. Whenever a hint of pointy ear poked up over the table, she let fly with another shell. The Mossberg only held eight, so she was about to need a reload. I stepped up behind her and drew her service weapon from the holster.

"Reload, I'll cover you." She nodded and started pumping fresh shells into the gun from the bandolier she had slung over one shoulder. A dozen Wookie jokes came to mind, but since I was the one being rescued, I decided to give her a break this time. A guard peeked up over the table, and I shot off the tip of his ear. He fell back, screaming, and I grinned at Sabrina.

"Show-off." She grinned back. The Mossberg reloaded, she racked a shell into the chamber and blasted away at the table again.

I turned to check on Anna and my eyes widened. The witch had the chef and all his minions bound with glowing bands of blue fire, and from the howls coming from the goblins, it wasn't a comfortable captivity. She shot me a nasty smile and pointed a finger at me. I dove for the floor just as a yellow sphere of force came shooting out of her fingertips at me. I heard a gurgling croak from behind me and rolled over just in time to see the top half of a faerie guard fall to the dirt beside me. His legs stood alone for a second, then toppled over backward. The smell of burnt faerie seared my nostrils, and I waved my thanks to Anna. She grinned back at me, and I remembered how much she didn't like me. I was suddenly very glad she didn't have that kind of juice back in our world. At least I thought she didn't. Scratch that. I really, *really* hoped she didn't.

It looked like our side was winning the battle handily, despite the lack of notable contributions from me or Greg. Even Marty had a long dagger in hand and was beating the hell out of Abdullah the goblin with the flat of it, wielding the knife with both hands. I stood up, looking around for something that needed to be punched, bitten, or kicked, and saw nothing. I leaned against the center tent pole to watch the carnage, then froze as I heard a thunderous roar from just outside the tent.

I glanced around, but everybody else looked just as confused as I was. Except for Chef, who grinned like he'd just found a toy in his Cracker Jack box.

"That would be my bodyguard, Slim," he said with a smirk. Then the back wall of the tent tore away and the biggest ogre I'd ever seen charged us. He was all of eleven feet tall if he was an inch, with arms that hung almost to the ground. His fists were each bigger than my head, and his thick-browed head sat upon shoulders the width of three NFL linemen. Long tusks protruded from his lower jaw, and his bluish skin looked more like scales than flesh. All in all, he looked like ten miles of bad road.

I looked around to see what contingent of my army was going to take this guy on, and saw every one of my soldiers was otherwise occupied. "Stephen! I could use that pigsticker if you don't mind!" I yelled, and Stephen tossed my sword across the tent, bending down to pick up a discarded blade from one of the guards he'd felled. I snatched my sword out of the air and stepped into the monster's path.

"Slim, huh? I guess your mom had a flair for the ironic," I said, hoping to distract him with my witty repartee. The ogre just grunted and charged, his huge arms outstretched to bowl over anything in his path. I dove forward and slightly to the side, landing in a roll that took me under his wingspan and left his huge back exposed. I leapt and jabbed downward with my sword, which glanced off his scaly hide. I crashed into his back, and Slim reached around faster than I would have dreamed possible, snatching me off his shoulders and slamming me to the ground.

I lay there dazed for a second, then managed to pry my eyes open. I looked up at a huge foot rushing toward my face, and rolled to one side. Slim stomped where my head had been, and the entire tent shook with the impact. My roll put me directly underneath the beast, so I decided to take the lowest of the low roads—I thrust straight up with my sword, stabbing the ogre right in the family jewels.

Apparently ogre physiology is similar enough to human that certain parts are in the same place. Slim let out a high-pitched keening howl that was sure to have dogs all over the Market whimpering in sympathy. I almost felt bad for stabbing him, then remembered that he tried to stomp my face flat, and he worked for a guy who *ate my bicep*. I got over my guilt in a matter of seconds, and quickly slid out from under the collapsing monster before the ogre fell to his knees. Both hands were clutching his wound, which gave me the perfect opening to stab him through the throat and put him out of all our misery. I drew back.

"STOP!" Bellowed a new voice, and all activity in the tent ceased. We all turned simultaneously to see a familiar, and yet still very scary form standing over the tent. Yeah, *over the tent*. Tivernius the dragon had ripped the roof off and was glaring down at us from some twenty feet in the air. Nearby tents shook with every flap of his giant wings, and his golden eyes fixed me with a look that made my borrowed blood run cold.

"Put away your weapons or I will incinerate each and every one of you," the dragon said in a quieter voice. We all hurried to obey. I didn't have a scabbard for my sword, so I just kinda jabbed it through my belt and tried to look non-threatening. I suppose to the dragon I *was* pretty non-threatening.

Tivernius shimmered, and instead of a huge golden dragon floating above us, a handsome man with blond hair and golden armor stood in the middle of the tent. He stalked through the tent in a wide circle, taking in all of the different factions of combatants. The guards knelt and removed their helmets in his presence. Marty prostrated himself before the dragon-man, groveling in what sounded like five or six different languages. Anna released the goblins, who immediately knelt and bowed their heads. Greg and Stephen bowed deeply, Anna, Sabrina, and Abby curtseyed, and even I gave him a nod of respect. I probably would have bowed, but once you've been through a cage fight with a guy, he loses a little of his majesty.

Tivernius came to a halt in front of me and looked at the moaning ogre, who had fallen over on his side and lay there, clutching his sack. Tivernius shook his head at me and held out his hands over the ogre. Golden light flowed down onto the monster, and the lines of pain on its face eased. After a few seconds the light went out, and the beast rolled over and went to sleep.

"That was not very nice, stabbing him there," Tivernius said, turning back to me.

"It wasn't very nice trying to stomp my head into a pancake either." I felt no remorse.

"Still, Jimmy. You stabbed the guy in the jewels."

"Dude, he's an ogre, and he was trying to kill me. If there hadn't been armor everywhere else, I woulda stabbed him somewhere with a little more dignity. Besides, his boss ate part of me!"

"That's not the ogre's fault."

"I am not going to stand here in the middle of friggin' Faerieland debating a dragon about the morals involved in stabbing an ogre in the nuts! I refuse. I have to draw the line somewhere, and this is it! Now are you gonna kill me, or are you gonna let us go?" I heard the note of hysteria in my voice, but I couldn't do anything about it. I'd gone from entree to rescued, to battling guards, to stabbing an ogre in the balls, to facing down a dragon. I was absolutely on the edge of losing my cool, and didn't have the energy left to hide it.

"Neither. I'm bringing you before the Queen, who shall decide your fate."

Well, crap.

Chapter 18

I WAS COUNTING on the trek from the Market to Milandra's throne room to give me time to work on my rapport with Tivernius, to make sure we were still buddies, that sort of thing. I'd gotten along pretty well with the dragon on our last trip to Faerieland, and the meddling Greg, Sabrina and I had done in his love life had worked out pretty well for him in the end, so I had high hopes for getting the Faerie Queen's scaly husband on our side over the days it would take us to walk to the capital.

But my luck held, and as usual my only luck was bad, as we were teleported directly into the throne room. We weren't the first ones to arrive, of course. It could never be as easy as getting to the Queen, pleading our case, and then walking out with all our dangly bits intact, *ooooohhhhh nnnooooo*. We arrived in a rush of air and no small amount of Market-dust just as the guard captain finished explaining his side of events. He seemed to have covered most of the high points, including the part where I kicked him in the knee. He gestured with his cane as he came to that part of his report and almost fell over, which I felt was a little overly dramatic, but I wasn't the one whose knee bent backward now, so I guess I didn't get to be all judgy.

"I have heard your case, Captain, and am ready to levy my decision," Milandra said. The little Faerie Queen had none of the mischief in her eyes that I had seen on our last visit. She was seated on her silver throne, clad in silver armor, with a gold-and-silver twined circlet on her brow and long, silver hair cascading down her shoulders. Across her knees lay a silver scepter with a fist-sized diamond at the end of it. She raised it and stood.

I started forward, saying, "Don't we even get a chance to—" I was going to say something eloquent about defense and due process, but Tivernius wrapped a hand around my mouth and jerked me back. I struggled against his grip, but dragons are *strong*. I mentally put them on the "things that can kick my ass" list, and stopped fighting.

"Good. Now behave yourself and watch. We're invisible back

here, but if you get more than ten feet from me you'll be outside the range of my spell," he whispered into my ear. I looked around and saw that the others were standing still and watching our exchange. I raised an eyebrow at Greg, and he raised one back at me, as if to say, "Well, I wasn't going to run in there and get us all killed, now was I?"

"You couldn't have told me that before now?" I hissed back. "And please tell me you have a roll of quarters in your pocket." He let me go, and I turned my attention back to the Queen.

I started a little as I saw myself appear and kneel meekly before the throne. I looked around, making sure that I wasn't really there and that the whole Scooby Gang was still hiding in the dragon's invisibility spell with me, then watched as Greg, Abby, Sabrina, and Stephen all popped into existence in front of Milandra. The fake us all knelt, then the Queen held her scepter high and spoke.

"It has been proven beyond reproof that you have violated the laws and hospitality of our land and of the Goblin Market. As follows our treaty with the Goblin King and the other sentient species of the realm governing the Market, you shall be put to death forthwith and without hesitation."

She waved her scepter, and it morphed into a glittering crystal sword. The sword flashed through the air, catching light and flashing prisms across the floor as it swung down, parting "my" neck like it was a sheet of paper. It was more than a little disconcerting to watch my head part from my shoulders and *thunk* to the marble floor, and it was *way* disturbing to watch my body turn to dust and blow away. I looked at Greg, and saw him turn even paler than normal. Sabrina closed her eyes as Milandra decapitated the rest of the fake us, and I put an arm around her shoulders. Anna was the only one who didn't seem fazed, and that creeped me out even more.

"Is that what really happens when you kill one of us? 'Cause it looks a lot like an episode of *Buffy*," I whispered to Tivernius.

"I know. Joss Whedon is very popular over here. And no, that's not what really happens. But it's what people expect now, so we have to give them a little razzle-dazzle."

Great. I'm standing here in Faerieland watching the Queen of the Fae chop off my head and a dragon is quoting musical theatre numbers at me. I turned my attention back to Milandra, who had finished decapitating my "friends." I kept looking back and forth between Stephen and Sabrina's "corpses" and the obviously not dead folks standing next to me. Somehow it was easier dealing with her killing me, Greg, and

Abby, since our bodies turned to dust.

Milandra sat back down on her throne and nodded to the Guard. "You may return to service with our thanks." The guards blinked out of existence at the wave of Milandra's scepter.

Then she shifted slightly on her throne and focused all her attention on the chef. "You, sir, are another matter."

"I just cook 'em, queenie. I don't got nothing else to do with 'em." He spat a glob of yellow something onto the throne room floor, and Milandra's personal guards stepped forward, hands on their swords.

The Queen held up a hand, and the guards returned to their positions. "And yet," she said, "You did kidnap two travelers from another realm and chop them up for stew. And then, when they tried to escape, you created a situation by which they had no choice but to break my laws."

"But I didn't break any laws." He paused for a long time before adding, "Majesty."

"No, you didn't. But you did require the aid of my Market Guard, did you not?"

"I did indeed. And they helped me out, like they would any law-abiding, tax-paying merchant of the Market. And I appreciates it." The corpulent little slime smiled and spat again.

"I'm sure you do. That's why you will now be providing free meals for any of my guardsmen that choose to partake. You reputation for fine cuisine has reached even my own palace, and I am sure that you would like to show your appreciation for the men who saved your business in any way you could."

"Of course, Your Majesty. Free eats for all the Guard. Absolutely! Anything they want on the menu or off the menu!"

"Thank you, Chef. You may go." Milandra waved her hand, and the throne room was missing a goblin.

"Come on out, Jimmy. And bring all your friends." Milandra raised her voice so we could all hear her, and we approached the dais. The throne room did that thing it does when Milandra wants it to be small, so what had been a distance the length of a basketball court only took us a couple of steps to cover. Abby seemed a little freaked out by it, but the rest of us pretty much took it in stride. I just hoped I wouldn't come home all glittery after this trip. That stuff takes forever to wash out of your hair.

Stephen looked the most amazed, and the most transformed by his entry into Faerieland. Any pieces of his mortal disguise were gone, and he was several inches taller than I was used to seeing, and he now had a pair of decidedly non-human pointy ears. He was a good-looking dude in our dimension, but here in Faerie, he was *beautiful*. He approached the throne and knelt like he'd been born in another time, all his dancer's grace flowing into a fluid bow at Milandra's feet.

"My lady." He lowered his head.

Milandra rose and stepped down from her dais. "Stephen, I presume?" The kneeling faerie glanced up at her and nodded. "It's a pleasure to welcome you home. Know that you and yours shall always be welcome here, even unto the end of your days." Her tone was strangely formal, and I almost felt a little energy pass between her and Stephen as she bent down and kissed him on the forehead.

I heard a little intake of breath and looked over at Tivernius. "Don't sweat it, lizard-breath. He's gay."

"I'm not 'sweating' anything, Jimmy, but she just bestowed on him something that few ever receive. The kiss of the Queen is a mark that one carries forever, and it shows him as favored by the royal house of the Fae."

"So with her lipstick on his forehead we're less likely to get chopped up for soup stock?" I asked.

"To put it in the crudest terms possible, yes."

"Awesome. Think I can get her to kiss me?"

"She can kiss you on the forehead right after I decapitate you," Sabrina cut in, her voice all saccharine.

"I'll settle for a kiss from you, then." I leaned toward her and puckered up.

"Not now, you smell like a goblin. Besides, we're in public." She pushed me away, and I turned my attention back to the Queen, who looked at me like a grumpy homeroom teacher staring down a kid who had just gotten detention. Again.

"James, Gregory, Sabrina," the Queen addressed us all. "So good to see you again. And welcome to your friends as well, especially the witch. Those of the Craft are always welcome within our halls. But James, why is it that every time I see you there is bloodshed?"

"For once it wasn't my fault, Your Majesty. I just take exception to being turned into an entrée." I shrugged, and Milandra laughed. I sighed a tiny sigh, relieved that the Queen still thought I was funny. If a woman who bends reality to match her moods stops being amused with you, your longevity is seriously compromised.

"Now, James, what is your side of the story? I've heard my

captain's account of the events in the Market, and while outlandish, they do sound very much like something you would be involved in. And please introduce me to your friends, particularly this well-mannered one? Rise, young Fae." She waved a hand at Stephen, who slowly got to his feet and stepped back with the rest of us. His eyes never left Milandra the whole time. I guess for me it would be something like meeting Robert Plant, or Clapton, only cuter and blonder.

I gave Milandra the shortened version of our trip to Faerieland along with the introductions, finishing up with our little run-in with the chef. "So, you see, it wasn't really our fault that we drew steel in the Market, it was more along the lines of an inevitability."

"Like it was an inevitability that your last trip to my realm would result in bloodshed in this very throne room and very nearly cause an inter-kingdom war across all of Faerie?" Her eyebrow crept so far up into her hairline that I thought it was going to come back around her head.

Milandra didn't seem to be the type to hold a grudge. Not like Greg, who'd been mad at me for seventeen years and counting. I'd killed him. He had a right to his anger, but Milandra was better off when we'd left than before we'd arrived. I wasn't truly worried that she was going to let the past color her opinion now.

"Yeah, sorry about that. But look on the bright side, nobody you like died." I gestured at Otto, her chief bodyguard, man-at-arms, and whatever else he was. He nodded back to me.

"So now what?" Milandra asked. "How do you intend to continue your investigation?"

"Well, I thought we'd kick, punch, and shoot everybody in the Goblin Market until we got enough answers to rescue a little baby's parents, then take them back home and let everyone live happily ever after," I said, ignoring the scowl on Milandra's face.

"And I thought that I'd go to the chef's supplier and cut off little bits of him until he told us where the people we're looking for are being held," Sabrina said from beside me.

"Well, that could work, too. But it takes some of the fun out of things. Can I at least beat people up until they tell me who the supplier is?"

"No need. I swiped the chef's ledger before we were whisked away. It shows us who he buys his meat from. That is, when he doesn't have a renewable source of it hanging in the back room. Why don't we start there?"

"That's kinda brilliant, Detective," I said.

"Thanks, I thought it was pretty good."

"I have known for many years who supplies the chef with his meat, but have had no reason to shut down his operation as long as the only humans killed were criminals, trespassers, or those who deserve it, as you would say, Jimmy. No matter my personal feelings about humans or how much they need to be protected from the more unsavory elements of the magical world, as long as no rules were broken, I could not act." Milandra's brows knit as she twirled her hair around one finger. I could almost hear the gears turning inside that gorgeous little head.

After a few seconds a pixiesh smile crept across the Queen's face. "But now they have kidnapped humans and endangered the whole of Faerie by their actions. We cannot allow knowledge of the Goblin Market to become widespread in the mundane world. Were all of your practitioners of magic to come flooding into Faerie for their charms and trinkets, our resources would quickly be depleted and our land destroyed."

"Not to mention what all those souped-up charms and spells would do back in our world," I added, thinking of how much more mojo Anna had on this side of the portal.

"Therefore, I shall empower you to act in my name and stop this unauthorized import of humans into the Goblin Market."

"We call that kidnapping back in our world," I pointed out.

Milandra just looked at me, and I shut up.

"There's just one problem," Greg chimed in. "Milandra just killed us. Or at least as far as anyone knows."

"That's simple enough to fix," Milandra said.

We all turned to her. She smiled at us. "I killed illusions that looked like you. It won't take much to make you look like someone else." She waved a hand and pink glitter settled over the lot of us.

I looked at Greg, but nothing seemed different. "Um, Your Majesty . . ." I raised a hand, noting that she still had that crystal sword leaning next to her throne.

"It worked, Jimmy. Have a little faith. You can't see the difference because you know it's Greg. If you didn't know him, he would look like one of my Guard. But this glamour will not work on the Fae, so wear these." She held out her hand, and it was draped with necklaces. Dangling from long silver chains were seven-pointed stars with pink diamonds at each point.

"These are emblems of my service. Now, if I might borrow your sword?" She held out a hand to me and I put my sword in her hand. The sword looked like nothing special, but it had originally belonged to Milandra, and something about it looked *different* here.

"Kneel." I hit one knee without ever thinking about disobeying. I looked from side to side and saw Greg and Sabrina kneeling beside me. I gave Sabrina a look that I hope said, *If this kills us, I really liked you.* She smiled back at me, and I swear if it was possible my heart would have skipped a beat.

"By the power vested in my by the Lords of the Fae, the Gods of the Realms, and the Dragons of Tivernia, I hereby declare you to be Knights of the Fae, with all the authority and power therein. Serve me well, Sir James Black." She tapped me on each shoulder with the sword, a little harder than I thought absolutely necessary, but a far cry from taking my head off. Milandra stepped left and repeated her declaration over Sabrina's head, then stepped right and did the same to Greg.

She stepped back and addressed us all. "Rise, my knights. You now speak with my voice, and act on my accord. You may bare steel in the Market if necessary, and may act in any fashion you see fit to uphold the laws of the land and the conscience of your Queen." She smiled, and suddenly she was the little girl playing at Faerie Queen again, complete with dimples deep enough to make a dead man weak in the knees. I know—I watched Greg's legs buckle when she turned that dazzling smile on him. "Just try not to embarrass me too badly, Jimmy."

"I make no promises, Your Majesty." I returned her grin with a lopsided one of my own, and we all broke up laughing.

Milandra handed the sword back to me with a slight smile, and I shoved it through my belt. I heard a sharp intake of breath from Tivernius and turned to the dragon.

"What's up? Was this your sword? You can have it, bro." I reached to take it out of my belt, and Tivernius held up his hands.

"No, it is not mine. I simply had not recognized it before that moment, is all."

"Recognized it? I've had it since the last time we were here, since the fight with the Unseelie."

"I remember," Tivernius said. "But at that time it had been only loaned to you. Now it has been bestowed upon you as a knight, which has certain other properties."

"Dude, what are you babbling about? It's a sword. It had properties of chopping people up, properties of poking holes in them, and if I'm feeling particularly generous, properties of slapping them around with the flat or the pommel. That's about it." I looked back and forth between him and Milandra. "Unless there's something you guys aren't telling me, that is?"

They shared a couple of those meaningful glances people like to throw around when they know something that you don't and they're deciding whether or not to tell you about it. I usually shortcut those glances with a punch or two, but since I'd already avoided one fight with a dragon today, I decided to wait things out and not start another one.

After a few seconds, Milandra took a deep breath. "I wasn't sure I was going to tell you this, James, but that sword is a little more than just a sword."

"I'd figured that out all on my own, Your Mysteriousness," I snarked back.

"You've probably heard of it, but likely regarded it as just a legend," she continued slowly.

"Once upon a time I thought the same thing about dragons, faeries, witches, vampires, and intelligent police officers. But look at us all now!" I held my arms out wide, and Sabrina stepped up to smack me in the back of the head.

"Shut up, Jimmy. She's trying to tell you something important," Sabrina hissed at me.

I rubbed the back of my head and looked back at Milandra. "So tell me. What's the deal with this legendary sword? Unless you're telling me it's Excalibur and I'm wielding it because the world is reaching a time of supreme peril again, I'm probably not going to be suitably impressed." I chuckled at my joke until I noticed that Milandra wasn't laughing.

I looked hard at her, but got nothing. I looked over at Tivernius, who wouldn't meet my eyes. "Is this sword Excalibur? *The* Excalibur?"

Milandra nodded. "Merlin brought it to us here for safekeeping at Arthur's passing. We have held it until a worthy bearer could be found."

"And until you find one you decided to let me use it?" I asked, trying to keep the mood light.

Milandra just shook her head.

"You think I'm worthy of carrying Excalibur, the sword of King friggin' Arthur?"

The Faerie Queen nodded. "I have seen your heart, James. What lies within you is more than even you suspect. More than you allow others to see or yourself to believe."

"No, wait. I know who and what I am. And I know that I have already stopped a Big Bad from destroying the world once. It's someone else's turn if things are coming that are so bad that this heavy-duty mojo needs to come back to our world to stop it."

"Mojo, as you call it, is needed." She nodded again. "All the auguries and signs point to a time of great upheaval, James. We don't know when it will happen, but something very bad is coming. And you and your friends must stop it."

I took a deep breath, then shook my head to clear it. Didn't help. I did it again, then once more. I'm sure I looked like a terrier with a nose full of cayenne pepper. I glanced from Tivernius to Milandra, then back again. "Is it coming today?"

"No," Milandra said. "We do not know when the attack will come, or in what form. But it will not begin for some time yet."

"Then we still have work to do. There's somebody in the Goblin Market kidnapping humans and selling them to the chef for soup stock. We've got to take care of that, then we'll worry about whatever this Big Bad is going to look like and how I'm supposed to use this pigsticker to stop him. So Scaly-butt, you wanna magic us back to the Market so we can go back to kicking ass and taking names?"

Greg tapped me on the shoulder. "Dude, I think I'd better sit this one out. It's going to take several regular feedings to regrow my leg muscles and if you run into anything dangerous, I'd be more of a liability than a help."

I nodded to him, then turned to Stephen. "And I'm guessing you have a lot of questions you'd like to ask the fine folk of Faerie about yourself."

He nodded, and Milandra motioned for Sabrina. "You should stay as well, Detective. There are certain events and auguries we need to discuss with you."

"Sorry, Your Majesty, but I can't let this civilian run my case, no matter what kind of magical sword he's packing." Sabrina crossed her arms across her chest and actually tried to stare down the Faerie Queen.

It didn't work. "I'm sorry, Detective. You were obviously under the impression that I was asking you to stay. There are things we need to discuss with you, and we need James out of the way to discuss them. So you will be staying here while he returns to the Market."

Sabrina's eyes got big, and I stepped up before she opened her mouth and got us all killed. "Sabrina. It's cool. I can handle this. You stay here, find out how to save the world, and I'll go chop the bad guy into little pieces and feed him to the dogs." I saw Greg wince out of the corner of my eye and flashed back to what had just happened to my leg muscles. Suddenly the concept of being fed to things wasn't funny anymore.

"Fine," Sabrina said between gritted teeth. "But don't do anything stupid."

"No promises. Okay, then, Big T. How about sending the rest of us back to the Market, unless you ladies would rather stay here?" I looked at Anna and Abby.

"There is no way I am letting you run around a magical marketplace unescorted while wielding one of the most powerful magical swords in history. Goddess only knows the trouble you would stir up," Anna said, crossing her arms and giving me a glare.

I looked over at Abby. She shrugged and said, "You did mention there was ass to kick, right? Then I'm with you. I'm not much for big houses with marble decorations anyway."

I nodded to Tivernius and said, "You're welcome to join us, pal. Might even be fun."

He shook his head with a little regret and said, "As much as I might enjoy it, goblins give me indigestion, and that's terribly inconvenient when one no longer lives in a cave."

"Fart fireballs, huh?" I asked. The dragon in human form ducked his head and made some funny gesture with his hand. Everything went dark, and we were gone.

Chapter 19

I BLINKED, AND we were back in the Market. I looked around for Tivernius, but the dragon was gone. There was no evidence that we had gone anywhere, except for the marked lack of Market guards milling around wanting to poke holes in us. I looked around, and Anna and Abby were there with me. Abby was scanning her surroundings for threats, while Anna was gaping at all the different types of creatures strolling through the Market.

I waved Abby over and said, "I've been meaning to ask. How did you guys connect with Marty anyway?"

"I approached them, Sir Sanguine. More mundane, searching humans at the Market? They had to be your people. I found them. Led them to you. How else would they have found their way to you?" I turned at the familiar voice and saw Marty leaning by a tent pole.

"Marty!" I exclaimed, holding my arms out. The little lizard ran to me and jumped into my arms. I gave him a hug, then promptly dropped him on his back in the dirt when he licked the side of my face. "Too much, dude. Too much," I said as I reached down to help him stand.

"My apologies, sirrah. I was overcome with the moment. I feared that I would never see you again once you were taken by the dragon."

"Yeah, I had a moment or two of concern myself. Wait a minute. How did you know it was me?"

"Your voice, sirrah, and your scent. Your appearance has been altered, but not the most important aspect of yourself."

"Yeah, most folks only use their eyes. So you led my friends to us?" I waved at the women.

"Yes, but there were more humans then. The dragon didn't eat your friends, did he?" The little lizard actually looked concerned.

I patted him on top of the head and smiled. "No. Tivernius is a friend. Most days, anyway. He wouldn't eat any of us. Greg was too injured to fight, and the others had things to discuss with the Queen."

"Oh, they must be important nobles, then."

"No, just a cop and a dancer. And I'll let you figure out which is which. Thanks for bringing them to our rescue. But how did you find them?"

"When I saw you were captured, I returned to the entrance to the Market, where we first met. I thought that eventually someone would come looking for you, and that would be the best place for me to find them. I knew the chef wouldn't kill you, because he wanted to use your regenerative powers for a never-ending food supply. I'm sorry it took so long, but I brought them as soon as I could."

Anna chimed in, "If I had my way, we'd still be on our side of the universe, but Sabrina and Stephen finally convinced me that you were worth coming after. Creating a portal from scratch is difficult, so we needed Stephen's blood to open a gate to Faerie." At the look on my face, she held out her hands. "No, no, we didn't spill his blood to open the gate, we just had to have a native of Faerie with us. Otherwise the gate wouldn't open where we wanted it to."

"And where did you open this gate? And is it still open?"

"In your living room. And no, we closed it behind us. But I can take us home easily enough, and anywhere I open a gate to from this side will tie to the gate in your house. As long as Stephen is with us."

"Okay then, so we can get home. Good. Now let's get this rescue underway. We need to find the chef's supplier and get to him, preferably unseen. I don't have my heavy hitters with me, so going in guns blazing is a bad idea."

"What's that supposed to mean, Jimmy? We're just as capable as Greg and Sabrina." An indignant Anna stepped in front of me holding her hands in front of my face. Her argument was made more persuasive by the fact that her hands were glowing with a nimbus of blue fire.

"Point taken," I said, taking a step back. "And what exactly is that, anyway?"

"I have no idea," she admitted. "As soon as I set foot in Faerie I felt my powers grow exponentially. I can do things here that I only dreamed about in the mundane world."

"Beware, human witch," Marty said, tugging on her belt loop. "That is the temptation that leads many of your kind to forsake your world entirely."

"Is that really so bad, Marty?" Anna asked him. "It might be nice to live somewhere that my people are respected, instead of ridiculed or feared."

"That may be true, miss, but there are many things in Faerie that feed on magical energy, and not all of them are content to take that energy from willing or inanimate donors. And while you are more powerful here than in your world, so are the dangers you face."

Anna's face betrayed her emotions, and I watched her struggle with those ideas for a few seconds. Then she sighed, extinguished her hands, and straightened her shoulders. Apparently a decision had been reached, and I wouldn't have to tell Mike that I'd left his kinda-girlfriend witch in the Magic Kingdom.

"Let's chat about Anna's relocation another time. When lives aren't at stake. Marty, do you know where this is?" I asked, handing him the ledger Sabrina swiped from the chef.

The lizard shuddered and looked up at me. His head-ridge was standing straight up and quivering, and his eyes were wide. "Are you sure this is where the chef gets his humans from?"

"Why? Is it another bad neighborhood?"

"No, Sir James, I know this address. It is the home of the Dream King. He is a very powerful wizard, and one that doesn't like outworlders at all. I have never known him to allow a human to leave his shop alive, but I have never heard of him trafficking in human meat, either."

"Why do they call him the Dream King?" Abby asked.

"He sells dreams, lovely Sanguine. He takes dreams from other creatures and sells them in his store. He is one of the strangest creatures I have ever encountered, and I admit to having no little fear of him."

"A four-foot-tall talking lizard thinks something is weird. Now this I gotta see," I said. "Lead on, Macduff!" I gestured as grandly as I could in the crowded thoroughfare.

"It's 'lay on, Macduff,' moron," Anna grumbled at me, but I would almost swear there was a teensy bit less hatred in her voice than normal. Maybe my charm was starting to have an effect on her. Or maybe she just couldn't be bothered to think as much about me. Either way, I'd take an early thaw any day.

Marty turned left down a less crowded alley, and we were off to see the Dream King.

Chapter 20

THE DREAM KING had a full building with real stone walls rather than a stall. His shop was smaller than the chef's serving tent, but larger than his prep area, so maybe the size of the living room in our new house. There were no other vendors around the shop. No stalls, no carts, no vendors hawking the wares on their backs. The King's establishment butted up against the hedge that formed the outer wall of the Market. A sense of isolation loomed over the whole place, made deeper by the run-down outer facade. There were no windows, and only one door on the front, with a sign hanging by it that read "DREAM KING—APPOINTMENT ONLY—GO AWAY!" The door had no knob, no knocker, no doorbell, or anything designed to welcome guests and facilitate entrance.

Fortunately, I excel at announcing myself with authority. I walked right up to the panel and knocked. I got no response, so I knocked again. The door opened a crack and a skinny white hand crept out and extended an index finger to the sign, tapping on the "Go Away!" part, then withdrew back into the murk of the building. I knocked a third time, but the hand didn't reappear. Nothing happened.

"It appears as though no one is home," Marty announced. "Perhaps this would be a good time to return to my other business endeavors. I have led you this far—I'm sure you can find a way in to see the Dream King without my assistance." The little lizard turned to head back into the Market, but I put a hand on his shoulder to stop him.

"Hold up a second, Marty. What about getting out of Faerie? Seeing a little mundane world lizard loving? What about all that, pal?"

"Honestly, Sir Sanguine, I might not have been completely honest with you regarding my motives in leaving the Market, and Faerie altogether."

"Color me shocked, the lizard lies," muttered Abby.

"What do you mean, Marty?" I asked.

"Well, it might be that my debts to Lord Buterin Great-Teeth had more to do with my desire for relocation than an actual—ahem—desire to relocation, if you understand me. And since you have asserted such an authoritative protection of mine person on Lord Buterin's enforcer, I have no doubts that I shall now be able to refinance and repay my debts in a reasonable fashion."

"So now you don't want to leave?" I asked.

"Leave all this? Why ever would I?" Marty gestured around him.

I looked at the dirty stalls, the monstrous beings wandering the aisles, listened to the bellowing shopkeepers, and tried very hard to ignore the stench of various animals and other unidentifiable things that wafted through the air. "Why, indeed. Well, then, Martifluousyntherianthemum Gregorovichinglingaringdingdingdong, I hereby release you from my service, and give you this token of my appreciation for your deeds." I reached in my pocket and handed him my pocketknife. "Take this blade as my gift to you, Marty. Use it well, but use it only in the cause of justice. And try not to lose it in a card game."

"Thank you, great Sanguine, for everything. You shall always have a friend in the Market." With that, the little lizard tucked my pocketknife into his belt like a sword, then turned and ran off into the Market.

I looked at Anna and Abby and said, "I guess his work here was done."

"Or he'd seen what kind of trouble you caused with a guy called Chef and was terrified what would happen when you messed around with a King, even a Dream King," Abby said.

"Point," I replied. I poked around at the door again, trying the knob and checking the solidity of the frame. Everything looked pretty solid, which was to say not vampire-proof.

I turned back to the others and in a spectacularly loud voice said, "Doesn't look like anybody's home. I suppose I'll just have to see if I can pick the lock on the front door." I leaned in next to the door when I almost shouted that last bit. Then I reared back and kicked the door in.

The door was stronger than it looked, but so am I. It flew into the room and fell flat, kicking up an enormous cloud of dust. Abby and I stepped in first, since we didn't need to wait for the dust to settle for the sake of our tender lungs. Apparently the Dream King ran enough business out of his home for it to count as a public place, because I could enter without being invited. Or maybe that was just another rule that didn't exist in Faerieland. If I could actually eat food here, I'd consider relocating.

I drew my Glock and looked over to the right of the door and tried to get my eyes to adjust to the gloom as quick as possible. I should have done that trick where you close your eyes for a couple of minutes before you rush into a dark place with things that might try to kill you, but I'm impatient. And a slow learner judging by the times screwed-up night vision had cost me a half step on my opponent. Today wasn't going to be one of those lessons. I could see nothing threatening in the gloom, so I called out "Clear!" over my shoulder.

"Clear!" Abby's voice came back, and Anna came through the door, hands lighting up the room with their blue glow. She was getting creepier by the hour in Faerieland, but I had to admit she made a great flashlight. And target, apparently, because something came barreling out of the darkness, heading straight for her, the second she crossed the threshold. I couldn't get a good look at it because it was dark, and the bundle of fur and claws was moving crazy fast. I stepped between Anna and the whatever-it-was.

It hit me high in the chest, knocking me off-balance and tumbling me to the floor. I wrestled with the thing, trying to keep its jaws from my throat even as I felt its claws pressing into my chest. Not ripping, just looking for purchase in my leather jacket. I wrestled with the thing for several long seconds before I felt something warm and wet on the side of my face. I squeezed one eye shut to try to see what I was dealing with, when the other side of my face was covered in moisture. Suddenly images from my childhood flashed into my head, moments of summer break and tennis balls before I ever knew what it was like to be trapped in the night forever. With a rush I recognized the deep, earthy, musky smell of a dog that hasn't been bathed in a long time. That's when I realized that I was lying underneath a very large, very happy Labrador that was trying its best to lick me to death.

"I think it likes you!" Abby said with a laugh.

"No accounting for taste," Anna added.

"Shut up and get this mutt off me," I snapped, rolling over and trying to get out from under the dramatically overweight dog. "Hasn't your master ever heard of taking you for a walk?" I muttered, ruffling the fur behind the dog's ears. It gave me one last lick and backed up a few steps, allowing me to scramble to my feet. I backed up and straightened myself the best I could.

I looked over at Anna, who was still standing by the door. "You okay?"

"Oh yeah. My hero. Saving me from the vicious licking Lab. If not for you I could possibly be writhing on the floor being loved to death."

"Well, there's a first time for everything, lady." I reached down and patted the dog's head. "Where's your master, puppy? We need to see this Dream King and have a little chat with him about some people he's kidnapped."

"That won't happen. You should just leave now while you still can, vampire," said the dog, tongue still lolling out one side of its mouth.

I jumped back several feet and looked around at the others. They were staring at me with big eyes and dropped jaws. "Did everybody just hear the dog tell us to leave while we still can?" Everyone nodded. The Labrador looked offended.

"With all the weird shit you run into every day, a talking dog has you hung up? Get over yourself, vampire. Now get out of my house. My master isn't interested in dealing with you." The dog turned and walked away, his tail wagging happily like a flag in a strong breeze.

"Seems the Dream King has interesting taste in butlers," Anna said.

"Yeah," I said. "I had one just like it when I was a kid." That led me to a chilling thought. I had one *just like* that when I was a kid, down to the splash of white on his front left paw and his big belly. Somehow whoever lived here had plucked that dog right out of my memories.

I looked at the others and said, "Let's go find this so-called Dream King and convince him that kidnapping humans and selling them for soup stock could be bad for his health." Not to mention how unhealthy it was to poke around in the childhood memories of a heavily armed vampire.

I stepped farther into the house and started looking around. My eyes had adjusted to the gloom by that point, so I could really see what was around me. It looked like something out of a remake of *Texas Chainsaw Massacre*, or maybe *Saw 27*. The walls were grey with grime, and the wallpaper was peeling all over the place. Squares of slightly brighter dirt outlined where pictures once hung on the walls, and the house seemed to go on forever. It was definitely bigger on the inside than it looked from the outside, reminding me again how much I hate magic.

I stepped through the foyer into a formal parlor, complete with tea service set for two. I lifted the lid of the teapot, then danced back as a spider the size of my fist crawled out. The spider reached up, grabbed the lid from my hand, and pulled it back into place. I gave the tea service (and anything else with a lid) a wide berth after that. There was a fireplace that looked like it hadn't seen use in centuries, and a layer of dust an inch thick on the sofa and two armchairs. I kept expecting Norman Bates or a random lunatic to burst out from behind the heavy curtains swinging a knife at my face.

I turned to say something snide to Abby, then saw that I was alone in the room. I walked back to the foyer, but no one was there. Even stranger, the door was back on its hinges. I grabbed the knob and turned, but the door didn't budge. I pulled harder, with no luck. I put one foot on the jamb and pulled on the door with all my strength, and the doorknob came off in my hand.

"Shit," I muttered. "Hey! Where did everybody go? Abby? Anna? Come on guys, this isn't funny!" I yelled into the apparently empty house. "Come on guys, we've got a job to do! We need to find this Dream King, kick his ass, and get those people back to their kid safely! We don't have time to dick around!"

Nothing. For all I could tell, I was completely alone in this apparently abandoned house.

"Okay, then. Something has snatched my friends and is now currently screwing with me. Probably something that calls itself the Dream King. So *something* is going to get the ass-whooping of its life when I find it." I stomped back into the parlor, looking for some hint that might get me out of this mess.

"Come on, Black. You are a detective, right? Then detect something." I scanned the room for anything that had changed since the last time I was in there. Everything looked the same. Same dusty pictures on the coffee table, same peeling wallpaper, same blank spots on the walls where pictures used to be. I turned in circles, looking for any clue to the whereabouts of the others, then sighed and moved on. Whatever had taken them, I was going to have to kick this Dream King's ass to get them back. As I walked through the parlor toward the back of the house, my knee bumped the tray holding the tea set.

When I did, the lid of the teapot rattled off, and I shuddered, remembering the giant hairy spider that was in there. My shudder shifted to a choked scream when *dozens* of big-ass spiders started crawling out. They boiled over the lip of the silver teapot like lava, a grotesque tide of legs and fangs. I jumped back halfway across the room, barely avoiding tripping over an ottoman that I swear hadn't been there before, and slammed my back into the wall. I felt the whole house shake with the impact, and something landed on my shoulder with a soft *thump*.

I turned my head to the side very, very slowly and saw out of the corner of my eye the biggest damn tarantula/black widow/brown recluse thing I'd ever seen. It was the size of a dinner plate. A dinner plate with fangs as long as my thumb. I screamed like a girl and swatted at the thing, spinning back into the room and hearing nasty crunching sounds as spiders exploded under my boots. I windmilled my arms and managed not to fall on my ass in the middle of the swarm of arachnids, but just barely. I put my arms out and steadied myself on an end table and three of the buggers ran up my sleeve quick as lightning, obviously aiming for my face. Any veneer of calm I had vanished at that point, and I sprinted further into the house, dashing into a formal dining room and slamming the door behind me. I brushed the spiders off my jacket and stomped them into paste, then dragged a heavy chair away from the table and used it to block the door shut. I could hear the scritch-scratching of thousands of little legs against the wood, but all of the spiders were too big to make it under the door. And that's officially the first and last time in my life I've ever been happy that a spider was *big*.

I leaned my head against the door, trying to get my breathing to slow to something resembling normal. I must have stood there motionless for a full minute before I heard the sound of people behind me. People breathing and rustling around uncomfortably, then the sound of someone stifling a laugh. Then came another, then another, then someone couldn't stifle it anymore and burst out laughing. First a polite little chuckle, then a titter, then a chortle, then a guffaw, then peals of laughter rolled over my back like a hailstorm. Each laugh hit me between the shoulder blades like a knife, because the second I opened my eyes and looked down I knew exactly who and what they were laughing at.

When I'd walked, or run screaming like a little girl, into the dining room, I'd been wearing my normal investigate-and-probably-kill-things wardrobe. That consists of a long black leather duster, jeans, a black T-shirt with a comic book character on it (Neil Gaiman's Death this time), a shoulder holster with my Glock 17, an ankle holster with my Ruger LCP, and a pair of motorcycle boots. And boxer briefs for the intimately curious. When I opened my eyes after deciding that I wasn't going to have a heart attack after being chased by giant spiders I saw something out of the ordinary. At least, out of the ordinary since I stopped going to college parties, and it became almost impossible for me to get blackout drunk.

I was naked. Not just missing an article of clothing or two. I was butt-naked standing in a formal dining room with what sounded an awful lot like a table full of people laughing at my skinny freckled butt. I turned slowly around, and the dining room had transformed from an empty, dusty, nasty shell of a formerly glorious place to a spectacular hall of culinary delights, complete with loaded table circled with guests. And by guests, I mean everyone who ever disapproved of me in my life. Anna was there, smirking at my hands clasped in front of my groin. She sat next to my middle-school principal, Mr. Whiteside, who told me time and again that I would amount to nothing in my life because of my flexible relationship with punctuality and attendance. Beside him was my Uncle George, who always thought that I went to Clemson for college because I couldn't get into the University of South Carolina. No matter how many times I told him I never applied to Carolina, he always bashed me for my choice of colleges.

Next to Uncle George was a string of girls stretching from middle school through the college girls I'd dated before I died. Every one of them giggled and pointed at my skinny frame. No small number of them had done the same thing in real life, leading to a series of unpleasant dates and a few downright disastrous ones. They were followed in the hit parade by Mickey Rogers, the guy who beat me up every day in fourth grade and stole my lunch. Next to Mickey was Jacob Riley, the guy who beat me up in sixth grade. Then there was Thomas Evers, who kicked my ass all through eighth grade. I never got beat up in odd-numbered years, or at least not enough to remember.

Anyone who had ever ridiculed or demeaned me was sitting around one fancy-dress dinner table, watching me clutch my jewels with both hands and scurry through the room butt-naked. As bad as the moment was, cavorting naked in this dining room wasn't the most humiliating event of my life, which says a lot of unpleasant things about my life. But naked cavorting definitely made the top five. I reached the far door and yanked it open, ducking through and only caring the slightest bit about what was on the other side. Until it tried to kill me.

Chapter 21

THAT'S THE STORY of my life, right? I barrel through the world yanking open doors and never thinking about what might be on the other side until it tries to shove a stake through my heart. Which is exactly what happened when I got through the door and slammed it shut, leaning my back against the door with my eyes closed. I heard the creak of a floorboard directly in front of me and opened my eyes just in time to see a stake headed for my chest. I dropped straight down onto my heels and then exploded up, launching myself at my attacker's midsection. He folded like a cheap suit, and I dumped him on his ass a few feet away. I stepped quickly back to give myself some room to work, happy to find myself clothed again, then froze at what I saw.

Lying on the floor in full vampire hunter regalia was the spitting image of Van Helsing. Or at least what I imagined Van Helsing would look like if he was alive today. He was taller than Hugh Jackman, but he had the leather duster, big hat, and flowing shirt going on. He was dressed all in black, with a closely trimmed beard and flowing dark hair. He put his hands back beside his head and performed a flawless kip-up to land on his feet, then lashed out at me with a vicious kick to my head. I ducked back just in time, a little stunned at the speed of the vampire hunter.

My surprise morphed into outright concern when he drew a pair of long silver daggers and came at me faster than any human had a right to be. I looked around me, taking in my surroundings for the first time, and realized I stood in an old-fashioned kitchen. I reached over to the cast-iron stove and grabbed a black iron skillet to use as a shield. I swatted away several of the hunter's strokes, but he was always advancing. I batted him aside time and again, but he kept coming. *So this is how most people feel about old age*, I thought as I dodged another thrust. *Inexorable and sobering.* I managed to get a punch or two in myself, but never connected with any strength behind it. The one good shot I got in, Van Helsing got one of his knives up and dug a deep furrow into my forearm.

I drew back my bleeding arm and said, "This is my favorite jacket, asshole. You're gonna have to pay for that."

"Let's see how much you worry about fashion when your head is hanging on my bedpost, bloodfiend."

I blanched a little at the image. "Dude, you are the worst interior decorator in the world." He had me pinned in a corner, with a refrigerator on one side and the stove on the other. Only a massive butcher's block separated the two of us, and he grinned as he sheathed his knives.

"You think that's a good idea, putting away your weapons in the middle of a fight?" I asked, secretly very relieved that he'd put the knives away. That cut on my arm *hurt*, and the silver meant that it wasn't going to heal very quickly. All my relief washed away in a tidal wave of fear when he picked up the butcher's block and swung it at my head. That thing must have been two feet in all directions and weighed a couple hundred pounds. I ducked, and a whole swath of cabinetry turned to splinters. I turned my duck into a forward roll and dove under his outstretched arms before he could regain his balance, and came up behind the hunter.

I put one hand on each side of his head, and with a quick twist of his neck, dropped his lifeless body to the kitchen floor. Van Helsing lay on the tile with his head facing the wrong way, and I reached down and relieved him of his jacket. I shrugged into the stolen leather duster and grinned. After all, he'd sliced mine open, so it was only fair. I looked around and saw two exits to the kitchen—one back the way I'd come and another one that looked like it led out into the backyard. I decided against walking back through the dining room and risking my clothes again. I turned the knob leading outside.

But instead of stepping out into the Market, or anyplace else for that matter, I stepped into my living room back home. Abby was standing in front of me, and it was all I could do not to throw my arms around her and kiss her adorable little vampire face.

"Abby! I am so glad to see you! Something crazy is going on here, and we gotta find Anna and get the hell outta Dodge."

I reached out to her, but Abby slapped my hand away. "It's not going to work, Jimmy. I'm really out of here this time. I'm tired of making up my mind just to get called back into another one of your schemes. I'm moving in with Greg, and there's nothing you can say to stop me." She turned and walked out the door, slamming it hard enough to rattle the glass on her way out.

I turned around a couple of times calling out for Greg, then Sabrina, but I was completely alone. I wandered through the house looking for someone to explain what the hell was going on, but there was no one there. No one. All of Abby's stuff was gone, all of Greg's stuff was gone, even the stuff of Sabrina's that she'd taken to leaving at our place was gone. The bottle of scotch I kept on the bar for Mike was even gone! I was completely alone, and I had no idea how to get back to my friends or how to rescue the kidnapped humans from the Dream King.

I heard a creak on the stairs and heard a *whoosh* as something heavy swung toward my head. I dove out of the way, then spun around and launched myself into my attacker. I heard a *"Whoof!"* from above me as I buried my shoulder in the other guy's gut. A fairly large gut, to be sure. I shoved the stake-wielding fatty off me and took a good look at who was trying to kill me this time. And almost ended up decapitated when I froze. It was Greg. My partner and best friend was trying to kill me.

He would have, too, if my self-preservation instincts hadn't outweighed my shock at the situation. He dropped the katana he was swinging at my throat, then stepped in and jabbed with a stake. Because I'm a lot faster than Greg I was able to get an arm up quick enough to block. I didn't manage to block the punch to the ribs that he followed up with, and I heard something crack low in my chest. Greg had always been stronger than me, and whatever rage was fueling him now had him jacked up beyond his normal strength. I staggered from the punch to the ribs, and he caught me on the side of the head with a looping roundhouse punch that would have killed a human. As it was, I spun completely around and went weak in the knees for a second. The only thing that kept me alive was the fact that I knew his style. I knew that Greg always follows up that right with an uppercut designed to finish the fight right there. Against an opponent who doesn't know it's coming, the uppercut usually does the job. But I did know it was coming, so I stepped inside his punch and blocked it with a forearm.

"What the hell, bro?" I exclaimed as I danced back out of my partner's reach.

"You're out of hand, pal. All your talk about being the 'apex predator' has gone to your head. You're killing things just to satisfy your bloodlust. You've turned into the monster we're trying to protect people from, and I've gotta put you down." He threw another punch at my head, but I knew the move was a patented Greg feint. I batted the attempt aside and spun out of the way of his follow-up strike with the stake. A quick kick lashed out at my midsection, allowing me to trap his foot in the crook of my elbow.

"Greg, this is nuts. I'm the same guy I've always been. What are you talking about? Today I might have killed a goblin or twelve, but they totally count as monsters. And they were eating us!"

Then it clicked. Greg was still in Milandra's palace, recuperating. He was too injured to travel and had to drink faerie blood every couple of hours to rebuild his leg muscles. So how was he here trying to stake me? Simple answer—he wasn't. Fake Greg threw another punch at my face, and I caught his arm. Now that I knew it wasn't really Greg and was probably just a figment of my imagination, I didn't have to play nice anymore. I pulled hard on the arm, and twisted while I yanked. I planted a foot in the creature's chest for leverage, and after a few seconds, the arm came off with a wet ripping sound. I swung my improvised club around my head a couple of times, then made a "come here" gesture to the bleeding thing that was masquerading as my partner.

At least I really hoped it was a thing masquerading as my partner. Otherwise I was going to have to open every jar of peanut butter in the house for the rest of eternity.

I was right, because the air shimmered, Greg vanished, and the room we had been fighting in was suddenly the inside of a tent, very similar to the other tents in the Market. I was lying on a blanket on the floor, and I was covered in a cold blood-sweat from head to toe. Sitting in a chair on a small dais was a wizened little man with big ears and a couple of tufts of white hair dancing around his head. He saw me looking at him and began to do that really irritating slow clap thing that people do when you've figured something out, but they still want to make you feel obtuse about it.

"Well done, Mr. Black. You found me out. None of it was real, not even the icky-wicky widdle spiders." He grinned at me, and I worked really hard at not lunging up to punch his nose out through the back of his skull. I slowly got to my feet, shaking my head to clear the last of the cobwebs.

"Where are my friends?"

"Well, they haven't figured it out quite as quickly as you did. And they aren't having a particularly good time in my dreamland." He gave me a vicious grin and pointed to where Anna and Abby lay writhing on blankets. They both looked like they were trapped in their worst nightmares, which thinking back to what I'd just left, I supposed they were.

"Let them wake," I demanded, taking a step forward.

The little man held up a warning finger. "Ah-ah-ahhh. You behave yourself, or their dreams might take a turn for the worse. And you know what they say happens to you when you die in a dream, right? You die in real life."

"I've been dead for a while. It's not so bad. Now let my friends go."

"And if I don't?"

"Then I wring your scrawny neck, Yoda." I stalked to the dais and put a hand on each side of the little man's head. As soon as I touched him, he vanished in a flash of light and a puff of smoke.

I heard a cackling laugh float through the air, and the obnoxious little man's voice came back to me. "It's not that easy, Mr. Black. You don't get to steal my dreams without a fight!" I felt a breath on the back of my neck, and turned to see an ogre standing there dripping sweat and spoiling for a fight.

I looked up, up, and up at the beast, a twin to the one we'd fought in the chef's tent. It reached out with a furry paw, and I ducked, lashing out with a kick to one knee. I bounced off, my foot hitting the beast in the leg and launching me backward instead of doing any damage to the ogre. I landed flat on my back in the center of the tent, and the ogre stalked me while I scurried around backward like an oversized crab. It stomped at my head, and I flipped over, jumping to my feet and running for the tent opening. The tent opening that oddly enough was no longer there. I turned back to the ogre and racked my brain for some weak spot in the creature. I saw nothing, just a big beastie with visions of picking its teeth with my shinbones.

Then it hit me—a vision. That's all any of this was, a vision. A dream. It wasn't real, it was all a dream. And if I could take control of the dream, I could take control of the ogre. It swung a huge fist at my head again, and this time instead of ducking I thought as hard as I could about being more powerful, trying to convince myself that this wasn't going to hurt, and I just stood there. I planted my feet and stuck out my chest, and the ogre's fist bounced off my jaw like a spitball.

The ogre's eyes widened, and I looked way up at its stunned face. "I'd run now if I were you," I said, and made a shooing motion with my hands. The ogre turned and dashed through the side of the tent, leaving a cartoon outline of its body where it went through the tent wall.

"Very good, Mr. Black. Very good. But you aren't out of the woods yet. You must still match wits with me, and I fear you are inadequately armed for that particular battle."

The little man stepped out of the blackness right in front of me, and I smiled down at him. "I don't have to be strong enough or smart enough to beat you, chump. She already is."

I pointed over the Dream King's shoulder at where Anna stood, her glowing blue hands held high above her head. She leveled her fists at the little man, and beams of pure magic shot from her hands and enveloped the little manipulator. He let out a scream as the blue fire enveloped him, and the tent flickered back into reality. The Dream King flung out his arms, and I watched as the fire flickered behind his eyes, rolled across his face, and finally covered his entire body in a flickering blue shimmer. The blue light flickered around him for long seconds, then a black fog began to ooze from his eyes and mouth. The smoke coalesced into a floating ball of blackness that hung in the air above the Dream King for a moment, then swirled in on itself until it finally winked out of existence. The little man's eyes opened wide within the nimbus of blue, then he floated up into the air about a foot, finally falling heavily to the dirt. He lay there stunned for a long moment before sucking in a deep breath and rolling over onto his knees. The little man gave Anna a terrified look and bolted from the tent.

"What did you do to him?" I asked the witch, who had sunk heavily onto a stool as soon as the Dream King fled.

"I burned out his magic. He'll never use his power to harm anyone again. Because he doesn't have any power left."

"Wow. That's pretty harsh," I said, poking around the tent looking for a back room.

"Especially since his magic was what had kept him alive for the last couple thousand years. He'll probably be dead before the sun sets." She put her elbows on her knees and sank her face into her hands. I patted her on the shoulder in what I hoped was an encouraging fashion. I knew what it felt like the first time you crossed a line, and how much easier it got every time you crossed it afterward. It was the kind of thing I tried not to dwell on, but something I hoped Abby would realize before she was too far over the line. Anna patted my hand in a kind of thanks, and I stepped away to give her a moment alone.

I stepped over to where Abby was lying. She was still out, but she wasn't thrashing around like before Anna took out the Dream King.

I reached for her, but Anna caught my arm. "Leave her. She'll come out of it on her own now, but you should let her find her own way back." I nodded and moved to check out the rest of the tent. My super-hearing could detect more people breathing, I just needed to find them.

I kept poking around, finding more and more vile substances in jars, books with indecipherable writing on the covers and human body parts labeled with uses I didn't want to know. Finally, in a back corner behind a stack of boxes, I found what I was looking for.

Chapter 22

TUCKED AWAY IN a dusty corner, hidden by a stack of boxes labeled "Records, Do Not Disturb," was a flap in the tent wall. I pulled it aside and saw a smaller room hidden from the main body of the tent. I ducked inside, holding breath I didn't need against what I might find. And there, sitting on the floor and trussed up like a Thanksgiving turkey in a whole lot of Eddie Bauer clothes, was our missing yuppie couple. The husband looked none the worse for wear, just a little dirty with a couple of bruises dotting his face. The wife was another story. Her makeup had seen better months, her hair looked like a rat had been breakdancing on her head, her clothes were torn almost to rags, and her nails were ripped off to the quick. But it was her eyes that told the story. The eyes always let you know just how bad someone has had it, and this lady had seen things that most humans think only exist in horror movies. Whatever the Dream King had been doing to people, he'd done a lot more of it to Mrs. Carmichael than to her husband. I hoped we weren't too late to save what was left of her sanity.

I pulled the tent flap open and motioned for Anna to come in. She started to push her way past me, but I put my hand on her shoulder. "The wife is almost gone, Anna. I probably shouldn't be the one talking to her about safe passage home and all that jazz, what with the not breathing, pale skin, and more guns and knives than a Schwarzenegger movie."

"That's remarkably sensitive of you, James. Perhaps you're not a complete moron after all."

"At least not on alternate Tuesdays in Faerieland. The rest of the time I'm pretty much a moron by your standards." I grinned and stepped aside as Anna stepped over to the woman. I slid silently back out to the main section of the tent and knelt down beside Abby's prone form. I reached out and shook her shoulder, and she jerked awake. She woke up grumpy, and went straight for my throat with her fingernails. I caught her hands and held her fast for a long moment until her eyes cleared and she realized it was me. Then she suddenly relaxed and threw her arms around my neck, sobbing into my shoulder.

"Oh Jimmy, thank God you woke me up! I was in the middle of the worst dreams ever! I was back in school, only I was still a vampire, so I had to deal with classes, and my sorority, and eating people, and you and Greg and Lilith and the Master of the City, and everything. It was awful! I had just about decided to walk out into the sunlight when you woke me." She collapsed back into incoherent sobbing, and I put one arm around her and patted her head with the other one. I'm sure I looked like a parody of a guy who has no idea how to comfort a sobbing woman, but the fact is, I had no idea how to comfort a sobbing woman. I let her cry for a couple of minutes, and she finally pulled herself together.

She sniffled, wiped eyes on her sleeve, and pulled back to look at me. "Now where's that little dream-twisting bastard? He and I need to have a little conversation." She punctuated "conversation" with a crack of her knuckles, and I suddenly wished that the little magician wasn't off dead or dying in the Market so I could see just what Abby had in mind.

"No good, kiddo. Anna took care of him. Permanently."

"Anna? That sweet witch that's friends with Father Mike? What could she possible do to anyone?" I explained what Anna had done, and Abby shuddered.

"That's pretty scary. I guess she's got more on the ball than I thought. And she doesn't really like you very much, does she?"

"Most days that's an understatement."

"Doesn't that worry you a little?"

"Nope," I replied honestly. "I think my irresistible charm is wearing her down. But it's working really slowly. So the faster we can get the nice people behind the curtain moving and back to the mundane world, the better off I think I'll be."

"Well then get in here and talk to this guy. I've restored his wife to some semblance of sanity, but she's still really freaked out, and he's got a few questions he wants answered." Anna's voice came from the back room.

"Abby, poke around out here and see if you can find anything connecting our Dream King to the mundane world. I've got a bad feeling that there's at least one more player we haven't met yet." She threw me a half-assed salute and started poking around the tent.

I went back into the room where our hostages were now sitting unbound, rubbing their wrists and ankles where the ropes had left red marks. I walked over to the husband and stuck out my hand. He took it and said, "David Carmichael. This is my wife Elizabeth."

His wife focused on me and started firing off questions faster than I could answer them. "Where are we? Where is our baby? Is Patrick okay? How did we get here? What was that *thing* doing to me? Why us? Where is my baby?" She collapsed in a sobbing heap in her husband's lap.

I looked over at Anna, who shrugged as if to say "that's the best I can do." At least she wasn't zombified anymore. Her reactions seemed normal, if a little extreme.

I sat down cross-legged on the floor in front of them and addressed the husband. "I understand you have a lot of questions. I can answer them one of two ways. I can make up answers that will fit in with the way you looked at the world before you were kidnapped, or I can tell you the truth. If I lie to you to protect your feelings, we'll need to blindfold you to get you out of here. I can lie like nobody's business, but some things you just can't unsee. If I tell you the truth, you probably won't sleep very well for a long time to come. But it's your call."

"Give it to me straight, doctor. I can take it." He gave me a lopsided half-grin, and I thought for a second about how I was about to turn this guy's view of the world on its ear. But he asked for it, even if he didn't really know what he was asking for.

"Okay, here goes nothing. You remember all those faerie tale creatures you read about when you were a kid? Trolls, elves, dwarves, vampires, and witches? Well, they're real. Pretty much all of them. You're sitting in a tent in the Goblin Market, which is in a corner of Faerieland. You were kidnapped by an evil magician, and I rescued you with my witchy friend Anna and my protégé, Abby."

"Protégé? And what are you supposed to be, a mighty wizard and his apprentice?"

I looked at him for a minute, then willed my fangs to drop. Needle-sharp fangs slid into place out of the roof of my mouth, and I smiled at him. "Not exactly," I said.

He skittered back a little on his butt, and I held up a hand. "But this time I'm one of the good guys. I'm working with the Charlotte PD on a group of unsolved murders and disappearances, and you guys happened to get kidnapped right in the middle of our case. So here you are, all safe and sound thanks to your friendly neighborhood vampire detectives."

"What did he want with us? Why did he bring us here? What was he doing to Elizabeth?" David asked, keeping a respectable distance from me. I didn't bother letting him know I could cross the five feet between us in less time than it took him to blink. No need to terrify the poor man any more.

"I'm not exactly sure, Mr. Carmichael. We haven't figured—" Anna cut me off before I could sugarcoat things for the husband.

"He was stealing her dreams," Anna cut in. "His magic was based on dreams, and he'd lived too long to have any of his own left, so he had to steal them from others. He worked with them, spinning dreams into illusions and charms that he sold, and he traded them raw for other magical components." Her face was tight as she flipped through books on a table along the outer wall of the tent.

"How do you steal someone's dreams?" I asked.

"It's a very painful and invasive process, Jimmy. I don't think I want to describe it right now." She put a lot of emphasis on the last couple of words, and slid her eyes over toward where Elizabeth as staring at her.

"Does this mean I won't be able to dream anymore? Will I sleep? Don't people go crazy when they can't dream? Is that what this is, I'm going crazy? David, what's happening?" Elizabeth's voice rose in pitch with every question until she was almost shrieking. She collapsed in her husband's lap, and he looked up at us with pleading eyes. Anna knelt beside them and pulled Elizabeth upright. Anna put her arms around the other woman and whispered something in her ear. Then she put her hands on both sides of Elizabeth's head and pressed their foreheads together. Anna's hands glowed blue again, then yellow, then a pale pink. Elizabeth stiffened, and then collapsed, unconscious, back in her husband's lap.

David lay his wife gently down on the floor of the tent, and as Anna gave him directions, stretched her out into a comfortable position. Anna pressed her hand to Elizabeth's forehead. She reached the other hand out to me. "Jimmy, give me your hand."

I didn't budge. "Why?" It's not that I don't trust Anna, or witches in particular. I don't trust anybody. Too many movies about people poking folks like me with sharp pointy things, makes a fella a wee bit paranoid. And, with Anna, my paranoia was justified. The first time we met she'd tried to trap me in a magic circle with a dozen angry spirits.

"I've given her some of my dreams, now I'm going to give her some of yours."

"Why does she need my dreams? Won't she make her very own dreams whenever she sleeps?" I asked.

"I know what science says about dreams, but they're all wrong. Dreams are the psychic manifestations of ourselves—our hopes, our fears, our ambitions—everything that makes up who we are is contained in dreams. Dreams are what happens when our minds touch the magic of the universe and we see what can be when we stop overthinking everything. The Dream King didn't just take her dreams, he took pieces of herself, and there isn't enough left of her to rebuild itself. She needs some of our dreams to build on. If I take a few from each of us you won't miss them. I won't take any of the ones where you're having sex."

"That doesn't leave many," I warned, but I let her take my hand. That pale pink light tingled as it crawled up my arm, then swarmed over my face, then I gasped as I watched half-remembered snatches of dreams flash past my eyes and into nothingness. It seemed to go on for hours, but the awake part of me told the rest of me that it lasted just a matter of seconds, then I slumped sideways to the ground, trying to get my eyes to refocus.

Anna repeated the process with David, explaining that Elizabeth needed dreams, and that hers were stolen. This whole process was just to patch enough of the holes in her subconscious for her to begin to build new dreams of her own. Taking just a pinch of the dream energy from all three of us was enough to help Elizabeth, but not enough to cause any lasting harm to any of us. There might be a few sleepless nights in our future, but that prospect worried me less than most folks. The look in David's eyes said he might be lying awake a few nights regardless of anything we did.

After getting our dreams deposited in her head, Elizabeth seemed to be resting comfortably. Anna went back to poking around in the Dream King's books, and I started opening boxes and flipping through papers. There had to be a clue to the King's partner. Someone had to deliver the fresh meat. The King had been an obvious recluse, with no contact with the mundane world. I couldn't see him procuring his subjects himself.

"Nothing out here, boss," Abby said, coming in from the main tent. "A couple of customers came by, and they weren't real happy when I told them the dream shop was closed permanently. You find anything?"

"Yeah, I've got books and books of his records, but there's so much here I can't tell what's useful and what's not."

"What are you looking for?" Anna asked.

"Well, I'm pretty sure our mighty midget Dream King didn't hop over into the real world to kidnap these folks, and no one at the shopping center reported seeing anything out of the ordinary, so I'm wondering who did take them."

"And why? I understand what the Dream King got out of the deal, but why would anyone from our world join forces with someone so vile as this bastard?" Anna asked.

"Same reason people do nasty things every day, Anna. Cash. And here's that missing piece we were looking for." I pointed to a ledger I'd just opened on the table. "This shows a list of transactions, with money coming in for dreams, and money paid out for what he called 'raw resources.' The last resource purchase was three days ago, the same time that the Carmichaels were abducted. It looks like he bought 'resources' every four or five days, so we've got maybe two days before another couple is kidnapped. That's not a lot of time."

"Why the rush?" Abby asked. "Why not just wait here for the guy and take him out when he tries to make the next delivery?"

I thought about it for a minute, but then shook my head. "No. We haven't been exactly subtle in our search, and if our Igor gets here with a couple of people in tow and no place to sell them, there's no telling what he might do. Let's get this guy taken care of on our schedule, back in our world."

"Seems legit," Abby said. "Besides, these folks are gonna need to see a shrink, and pronto."

"Exactly. So let's get to detecting." I turned to the man sitting on the floor stroking his wife's hair. "David, how long do you think you've been here?"

"I'd guess a day, day and a half, maybe."

"Were you taken somewhere else before you were brought here? You've been missing three days," I said.

"Yeah, the guy who grabbed us kept us in his garage for the rest of the afternoon and moved us at night. I guess I lost track of the time we were in the garage if you say it's been three days."

"Don't sweat that," I said. "Time gets funky when you cross dimensions, and he probably kept you pretty well knocked out while he was working on your wife." I felt for the guy. Here he was, just trying to go through his day, get a little shopping done, and then he finds himself trapped in something beyond his worst nightmare. There were certain parallels between his situation and my own. I'd woken up one day to find my world changed into my worst nightmare, but hopefully his walk on the wild side would be over in a couple of hours.

Chapter 23

WE DUG UP WHAT information we could from the Dream King's tent, and Anna whisked us all back to Milandra's palace. She'd brought a trunk full of books with her, and when I asked about it, she just said some things shouldn't be left lying about. I didn't ask any more questions, because she still scared me. Not because she hated me, but because she treated me like a bug she could squash if it became worth the bother. I couldn't wait until we got back to our world where I was at the top of the food chain again.

Greg looked a lot better when we got back. Sabrina, Stephen, and Milandra all had that hint of red in their cheeks and eyes that hinted at a tearful reconciliation, probably followed by copious amounts of booze if my past experience with fae hospitality was any guide. Yep, Sabrina was a little unsteady on her feet when she ran over to me and threw her arms around my neck. I caught her before she ended up on her butt.

"Detective, I don't know if your lieutenant would consider you fit for duty right now, but I'm not complaining." I enjoyed the way all her curves were pressed up against me, but I might catch some serious ribbing from Greg and Abby about it later.

"I can think of a few things I'm fit for, big boy." Sabrina purred into my ear, then reached around and grabbed a handful of butt cheek with one hand. "Is that a Glock in your pocket or are you just happy to see me?"

"Oh, I'm definitely happy to see you, Sabrina." I leaned down and kissed her hard enough to leave *me* short of breath, then broke free to look her in the eyes. "But this is going to have to wait."

"I've never met a man so insistent on keeping me at arm's length. What's wrong, Jimmy? Don't you like me?" She gave me a little pout and batted her eyelashes at me. When she let a curl of brown hair fall down over her eye, I almost melted right there, but duty called.

"Boy howdy, I like you, but we've got another kidnapped couple. Or we will soon. And I'm afraid that when the kidnapper realizes he doesn't have anyone to deliver the goods to, he'll freak out and kill his latest victims to avoid getting caught with them."

I saw understanding flicker deep in Sabrina's wine-soaked eyes, and she heaved a deep sigh. She hopped up on tiptoes to give me another quick kiss on the lips, then turned to Tivernius. "Well, that will have to wait for another time, I suppose. Magic me sober, oh Grand Scaly One."

The dragon chuckled and waved a hand in the air. "You'd better catch her, Jimmy. This is going to hurt."

A greenish glow flickered over Sabrina, and she staggered against me. Her free hand flew to her head, and she buried her face in my shirt for a long ten seconds. I felt her shoulders heave once, twice, then settle down as the urge to puke all over me passed. I heaved my own sigh of relief at that, then barely stifled my laughter as Sabrina stood bolt upright and hurriedly removed her hand from my ass, tucking it into a pocket.

The newly sober and obviously brutally hungover Detective Law straightened her clothes and waved a servant over for a request. The faerie dashed off and returned a few seconds later with a pitcher of what smelled like grape juice. I put my hand on the handle before Sabrina poured her glass, and she stared up at me with pained eyes.

"Hold on for just a second. And you probably don't want to look." She closed her eyes and stood still as I poured her a glass, then pricked my index finger on a fang. I squeezed out a few drops of my blood, then shook the glass to stir it as well as I could. I handed the glass to Sabrina, who drained half the glass in one gulp.

"What is this? I thought you were bringing me grape juice. Are grapes different in Faerieland?" she asked the servant.

I coughed and raised my hand. "I added a little restorative agent to the juice. It'll help the hangover heal a lot faster."

Sabrina's eyes narrowed. "What kind of restorative agent? The kind that comes from that flask in your jacket pocket?"

"No, honest. There's no alcohol involved." I checked for my flask and realized it was still there. Good thing, too. If I'd really swapped jackets with that dream-Van Helsing I'd have been upset about losing the flask. And my car keys.

"So what is it? I know there was something more than grape juice in there?" Sabrina's eyes were starting to flash, and I knew it was about to get loud.

"Blood. I put a few drops of my blood in the juice. It'll help you heal faster."

She went pale and very, very still. She looked up at me, and her eyes were very wide. "What else will it do?" Her voice was low and a little shaky.

"Nothing. I put like three drops in there. Not enough to do anything but provide a healing boost. For it to have any effect on you other than healing you'd have to be almost dead yourself, and drink me almost dry. The drops will just help you heal and give you a little extra pep in your step. That's all, I promise."

"Are you sure? I'm not suddenly going to have to have all my steak *tartare*, am I?"

I pulled back, offended that she thought I'd turn her against her will, and barely caught sight of Greg out of the corner of my eye.

"I'd never do that. Not again. Not now that I know what it means," I said, trying hard to keep my voice under control. The idea that she thought I wanted to turn her hit me in the gut, and left me wondering how good an idea this whole "try to date a human" thing really was.

"No, don't worry, Sabrina. He only condemns people to eternal darkness and a limited diet when he's ignorant and really hungry." Greg picked the wrong moment to add in his two cents.

"You wanna go, partner? I've just spent the last half a day battling a guy who turned my head inside out and showed me my psyche, while you've been lounging around here snacking on faerie neck and laughing it up in the lap of luxury. I'm not exactly in the mood to have my motives questioned, especially from the guy who used to list his biggest goal in life as 'develop super-powers.' Well, I gave you everything you ever dreamed of, pal. So back off."

Greg and I had moved to where we were facing off just a few feet from each other. There was a wide circle around us, like a playground when a fight was about to break out. I took one step in, and then Abby was between us.

"God, I hate it when Dad and Dad fight!" she said, putting a hand on each of our chests. "This isn't the time. We've got to get these humans home and find the kidnapper before he grabs another pair, remember?"

I nodded and stepped back, turning to Sabrina. "I'm sorry. I didn't mean to scare you."

She didn't look in my eyes, just said, "I'm sorry, too. It's been a tough week."

"Tell me about it. I had a goblin eating my arms, remember?"

"You've got a point there. And my head really does feel a lot better. Thanks."

"Anytime, babe. Anytime."

I turned to Greg. "Can this be over?" I asked.

"No, but it can be over enough for now."

"I'll take it. Here's what we've got so far. We beat the bad guy here, but I'm afraid there's at least one more guy back in our world that needs an extra-large can of whoop-ass opened on his head," I said, cracking my knuckles.

"I can do that. I've really wanted to hit something ever since we got out of the chef's tent."

"I'm pretty sure we can arrange that. So what are we looking at?" I asked, trying to get a good look at the paper he held.

Abby stepped forward and grabbed the page. "Well, I'm no Picasso, but I came up with a rough sketch of our bad guy based on Mr. Carmichael's description." She turned the picture around, and I immediately disagreed with her. It might have been a Picasso. From the cubist period. Or a Dali. Or a Pollock. What it was not, was a useful sketch that we could compare to the features of any living human being, unless their face was first run through a meat grinder and then spit out the ass end of a wood chipper. I tried to hide my reaction, but I was all out of subtle for the day, apparently, because Abby's face fell to somewhere around her kneecaps.

"Why not simply pluck the image from his mind and transfer it to the page?" Milandra asked from behind me. I jumped a little and whirled around.

"How did you get there?" I asked. "Nobody should be able to sneak up on me!"

"I'm the Queen of Faerie, James. This is *my* realm, and I get to do whatever I please. Including mask my approach from the legendary senses of the Sanguine."

"One of these days I'm going to get you to explain that whole Sanguine thing. Seems to be a little bit more than a title around here," I grumbled at her.

"One day I shall. Now back to the matter at hand. You have a powerful witch with you, why not simply transfer the image from Mr. Carmichael's mind onto the page. And welcome to Faerie, Mr. Carmichael. I apologize for the wrong done to you by the denizen of the Market, and promise you and your wife the protection of my

consort Tivernius and all the legions of the Fae while you are here."
She gave him a courtly curtsey, and David stood up to offer the best
bow he could manage, which was good for a guy raised in
contemporary America.

Anna stepped forward and curtseyed to Milandra. "Thank you for
the kind assessment of my meager abilities, Your Majesty, but I have
no idea how to do this thing of which you speak. I fear Mrs.
Carmichael is far too fragile to attempt any tampering with her mind at
this time, and I would hesitate to put Mr. Carmichael's mind in
jeopardy by attempting an unfamiliar spell."

"A wise response, Madame Witch. I believe Tivernius may be of
assistance. Dear?" she called, and Tivernius came over. He was less
terrifying in human form than when he was a twenty-foot-tall dragon,
but he was still better than six and a half feet of pure muscle and
chiseled jaw. I reflexively tightened my grip on Sabrina's hand when
the paragon of manliness strode over to us. I noticed that Tivernius
never walked, he always *strode*. I wondered a little if I could stride, then
remembered that I tended to trip over things when I took long steps. I
sighed a little and focused on what the magic-users discussed.

"I believe I can help. Mr. Carmichael, did you get a good look at
the man who abducted you?"

"Yes, I'll never forget his face."

"If you concentrate on that image to the exclusion of anything
else, I should be able to peer into your mind and transfer that image
from your mind to paper by magical means." Tivernius snapped his
fingers and a servant ran over to him. "Paper, please."

The servant returned moments later with a sheaf of thick paper,
and Tivernius led David over to a small round table with two chairs.
He sat opposite David, and instructed him to lean forward with his
elbows on the table and head in his hands. "There should be no
discomfort associated with this spell, but I cannot promise it. I do not
completely understand the magic of this so-called Dream King, so
there may be damage to your brain of which we are not currently
aware. I can only assure you that I will attempt to cause you no undue
pain, and that this is the most accurate method for creating the sketch
that could bring your abductor to justice."

David nodded, then assumed the position. Tivernius mirrored his
posture, and leaned forward until their heads were almost touching.
The dragon-man shifted until his head was supported by one hand,
with the other hand touching the stack of papers. He closed his eyes,

and the pair were enveloped in a warm yellow glow that flowed from Tivernius across the air to David, and down over the man's head and shoulders.

Sabrina leaned over and asked me, "Do you know what he's doing?"

"I have no idea. I can't even program my DVR, much less do magic on this scale."

She grinned at me. "Yeah, good point. You're more the hit-things-until-they-work guy. Anna?"

The witch turned from where she had been closely studying the process. "It seems that there are two spells layered on top of each other, maybe even more. The first spell allows Tivernius to see an image that David has fixed firmly in his mind's eye, a type of magical clairvoyance, if you will. Then there seems to be another spell on top of that one which gives Tivernius significantly increased artistic ability, to let him draw anything that he holds firmly in *his* mind."

"So it's using magic to create psychic abilities?" Greg asked. "Because I've heard of people doing that before. Drawing things they've never seen."

"Automatic writing, I chimed in. Everyone turned to look at me like I had three heads. "What? I read."

Anna continued. "He's right, for a change. It's also called psychography, and it's the principle on which a Ouija board works. Something outside the person holding the pen, or planchette, takes control of their body and writes, draws or moves a pointer through them. That's what Tivernius is doing—he's using magic to move the pencil and create a drawing based on what he sees in David's mind."

After a few minutes, Tivernius' hand started to move across the page. I tried to peek at what he was drawing, but his hand was moving too fast for me to get a good glimpse. It took him another five minutes or so, then he leaned back in his chair and the glow faded from around the two men. I walked over and picked up the paper.

I showed it to David, and asked "Is this the man that kidnapped you?"

He gasped and nodded. "That's him. That's him exactly."

I walked over to where Elizabeth was sitting and showed her the picture. "Is this the guy? Take your time, we want you to be sure."

She didn't take any time. "That's him. That's the bastard. He pulled out of a parking space right in front of us, and when we stopped, he jumped out of his car with a gun in his hand. He pointed the gun right at David's face and made us get in his van. When I tried to go back to Andrew, he grabbed me by the hair and threw me in the back of the van. David tried to fight him, but he sprayed something in his face."

"Probably mace or pepper spray," Sabrina said, her tone now back to business. "Traces of capsicum spray were found at the scene. We figured that was what he used to subdue his victims. Can you describe the van for me?" This was the first we'd heard from Elizabeth since we got her free of the Dream King, and she was proving a lot more helpful than I'd hoped.

"It was white, with a rack on top, like the ones that carry ladders? There was nothing in the back, no windows, no seats, just a big empty space with a cage between the back and the front seats. We tried to get out, but there weren't any door handles on the inside."

"He modified a normal work van into a kidnap vehicle," I muttered.

"Makes you wonder how often he did this kind of thing," Greg added.

"I'll put that on the list of things I need to ask our friend when we find him," I said.

"What if he doesn't feel like talking?" Greg asked.

I smiled at him and said very quietly, "He will."

Tivernius stood and turned to us. "I hope that drawing will be of assistance. I am afraid that I will not be able to travel with you and provide direct aid in apprehending this foul villain. We have much work to do in restoring the Goblin Market to normal business conditions after your . . . visit."

"Yeah, sorry about that. Maybe someday we'll come to visit and not start half a dozen inter-dimensional wars." I gave Milandra a sheepish grin. "Thanks for not killing us, Your Majesty. It was good to see you again."

"And you as well, James. Now it is time for you to return home, and finish this unpleasant business once and for all." She waved a hand, and a golden circle of light opened up in front of us. I had just enough time to wonder if it was daytime back in our world before the circle passed over me and I was home.

Chapter 24

FORTUNATELY FOR MY lily-white complexion, I was *really* home. As in, in our basement den, right where Anna said we'd reappear. Even better, it was just about sunset. The room was pretty full with me, Greg, Abby, Anna, Sabrina, Stephen, and the Carmichaels, but as soon as we all realized where we were, people jumped into action. Sabrina whipped out her cell phone and called into her boss, Lieutenant McDaniel, telling him that we had recovered the Carmichaels safe and sound, then asking him to send a couple of patrol cars over to our place to take them home and to bring her cruiser to her from Anna's. McDaniel didn't ask any questions, just went along with it and sent the cars. That worried me a little. I didn't want to think too much on what Sabrina's boss did or didn't know about the help we gave Sabrina from time to time.

She got off the phone and turned back to the rest of us. "There have been no other reported missing persons since the Carmichaels, but that doesn't mean anything."

"Yeah, it's the weekend. He could have grabbed a couple of kids from the college and nobody would know they hadn't gone to visit their parents or just gone off on a bender."

"I don't think they call them benders anymore, bro," Greg said. He seemed to have decided to let me off the hook, at least for now.

"Regardless, Jimmy's right for a change. We have to assume that he has hostages until we know different, regardless of the police reports. He could have taken a couple that lives alone, people vacationing, or any number of people that wouldn't be missed quickly. When I get back to the station I'll go over any reports that may have come in and not been filed yet because of the forty-eight hour limit." Technically, people weren't declared missing until they'd been gone two full days, but with our timeline that could be way, way too long for safety.

Greg hopped on the computer and scanned the sketch into his hard drive, then started poking around databases to see if he could pull a facial match off the drawing. I wandered over to where he was working, but he waved me off. Abby settled in beside him at the big monitor and started surfing social networks, posting the sketch as a "possible sexual predator—call police immediately" alert on every website she had access to.

Anna took a look around the room and shrugged, then pulled out her own cell phone and called a cab. "I've done all I can do here. My magic is down to normal levels now that we're back in the mundane world, so I won't be any good in a fight. And I do not want to be here when the police start asking questions about how you found these two."

"Can I catch a ride back to your place?" Stephen asked. "I'm in the same boat. I don't think the Scoobys need me to take down one human, and I'd really like to go home and cuddle on the couch with my husband. It's been a long day. Or week. Or however long we were gone." I thanked both of them and led them upstairs to wait on the cab. After they were gone, I went back downstairs to see Sabrina talking seriously with the Carmichaels.

"No, there is absolutely no reason for this man to ever come after you again." Sabrina was saying in a low, reassuring voice. "He thinks the Dream King killed you. And besides, we have no reason to believe that you were anything more than a crime of opportunity to him. We know that he always took people in pairs, and the pairs were married couples, friends, co-workers, any kind of pairing of people that happened to be together."

"Besides," I chimed in, "I'm going to kill him tonight. So you won't have anything to worry about."

"How are you going to do that?" Elizabeth asked. "You don't have any idea where he is."

"I have a few resources the police typically don't have," I replied.

"Like what?"

"Like my enhanced senses. I visited the abduction site before we went to Faerieland, and I took a good look around and catalogued the scents of the crime scene. Now that I've been around you two for a while, I know which scents are yours, and which ones belong to your kidnapper. We can use that to track him, and when we find him, I'm going to kill him." That was complete BS. I was counting on Greg's computer-fu to find the guy, but no point in making myself seem less mysterious and omnipotent to the mortals.

"Enhanced senses help with the police work. I can see that,"

David said. "That's really handy, I bet."

I stared at him for a second, but he gave no indication that he understood. "Absolutely handy. I hunt by scent, David."

He went a little pale when he realized that I meant hunting people, but I couldn't afford to sugarcoat anything for him. "Yes, I hunt people. Nowadays I do it for my job, not for my dinner, but the principles are the same. So I'm going to use the abilities that nature has given me to track my prey to track the man who abducted you."

"And kill him," David said, looking me firmly in the eye.

"Yes, and kill him," I confirmed.

Sabrina stood up and said, "Can I talk to you for a moment?" She grabbed me by the elbow and dragged me off to a corner of the room.

"Are you crazy? Telling these people that you're going to kill the man who kidnapped them? At first I thought you were just grandstanding, but now I think you mean it."

"I am going to kill him."

"Jimmy, in case you've forgotten, I'm a cop. We don't kill the bad guys, we turn them over to the courts and let them do their job. That's the way the justice system works."

"Not this time. This time we know who the bad guy is, and exactly what he is doing. We're not going to trust your so-called justice system to make sure he never, ever gets out of the hole he deserves to be planted in. So we're going to take care of that for them."

"That's vigilante justice!"

"And some days that's the only kind of justice there is. Look, Sabrina, *that little spider in his web of dreams* went into the heads of who knows how many humans and stole their dreams. Then he sold those dreams to other magicians to be used in God-knows-what. And when he stole all the dreams they could ever have, he sold them off to be cooked into stew by goblins! How do you think you're going to explain that to a judge so the bench will understand just how heinous trafficking in *raw materials* is? Would anyone believe us? Can we even tie our guy to the disappearance with only the word of very shaken victims? You think they'll hold up to a cross? You think they'll sleep nights ever again if our guy is still alive?"

Memories came flooding back to me as I talked to her: hanging there waiting for Abdullah to cut off more bits of me to throw in the pot, listening to Greg screaming as the sadistic little goblin worked on him, the look in Elizabeth's eyes when she woke up in the Dream King's tent, the bookcase full of heads in the back of that tent—no books anywhere—just shelf after shelf of heads magically preserved to look almost alive, except for the look of horror on the faces and the missing eyes.

I put my hands on Sabrina's shoulders and looked her in the eyes. We both knew I couldn't mojo her, so it was just to make a point. "Sabrina, this guy is giving people to monsters. That makes him a monster. And we don't try monsters in a court of law. We kill them. This time the monster happens to be human, but only on the outside. On the inside, this bastard is as evil as any demon, ghoul, or beast that we've ever faced. And we have to put him down, once and for all." I looked her in the eye again, trying to see some hint of agreement.

"You with me?" I asked.

"I don't know yet. But I'm not going to say no. That's as good as you get right now."

"I can live with that. Now let's get these people home. Their ride's here."

Sabrina began to move, then looked back at me.

"I know, you can't hear anything yet. You will." A few seconds later the sound of gravel grew louder, and Sabrina shook her head at me.

I went back to where the traumatized couple was sitting on our sofa. "The police are here to take you to the station for some questions, then home. Sabrina's right that you shouldn't have anything to worry about, but I'm sending Abby with you just in case."

"Why me?" Abby protested. "I wanted to help kill the bad guy!"

"I know you did, but it's his fault that goblins ate parts of me and Greg, so we get dibs. Sorry." She thought about that for a second, then nodded. "I promise to bring you a present if he's got anything good lying around."

"Oooh, that's good. Remember, I want a puppy!"

"Not on your life, chicklet." I hugged her and whispered in her ear, "Keep sharp. If this asshat makes an appearance, don't screw around with him. Put two in his face and then decapitate him."

"But he's human, right?" she whispered back to me.

"Who know what kind of upgrades he got from the Dream King. Don't take any chances."

"Deal." Abby led the couple up the stairs, and in a few seconds I heard feet coming down.

Sabrina came over to me and said, "I've got to go with them to the station. Even with McDaniel running blocker for this, I'm going to have to do some fancy footwork to keep the feds off your back."

"Give me until the morning, and then they can come in guns blazing. If we can't settle this thing by then, we've got bigger problems."

"Where are you going? Do we know where this guy lives?"

"Not yet, but we'll find him. Track Greg's cell if you need to find us."

"Why his cell?"

"Because I broke mine again."

We stood there, looking at each other for what felt like a year. Finally I said it. "You know I'd never hurt you, right?"

"I know." She didn't quite look in my eyes as she said it.

"Sabrina, I don't know where we're going, but I just want you to know . . ."

"I know." This time she looked in my eyes, and what I saw there was a mirror for what I felt—a little scared, a lot worried about the future, but either crazy in love or damn close to it.

"Okay. Well, let's talk after this is all settled. Figure some stuff out," I said.

"I can live with that." She took a step, then turned around and threw her arms around my neck. Our lips met, and it was better than the first time I tasted blood after being turned. It was even better than drinking faerie blood, and that stuff is *amazing*. I felt her warmth flow into me all the way to my toes, and as she stood there wrapping her arms around me, I almost felt alive again. After our little scene in Milandra's palace, my head was all in knots about Sabrina, but the rest of me knew exactly how I felt about her. And apparently, with that kiss, a few parts of her were still into me, too.

Sabrina pulled back and looked me in the eye. "Don't get dead. I need you in one piece."

"I'm already dead, but I'll try to not get any deader."

"I'd appreciate it." Then she leaned in and gave me another quick kiss, just a brief meeting of our lips, but the tingle it sent down my everything was intense. I watched her walk to the stairs, then she stopped and turned back to look at Greg.

"If anything happens to him, I'm putting a stake somewhere the sun doesn't shine, Knightwood." Then she turned and walked up the stairs.

Greg looked over at me and said, "Dude, I'm a little scared of your girlfriend."

I looked back at him and said, "Dude, sometimes *I'm* a little scared of my girlfriend, and I'm pretty sure she likes me. No telling what she'd do to you."

Then there were male footsteps on the stairs, and I snapped to attention. I wasn't expecting anyone to come back in, so Officer Nester found himself with a Glock leveled at his face when he stepped into the room.

"What are you doing here, Officer?" I asked without moving the pistol.

"I brought Detective Law's car keys. And I'm here to help finish things."

"I don't remember asking for your help."

"You didn't, but I can be useful. And I haven't spilled the beans on you guys so far, have I?"

"Spilled the beans? Who says that? What are you, Officer Howdy Doody?" I asked, looking at the kid.

"I'll be Officer Fozzie the Bear if I need to, but let me help. This is why I became a cop, this is what I've dedicated my whole life to doing." He looked so sincere I couldn't help it. I put my arm around his shoulders and walked him over to the sofa.

I sat down next to him and said, "Look, kid. I know this is important to you. But you've got too much tied up in this thing, which is why I can't have you around. When people are too close to a situation, they miss things. And with the kind of fights we get into, if you miss something, there's a good chance you're going to end up dead. Or worse. And trust me, I've seen what 'or worse' looks like."

He sat there for a minute, then looked at me, eyes cold. "Is it worse than lying awake every night listening to your mother cry because her baby girl's gone missing and she doesn't know what happened to her? Is it worse than watching your father drink himself to death while you're still in high school because his wife cries every time the phone rings? Is it worse than dedicating twenty years of your life to something, only to be told that you can't take the last two steps to get there because it might be too dangerous? If you can tell me how anything is worse than that, I'll go home."

I couldn't. He had me, and he knew it. I'm a sucker for the whole unfulfilled destiny thing, and it sounded like his sister had it in spades. I was just about to open my mouth and tell him that he could ride along when Greg spoke up.

"Officer, was your sister with anyone when she was abducted?"

Greg asked from his computer command center.

"Yes. She was with her best friend from school, Jenny. They were going to the mall to try on shoes. At least that's what they'd told our parents. I don't know if they were meeting people, or what. But they left school and were never seen at the mall. Jenny's car was found at school that night when they didn't make it home."

"It checks out, Jimmy. I've got a Lisa Nester and a Jenny Grant among the list of missing persons taken in 1991. There were sixteen abducted between South Meck High School and SouthPark Mall."

"Pretty swanky part of town for kids to go missing," I mused. "Why don't I remember anything about it on the news?"

"Jimmy, we were seniors in high school. All we were thinking about was graduating, moving out, going to Myrtle Beach that summer—"

"And all the parties we'd be going to at Clemson that fall. Yeah, that makes sense. All right, Nester, you can come along. But I hope to hell you brought a change of clothes. We are not riding around town with Deputy Dawg in the backseat."

"I figured. I'll get changed." He ran up the stairs, and I heard the front door slam. A few seconds later he was back, clumping toward the bathroom to get changed.

"So . . . are we good?" I asked.

Greg didn't turn around. He didn't say anything for a long time, but finally he sighed and said, "Yeah, we're good. It's just been a lot, you know? Seeing my sister again after all these years, getting pieces of myself chewed on by goblins, drinking faeries to heal, watching you and Sabrina do whatever it is you're doing, Abby . . ."

"You know I'd take it back if I could, right?"

"Yeah, I know. It's just . . ."

"A lot. Yeah, I know." I walked over to where Greg's enormous monitor hung on the wall. He had a map of Charlotte displayed there with dots of different colors blinking all over the town. "Okay, Boy Wonder, feel free to explain how we're going to narrow our search from the entire Charlotte metro area and find this jerkoff before he takes someone else."

"Or kills someone he's already taken," Greg added. "I've done a geographic profile of his victims. You can look at the map and see that they were all taken from high-traffic areas in a couple of sections of town. It seems like his preferred hunting grounds are the SouthPark and Cotswold areas. He's taken several victims from the parking deck at SouthPark, but never more than one set per abduction period."

"And since that's where he took the Carmichaels from, he probably won't go back there this soon."

"Exactly. If I add the sequence in which he hit each area into the profile, you'll find that he took his first victim near the Cotswold shopping center, then the next pair in the SouthPark garage, then his third and final set each time came from a movie theatre."

"But they closed the movie theatre at SouthPark."

"Yes, but they opened the new one at Phillips Place," Greg replied.

"Which is less than a mile from SouthPark Mall," I said.

"Still well within the kidnapper's comfort zone."

"Do you think that he'll be more nervous since he's taking someone from a new place?" Officer Nester asked from the stairs.

Greg swiveled around in his chair to face the young cop. "I don't know if he'll be more nervous, but I definitely think he'll have spent some time scouting the area. We should show the sketch to the kids at the ticket window, and ask them if they've seen a white van with no windows cruising the parking lot recently."

"Yeah, because there aren't a lot of blue-collar types hanging out at Phillips Place," I agreed. "Let's roll, kids."

Chapter 25

IT TOOK US BETTER than half an hour to get across town from our place in the university area north of town to Phillips Place, down by SouthPark. Phillips Place is one of those sparkling new "mixed-use" developments, which means that when they get home from their soul-sucking job at the bank, the yuppies don't have to leave the neighborhood to do anything they want. Condos are sprinkled around high-end retail shops, and shiny grocery stores offer the latest organic whatever in the windows. The limited parking is heavily populated with Mercedes and Beamers, and in the middle of the day you could sit for hours and watch the trophy wives walk by with their trophy dogs in tow.

Fortunately for Greg and I, it wasn't the middle of the day, but the sun had just set and the place was jam-packed with people. We stood out a little in our work clothes of long coats, ass-kicking boots, and sunglasses, but I was used to getting weird looks from people. Officer Nester didn't seem bothered by it either, but then I remembered that he was used to getting stared at because of his badge. We took a couple laps around the parking lot looking for both a place to put Greg's newest acquisition—a candy-apple red 1973 El Camino SS with a 454 V8 and Hydra-Matic tranny. The damn thing sounded like a thunderstorm on wheels, but it would move like a bat out of hell. Of course, fitting three dudes in the front seat of an El Camino took almost all the cool out of the car, but I made Nester ride bitch, so we survived.

We didn't spot a white panel van in the parking deck, so we took copies of the sketch and split up to check out the different businesses. If anyone had been loitering around looking anything but rich and snobby, someone would have noticed. Greg checked out the movie theatre, while I headed to Dean & DeLuca. The upscale market and coffee shop had a wine bar attached, so I started there. I flagged down a cocktail waitress with a nametag that read "Cindy" and showed her the sketch.

"Cindy, I'm a private investigator working with the police on a string of kidnappings. We think this man might be looking for his next victims in this area. Have you seen him?"

She took a step or two back and shook her head. "No, I haven't seen him. What does he drive, maybe I've seen his car?"

"He drives a white van with no windows and a ladder rack on top. Have you seen anything like that?"

"I'm sorry, but they've been doing construction over at the hotel, so there are a lot of those kinds of vans driving through here lately. Wish I could help!" She backed away hurriedly and dashed back inside. I went back to the car in time to see Greg leaving the theatre.

"Anything?" I asked.

"Nothing. One—the quality of movie theatre employee has gone to shit since I ran the candy counter."

"You mean two decades ago?"

"Yes, but that's beside the point. Two—these little morons couldn't be pried away from texting, Facebooking, or Angry Birds long enough to know if they'd sold a ticket to Freddy, Jason, *and* the thing from *Predator!*"

"Well, then I guess it's good you brought me along, isn't it?" Nester asked, walking up with a huge grin.

"Spill it, Little Boy Blue," I growled.

He didn't stop grinning. "After you guys took the good spots, I looked around and saw the women at the salon standing out front having a smoke break and gabbing. I walked up to them and asked if they'd been busy lately. After listening to them bitch about having no business for the past week, I showed them the sketch."

"And?" Greg asked.

"Nothing. But when I asked about a van, they remembered seeing one parked right in front of Via Veneto for three days this week. One girl thought it was strange, because they never let service vehicles park out front, so she wrote down the plate number."

"Tell me you got it," I said, barely letting myself hope he'd actually pulled it off.

"Not only did I get it, but I've already called in, run a check on it, and gotten the address. It's on Red Fox Lane, off Sharon Amity."

"Right between here and Cotswold Mall," Greg added.

"We can be there in less than ten minutes," Nester said, but I already had the door open for him to slide into the car. "Come on, I found the address. I still gotta ride in the middle?"

"Until you've been dead at least a decade, you're still low man on the totem pole," I replied, bowing to the door. "Your chariot awaits."

RED FOX LANE was a quiet city street. Nice houses, clean lawns, moderately expensive cars, but nothing too flashy floating around. There was nothing about the neighborhood that screamed, "Serial Kidnapper Living Here." Which was probably what made the place appealing to a serial kidnapper. We found the house quickly enough, then parked the El Camino a couple blocks away. My ride had serious badass capacity, but the car was for shit on stealthy approaches. Some things you just can't do with a 454 Big Block, and sneak up on somebody was one of those things.

I took point, with Nester behind me and Greg as rear guard. The problem wasn't that I trusted Nester less; I put Greg at the back of the pack so that when the inevitable happened and he tripped over something, no one would trip over him. I just hoped that he got the whole falling down thing out of the way quickly, before we were close enough for the suspect to hear us swearing.

Nester filled us in on the suspect on the way over. Richard Asa was a retired electrician, which explained the van. He was an oddity in Charlotte these days, a native Charlottean. Never married, no relatives that Nester could find a record of, no church affiliation, no social groups, nothing. Basically, he was a hermit these days. His house was a standard ranch three-bedroom affair, but we were more interested in the shed he'd built back in the late eighties. Set almost a hundred yards back from the house in a neighborhood where most of the lots aren't anywhere near that long, tax records showed an outbuilding of six hundred square feet. If he had anybody tucked away, that's where they'd be. Or at least where they'd been.

Starting our search with the shed had the added bonus of avoiding our little threshold problem. Storage buildings weren't an issue for us, but we had to be invited into homes or permanent dwellings. If Asa was in the house, either Nester was going to have to take him down alone or we'd have to wrangle an invitation. And with us in full tactical gear, I didn't see an invitation forthcoming.

So we split up, sending Nester to cover the entrance to the shed while Greg and I made a quick scout of the perimeter of the house with our vamp-senses and regrouped at the back door. "You hear or see anything?" I asked Greg.

"Nada. You?"

"Zip."

Nester stood on the back porch, his gun trained on the shed's front door. "There was movement in the shed a second ago, but I can't see any details."

I put a hand on his shoulder. "Good deal. Now put your gun away, and pull out your Taser." He did as I asked. "Remember not to shoot me or Greg. Because he'll be upset if you shoot him."

"And you won't?"

"No, I'll just very calmly rip your arms off. I believe in consequences as life lessons."

He pointed the Taser at the ground.

"Good boy," I added, patting him on the head.

I waved Greg over, then continued. "Here's the plan. Greg's going in first, because he's the strongest. He'll take down the door, and I'll go in over him."

"Over him?" Nester asked.

"Don't interrupt unless it has to do with what you're supposed to do. You don't have to understand what we do. You just have to do your part and NOT shoot me in the ass with a Taser. Clear?"

"Crystal." He didn't look very happy at being talked to like a four-year-old, but I didn't have time to worry about his feelings.

"You will stay outside securing our perimeter until you get the all clear from our sweep of the shed. Then you will come into the shed and take up a position opposite Greg, who will make sure that no one gets out of that room without my approval. If this guy somehow manages to overpower Greg and I, you call for backup and pursue. Do not engage this man. If he can take down two vampires, you have about as much hope bringing him down as a snowball in a microwave. Do you understand me?"

"Yes, sir."

That's what I love about working with trained professionals. Once you lay the whole plan out for them, they do what they're told. Even if some of it is completely batshit crazy, they'll go for it.

We crept to the door of the shed, and I looked back to see that Nester was in position. He nodded to me, and I tapped Greg on the shoulder. He and I stood up at the same time, and he charged the door. He hit that shed door like a fanged rhinoceros, and it exploded inward in a shriek of mangled aluminum and a cloud of splinters. Greg dropped flat as soon as he was past the doorway, and I dove in over him, tucking into a forward roll that carried me into the center of the room. I rolled to my feet and spun around, gaze finding and locking onto Asa almost as soon as my roll was complete.

He stood against a wall, ten feet away, unarmed. He was a big man, run slightly to fat as he aged. A shock of white hair swept back from his brow, and thick grey eyebrows stuck out wildly. He wore jeans and a tattered work shirt spattered with blood and grease. I hoped the blood didn't belong to the two bodies hanging from the wall.

They were alive; I could smell that from where I stood. I couldn't tell much about them except that they were female. Asa had black pillowcases over their heads, and judging by the noises coming from under the makeshift hoods, he had taped their mouths shut. They dangled from handcuffs which were attached to chains hanging from the rafters. Their feet could touch the ground, but just barely. Having recently been tied to something and forced into one position for a long time, I felt a burning in my own arms and legs in sympathy.

As much as I wanted to pull them down, I had to deal with Asa before I freed the women. I turned my attention back to him, and was amazed to see him striding toward me, holding his hand out for me to shake.

"You must be the Dream King's Honor Guard. At last! You're here to bring me over to the Other Side for all my years of loyal service. I am so pleased to finally meet you. I'm Richard, Richard Asa, and I have been the King's supplier of dreams for this Market location for forty of our years." I shook his hand, mostly because I didn't have any idea what else to do. Then I punched him in the side of the face and knocked his ass out cold.

Chapter 26

ASA CAME TO A few minutes later, after a little slapping and a little water thrown in his face. Plus, I finally got frustrated with his sluggish response and punched him in the testicles a little. That got his eyes wide open, and his hands clutching convulsively around his privates. Or they would have been if Asa hadn't been handcuffed, arms over his head, and suspended from the rafters.

We'd cleared the girls out of the shed and sent them home with a very satisfied Officer Nester, leaving just me and Greg to interrogate our kidnapper. I had Greg lean what was left of the door back against the hole in the wall, just to muffle the sound of the screams. I figured we were probably far enough back from other houses to question our prisoner without disturbing anyone's rest, but I wanted to be sure.

Once we had him awake and had his undivided attention, I pulled a chair over and sat down in front of him. I had an inkling this guy's elevator didn't stop on all the floors, so my best shot at getting information out of him might be to play into his psychosis. "You're Richard Asa, the Dream King's faithful and loyal servant. As the Dream King's envoys into the mundane world, we must test your knowledge before you are allowed to cross over. So tell me all you know of his need for humans."

"He requires human sacrifice of dreams to keep his Land of Nod running smoothly, so I help him by selecting appropriate sacrifices."

"Land of Nod?" Greg asked. He was busy searching the shed, and kept adding things to a small pile he was building on a workbench. I hadn't taken a good look at the pile yet, but the items looked like random crap you'd find in an old shed. Watches, a wallet, a bracelet—weird tchotchkes and shit like that.

Asa smiled like a loon, making me glad he was in handcuffs. "Nod. Where the Dream King keeps his castle. He lives there in the clouds and walks through our dreams every night, keeping order in the mortal realm by making sure our dreams are perfect and happy. Unless you're bad, then he sends you nightmares." That last bit was in a whisper, and he gave me a nasty wink, like we were conspirators or something.

I lost it. I tried, but I couldn't hold onto the ruse of working with the Dream King anymore. I stood up, waving my arms as I shouted at Asa, "I can't tell if you read too many *Sandman* comics, did too many drugs, or are just the stupidest human I've ever met. The Dream King didn't live in the Land of Nod. He lived in a shitty little tent in the middle of the Goblin Market, which is one of the nastiest places I've ever been in my life or death. He was a three-foot-tall Yoda-looking rat bastard without even the good graces to be green. And he sure as hell wasn't doing anything to help anybody but himself. He sold those dreams, you jackass! And when he was done selling the dreams, he chopped the people up into chunks and sold them off to a goblin. A friggin' goblin! A short, fat, smelly green bastard called the Chef! And do you know why he was called the Chef? Because he made the most popular stew in the Goblin Market. Stew made from people! People you kidnapped and sold to the Dream King!"

I was panting and red in the face from screaming at the stupid bastard, but then I took a good look at his face. He had no idea what I was talking about.

I took a deep breath and said, very quietly, "What did he tell you he was doing with the people you gave him?" I thought if he had been duped by the Dream King then maybe he was just another poor schmuck taken in by an evil wizard.

"He didn't really ever tell me anything. He just told me to bring him pairs of people, so I did." The dumb son of a bitch didn't seem to realize that lying might not be the best move for his longevity.

"Why pairs?" Greg asked. I looked over, and he was holding a small box with several high school rings glittering in it. I didn't want to think about how many rings there were or what that pile being amassed actually was. The rings alone would account for more missing persons than we had on our list.

"He asked me for them," Asa said, as if it made perfect sense.

Greg was on him before I could blink. He's not as fast as me, but he's still vampire fast. He was across the shed in half a second and had Asa by the throat. I grabbed his hand and pulled him back, trying to pry his fingers loose.

Finally, I pulled back and slapped Greg across the face. "He can't answer you if he can't breathe."

Greg dropped the guy, and he let out a little yell as his body dropped like a cement bag, almost wrenching his shoulders from their sockets. Asa had been pretty careful when he hung the girls from the rafters, making sure they could touch the ground and carry some of their weight. I hadn't been so careful hanging him. He could stand on tiptoes if he really stretched, but mostly he was just swinging. I looked around in the recesses of my soul to see if there was any sympathy floating around for him but came up empty.

"Why did you give those people to the Dream King?" Greg asked again, speaking very slowly and very clearly. Asa tried to dance back on his tiptoes to get away from the angry vampire in his face, but he had nowhere to go. The touches of his toes threatened to spin him in a circle rather than take him to safety.

"I wanted to go back," he finally whimpered.

"What?" I asked. "Go back where?"

"Faerie. I crossed over when I was a little kid, and all I've ever wanted to do since was get back. It's the most amazing place ever, and the Dream King told me that if I was a good servant here in the mundane world, that when the time came, he would take me back to Faerie. I was hoping this trip would be my turn."

"What do you mean 'this trip'?" Greg asked.

"The Market only comes here every twenty years. It moves around all the time, and this is the fourth time it's been here in my lifetime. The first time was when I was a little boy, about nine or ten years old. I found my way in by accident. I was playing in the woods and crossed over into the Market. I spent days in the Market wandering around, exploring. It was the most amazing place I'd ever seen. Then, after I'd explored a lot of the Market, I found an exit to Faerie proper, and I went through. I couldn't believe what I saw—the creatures, the colors, the food, the plants—everything was so wonderful I never wanted to leave. But when the Market moved, I found myself thrown back here. Back here, where everything is dull and grey and boring and there isn't any magic or any cool monsters or anything. And nobody believed me, not my parents, not the kids at school, nobody." He looked so pathetic I almost took pity on him and reminded him that he was currently being held captive by two real monsters, but decided to just let him keep going.

"I kept trying to go back. I went back to that same spot every day that summer, then once a week, then once a month. Finally, I just went back on the day I first found the path every year, until one day the way was open! I was older then, and that time when I wandered the Market

I found more information. I met the Dream King. He showed me such wonders in human dreams that I'd never even contemplated before. The things he could do were amazing. And all he needed to make his magic and keep the Land of Dreams running properly was a sacrifice of a few dreamers each time the Market stopped near me. He was growing old, and couldn't venture from the Market to collect his own sacrifices, so he needed worshippers like me to collect the offerings for him." His face glowed with a religious rapture, and I knew without a doubt that this guy was around the bend a long time ago.

"And I was happy to do it! There are so many people, and they all want to follow their dreams. I just gave them the opportunity to *become* dreams, to serve the greater good. That's all I ever did—I helped people live out their dreams and grow the dreams of others."

I felt sick to my stomach. I leaned forward and grabbed his face in one hand. "You gave people to that sick bastard so he could reach into their head and yank out their dreams. Even if they lived, they would have been mindless shells. You gave them to this sicko to be destroyed, even if he didn't kill them. Who knows? Maybe by the time he was done with them, killing them was a mercy, but nobody deserved to end up in the Chef's stew pot!"

"Most of all not us, asshole," Greg grumbled. I looked over, and his pile of trinkets was really big now. There were enough rings, watches, and necklaces to open a small jewelry store.

"But it was the only way he'd take me with him. To let me stay in the Market forever and live out the rest of my life in Faerie." He grinned that beatific smile again, and I could see the madness in his eyes. This moron not only believed the Dream King was going to take him into Faerieland, he still believed the little bastard was coming for him.

"News flash, dumbass. We killed the Dream King. Actually, a witch friend of ours did. He's dead, his shop is closed, and now it's time for you to pay for all the pain you caused." I moved in, ready to end it right there, but Greg held up a hand.

"But first, how many people did you give to him?" my partner asked.

"I was to provide him with eight sacrifices each time the Market stopped here. I only managed six the first time I went in as an adult, and this time you spoiled my last two sacrifices, too."

"Last two?" Greg asked. "We only know about six people you took recently. There was a bartender and her friend that you kidnapped downtown."

"Then the Carmichaels," I chimed in.

"Then the women we rescued today. Who are the other two and where are they?"

"I don't know who they were. I never knew who any of them were. That would have been . . . uncomfortable. But they were a couple. A man and a woman in their thirties. I found them on the interstate. Their car had broken down, and I offered to help. They were my first sacrifices this year." He didn't even talk like he'd done anything wrong. I felt chills run along my arms as I listened to him. I'd fought monsters, humans and demons, but this guy was creepier than any of them.

"How many others?" Greg asked.

"What do you mean?" Asa didn't look at my partner.

"How many others? I've got a pile of jewelry and wallets here, and I bet none of them are yours. There's too much stuff to all have gone to Faerieland. There must be thirty different sets of stuff here. So I'm going to ask you one more time, then I'm going to pull your big toe off. How many others did you kill?"

"Oh good God, who counts? I don't know, and I don't care. So I started to take an extra here and there. The Dream King never cared if they were beat up a little when I delivered them, so I started to play a little before he got them. Then I took one between visits to the Market, and I realized I had a knack for it. It's easy, once you get the hang of it. You just make yourself look as harmless as possible, then when they least suspect it, BAM!" He yelled that last part and jumped forward. I didn't blink. I wasn't going to give him the satisfaction.

"Is this everything?" Greg asked, waving to the pile of stuff on the workbench.

"There might be a few samples still in the fridge." Asa smiled up at me and my blood ran cold. I really, really did not want to open the big freezer he had chugging away in a corner of the shed. But I did. I walked over to it and flipped up the lid. I didn't scream, and I didn't puke. I was pretty proud of myself for that. I looked inside the freezer, and stacked neatly along one wall were small clear Tupperware containers. There must have been five or six dozen containers. And in each container was a neatly severed pair of thumbs. Taped to the top of each container was a Polaroid picture. And in each picture was a face. A terrified face.

I whirled back to where Asa dangled, grinning. I was close enough to feel his breath on my shirt. I could hear his heart pounding, and he looked up at me and said, "The Dream King told me I could keep the thumbs. No meat on those, you see, no resale value to the Chef."

"You sick bastard . . ." I started, but turned away before I could finish the thought.

I didn't turn around as he talked at my back. "I'm an old man, what do you think they'll do to me? Put me in prison for the rest of my life? I'm already there. What do I care? You can't touch me! Nobody can touch me! I'm the Dream King now!" He started to laugh, and I looked over at Greg.

Greg shook his head, and said, "No. We need to let the police handle this, dude. You promised. We aren't monsters. We're civilized. He's human. The cops can handle it."

"You got that right. They work crime scenes all the time," I said, then turned around and put my hands on the side of Asa's face. "See you in Hell, asshole," I said, snapping his neck. He sagged against the chains, let out a long sigh of breath, and was still.

I turned back to Greg. "Let's get out of here before he craps himself and it stinks even worse." I tossed the door aside and started for the car.

Chapter 27

AN UNDERSTATEMENT would be to say that Sabrina was not happy with the way I handled the Dream King's mortal minion. Apparently "he deserved killing" is not considered justification in the eyes of the law these days. I didn't really care. I looked in David Carmichael's eyes and told him that I watched his kidnapper die, and the relief that I saw there was worth a couple days of a pissed-off girlfriend. And I was right—after a couple of days she showed up back at the house with a six-pack of Miller Lite and made no further mention of my twisting the bad guy's head completely around.

I was a little surprised that she brought Nester along, though. Wasn't exactly thrilled about it. He was young, handsome, and able to move about freely in daylight—several things I'm not. I felt a lot better about his presence when he plopped down in front of Greg's computer and starting pressing buttons like a psycho concert pianist tearing into "Flight of the Bumblebee."

What? I like classical music. Lay off.

Anyway, Nester backdoored his way into the Charlotte-Mecklenburg PD computer system and brought up a series of case files on the bug monitor. I pulled the couch around for me and Sabrina to sit on, and called Greg and Abby down to watch the show. Greg grabbed a chair for himself, and Abby plopped down cross-legged on the floor in that casually sexy way smoking hot young girls have, no matter if they're dead or alive.

Nester turned to us and said, "So I hacked into the CMPD database to show you these case files."

Greg interrupted him. "If you'd *asked* before you went poking around in my computer, I would have shown you the shortcut on the desktop that gets you there quicker."

"You have a shortcut into the police computer system?" Abby asked. Greg shrugged like it was no big thing. He didn't want to admit that it took him three weeks of Red Bull–fueled twenty-hour days to get that hack set up and stable.

"That is so cool," Abby said, and leaned her head on Greg's knee. If he wasn't already a walking corpse, I think he would have dropped dead right there.

"Anyway," Nester continued, frowning a little at the incongruous picture of the hottie and the notty sitting there being all lovey-dovey. "This is a list of eighteen missing persons cases that we were able to resolve based solely on the evidence discovered in Asa's house, particularly the class rings. This includes the Carmichaels and the two girls that we were able to rescue from Asa's house before they were sent into Faerie."

Nester took a deep breath and looked down for a second. "It also includes my sister. One of the necklaces you found in that shed was a birthday present my mother gave her. I gave it to her yesterday." The young cop looked down again, then squared his shoulders and plowed ahead. I saw a little sheen of moisture in his eyes, but that was all.

Nester moved the wireless mouse around and clicked it a couple of times. "This is a list of thirty-seven other missing persons cases that we were able to close because of evidence recovered at Asa's home and shed. Some of this was the jewelry from the shed, some was from a collection of wallets under his bed, and some were bodies recovered from his backyard."

"He buried people in his yard?" I asked. I thought back and didn't remember seeing any turned earth, or smelling any decay. "That must have been years ago."

"Our best estimates are that he stopped burying people in his backyard more than twenty years ago, when the lots around his property were purchased and houses were built closer to his own," Sabrina chimed in.

"So this son of a bitch killed more than fifty people over the past forty years right under all our noses?" I took a long pull of my beer to wash the bad taste out of my mouth.

"And if a kid and his dog hadn't found a random jawbone in the woods we might have never known about it," Greg almost whispered.

"Can I get a pass for ripping his head off now?" I asked. Sabrina gave me a tight smile and punched me in the arm.

"If you'd like to do it again, I'll loan you a shovel," Nester said. I looked up at him, but there was no smile on his face. He nodded solemnly at me and lifted his beer. I raised mine in an imaginary toast, and we both drank.

"Alright, kids," I said, standing. "It's Friday night, we all survived our latest trip to Faerieland, and none of us came back sparkling. I say we celebrate! So what's the plan?"

"Sorry, Jimmy, I've got to work," Abby said, getting to her feet.

"Work? What are you talking about?" I asked.

"Remember that little deal I cut with Lilith that you were so pissed about?"

"Yeah," I glowered at her, remembering.

"Well, I start tonight. I'm the new bouncer at the Angel. You broke a few of her old ones, remember? Lilith thinks that having a bouncer that looks more like one of the girls than a linebacker might cut down on the property damage."

"I don't like it," Greg said, and I nodded.

"Doesn't matter. I made a deal, and I don't think any of us are dumb enough to want to break a deal with Lilith. Now I've got to go change. Somehow I don't think a ratty T-shirt and sweats is what she had in mind when she told me to wear something short and sexy to work in." She turned and headed upstairs.

Nester smiled and said, "Thanks for the invite, but I've got more paperwork to catch up on."

I looked over at Greg, who said, "Nah, man. I haven't made game night at the comic shop in a month. If I miss tonight they're going to kick me out of the Magic: The Gathering league."

I wasn't even sure what that meant, but it sounded like nothing Greg wanted to happen. A few seconds later, I looked around and I was alone in the den with Sabrina. I sat back down on the couch and looked over at her. "So . . . is it time to have that talk?"

"I think so," she replied. "Let me start. You drive me nuts. You're immature, reckless, half-crazy, and one of the two biggest geeks I've ever met."

"And those are my good qualities."

"Yes, exactly, those *are* your good qualities! You rush into things unprepared, you get hurt more than any man should be able to survive—"

"Well, technically—"

She put a finger on my lips. "Shut up, I'm talking. You're infuriating, irresponsible, and you look like a twenty-year-old! In short, you're nothing like what a responsible career woman in her mid-thirties should be interested in. So why in the world can't I just be through with you?"

I shrugged. "World's funny that way. I mean, look at it from my perspective. I'm immortal, young forever, with mental powers that can make any woman fall at my feet in a swoon, and I'm nuts about the one human I've ever met that I can't use my mojo on. And why the hell should I be falling in love with somebody that I'm eventually going to have to watch die of old age?"

We just sat there staring at each other for a long time. "Well, I guess I finally pointed out the elephants in the room, huh?" I asked.

"Which ones?"

"Well, there's the whole thing about not wanting to watch you get old and die—" Sabrina started to say something, but this time I put my finger over her lips. "And then there's the bit where I'm in love with you."

"Yeah, that." Her voice was low, but at least she was willing to look me in the eyes.

"Look, Sabrina, I know I'm not much of a catch. I'll get carded in bars until I'm a thousand, if I can avoid pissing off Faerie Queens that long. My nose is too big, my hair never does what I want, and I'm too skinny. Not to mention my fashion sense, or lack thereof. And that's before we get to the whole being dead thing."

We sat there on the couch in silence for a while, just looking at each other, until finally I broke. "So . . . *Doctor Who* marathon?"

She smiled at me, set down her beer, and scooted over closer to me on the sofa. A *lot* closer. "I didn't spend all that time making sure everyone but you and I had someplace else to be tonight just so we could watch TV." She smiled and leaned in, a curl falling loose from her ponytail to bounce across one cheek. I reached over and brushed it away, then pressed my lips to hers. She threw her arms around my neck and the kiss deepened. Her lips parted, and I felt her tongue flick across my lips.

I pulled back for a second and looked deep into her eyes. "This is nice and all, but the couch isn't exactly where all this played out in the movie in my head."

"Then what did you have in mind?" She asked with a smile.

I kissed her again, longer this time, wrapping my arms around her and standing up, picking her up with me as I stood. She wrapped her long legs around my waist and I carried her upstairs. I took my time, pausing at a couple of steps to set her down and kiss along her neck and nuzzle that spot behind her ears that makes her purr like a contented kitten. Finally, after what felt like a year, we were in my room. I looked around the room at the candles one of my helpful and interfering friends had lit as they were leaving, and smiled.

Then I laid Sabrina down on my bed and showed her exactly what I had in mind.

THE END

Acknowledgments

They say it takes a village, and it's just as true with books as it is with children, so I want to take this opportunity to thank some of the members of my village that have been instrumental in the development of this book.

First, I have to give a huge thanks to Deb Dixon and the whole crew at Bell Bridge Books. From the moment I signed on with them to rebuild The Black Knight Chronicles and release the rest of the series, they've been incredibly supportive, patient, and helpful. I knew going into this process that I had a lot to learn about writing professionally and the publishing business, and I couldn't have asked for better teachers.

I also have to give a huge thanks to my friends Faith Hunter, Misty Massey, Kalayna Price, James Tuck, Allan Gilbreath, Gail Z. Martin, AJ Hartley, Stuart Jaffe, and David Coe. I've always said that the best way to become a better writer is to surround yourself with better writers, so that's exactly what I've done. All of these folks have provided support, guidance, education, drinks, and most importantly, friendship.

I have to thank my con cohorts Davey Beauchamp, Emily Lavin Leverett, Vikki Perry, Stephen Zimmer, Sarah Adams, and so many more folks for the laughs, the drinks, and the good times. And the Wednesday night writers' bunch from Charlotte is the best bunch of friends I could hope for, so a huge thanks to Darin, Nico, Eden, Matthew, Jay, Margot, Traci, and Aaron. You guys rawk!

I have a great family that's always been very supportive and only rolls their eyes a little when they listen to my latest harebrained scheme, so thanks to them for their patience, love, and support.

And I have to thank you guys, the readers, because without y'all there wouldn't be a Black Knight Chronicles. I didn't start out to write a series, I just wrote one book about a couple of goofy vampire detectives. But you guys came along for the ride, and now we're four books into this journey. Thanks for coming along. I couldn't do it without you.

But all of that pales in comparison to the debt I owe to my wife Suzy, who stands by me through every crazy idea I've ever had for the last couple of decades. From theatre to poker to writing to job changes and life changes, she's been the one constant in my life for almost twenty years and for that I thank her most of all. Thanks honey, and I love you.

About the Author

John G. Hartness is a recovering theatre geek who likes loud music, fried pickles, and cold beer. He's also an award-winning poet, lighting designer, and theatre producer whose work has been translated into over twenty-five languages and read worldwide. John lives in North Carolina with his lovely wife Suzy.

Made in the USA
Las Vegas, NV
26 August 2021